The
Kingdom
of the Rings

The Beauty of Norway's Fjords

Praise for The Kingdom of The Rings

"Duane Lindberg's *The Kingdom of The Rings* is a powerful saga that takes the reader through many centuries and across the Atlantic. It reminds us that there are not two separate worlds, Europe and America. The author employs the symbolism of the three rings to capture our imagination as they are passed from generation to generation. We recognize individuals who are similar to our relatives and friends. One feels their joys and sorrows as their lives become links in a chain of spiritual continuity."

Dr. David Noble
Professor Emeritus, History and American Studies
University of Minnesota, Minneapolis, MN

"*The Kingdom of The Rings* is a brilliant story, tracing back to the Middle East and linked to Norway before ending in America. The Norway part of this fascinating story is from the time of the late Middle Ages, and very much related to Ringsaker area in Hedmark County, east of Lake Mjøsa and Ringerike County, west of Lake Mjøsa. The author, Duane R. Lindberg, PhD reveals a very good knowledge and insight regarding society and church of the time, and how faith and life traditions in Norway came to expression in everyday life and dreams.

"As the current Pastor of Ringsaker Church, erected ca. AD 1150, I am impressed with the story presented in this book, inspired by the entire concept, and moved by how emigrants from Norway with faith and courage might have left their homeland and finally found a new home 'over there.' I also read this book as a creative portrayal which illustrates how Christian faith and hope might influence. This book has my best recommendations."

Ole Amund Gillebo
Pastor, Ringsaker, Norway

"In *The Kingdom of The Rings*, the author combines the necessary ingredients in any good book: innovation, mystery, challenged characters, sweeping history, drama, insightful observations, plus twists and turns, all these as he spins with control the saga of The Rings and then craftily reveals the outcome as The Rings are nearly rejoined. As he moves through generations of Scandinavian immigrants, he challenges the standard concept of the American Melting Pot and convincingly replaces it with the 'Field of Rings.' One does not have to be Norwegian to appreciate this book."

Dr. Art Lee
Professor Emeritus, History Department
Bemidji State University, Bemidji, MN

Praise for
The Kingdom of The Rings

"Combining the best of Tolkien's *Lord of the Rings*, Rolvaag's *Giants in the Earth*, and Moberg's *The Emigrants*, Lindberg's saga spans nearly a millennium beginning with the last of the Crusades, on through the nineteenth-century Norse immigrants to America, their cultural acclimatization to America, and their struggle to maintain their faith in an increasingly hostile climate of the twentieth century. A connecting thread throughout the saga is the set of three interlocking golden Rings, part of the treasure given to the Christ child by the Magi." (From the Foreword)

John A. Eidsmoe
Colonel (MS), Mississippi State Guard
Senior Counsel, Foundation for Moral Law
Pastor, Association of Free Lutheran Congregations
Author, *Christianity and the Constitution*, **and**
The Historical and Theological Foundations of Law **(3 Vols.)**

"Author Lindberg has blended a fascinating tale of religious lore with snapshots of the Norwegian immigrant experience in America. It is a good story in and of itself, but should have special interest to persons interested in their Scandinavian affiliation."

Dennis Sorheim
Past International President, Sons of Norway

"Duane Lindberg's saga *The Kingdom of The Rings* is a story of expectation and hope. First, he sets the foundation of the story: the three Rings. Then we see the three Rings separated and how they are passed from generation to generation and how they affect those who possess them. Next, we move forward to the great migration to America, especially the Norwegians. Lastly, all three Rings are in America, two in the possession of Norwegian families, and one with a family descended from the Egyptian Mamelukes. Do the Rings come together? Almost. Along the way, the narrative reveals a depth of the author's scholarship, compassion, and theological background. His characters are real and exhibit their expectation and hope. *The Kingdom of The Rings* will cause us to reflect upon the expectation and hope that we have for our lives, just as the characters in the saga."

Jon Tehven
Secretary, Sons of Norway, International

"From back in Viking times, freedom has been a central issue in Norwegian history (I write of this in my novel *West Oversea*, published by Nordskog). The three elements in keeping liberty in balance are freedom, order, and the Word of God forming the central point of equilibrium. Dr. Duane Lindberg echoes this in his book. *The Kingdom of The Rings* reminds us that the Kingdom of God is among us, and is a mystery, and is revealed as determined by the Ruler of all things."

Lars Walker
Librarian, Association of Free Lutheran Congregations' Schools, Plymouth, Minnesota
Author of *West Oversea* and other novels.
Graduate student, Norwegian translator, and Viking re-enactor

"In *The Kingdom of The Rings* Duane Lindberg combines his life-long interests and studies in an intriguing combination of mystery, history, and theology. From his work as a leader of the Lutheran Student Association at the University of North Dakota, to organizing and leading a fledgling church body, he has always pushed the boundaries of imagination. From Minnesota across North Dakota, as a pastor he observed the results of the Norwegian immigrants' community building as well as their theological struggles. So much in this book is familiar to me—from the 'Melting Pot' in America to Hadeland, west of Lake Mjøsa in Norway, where ancient pilgrims, and I, have traveled. In all aspects, Duane is Right On."

Dean Sorum
Moorhead, Minnesota
Former Treasurer, Hadeland Lag of America

"In his book, *The Kingdom of the Rings,* Dr. Lindberg has skillfully entwined together three areas dear to his heart: his love of the promise of Christ's return, his love for the church, and his love for his Norwegian heritage.

"As a former colleague in church leadership with Dr. Lindberg and friend for twenty-five plus years, I highly recommend this book for enjoyment and encouragement to believe in the Promise of Christ's coming again."

Rev. Robert M. Dennis (Retired)
Chairman, Clergy Commission
The American Association of Lutheran Churches
Assistant Presiding Pastor, The AALC 1991–1995

Trondheim
(formerly Trondhjem)
A pilgrim's first view of the Nidaros Cathedral
seen at left in the distance.

The Kingdom of the Rings

Duane R. Lindberg, PhD

Ventura, California

The Kingdom of The Rings

D. R. Lindberg Books, LLC

Hardback: ISBN 978-0-9903774-1-2

Paperback: ISBN 978-0-9903774-2-9

LCCN 2014949390

Editing and Design by Vicki C. Weiland
Text Review and Proofing by (Mrs.) E. Mardell Lindberg
Image Director, Minette Siegel

Cover and Interior Design and Production, Desta Garrett, Managing Editor
Cover includes art by Erik Anundsen, Anundsen Design Group, Decorah, Iowa.

Original Maps by Forge Toro; "Timeline of Fictional Ring Carriers" by Erik Lindberg; Photograph "Prairie and Sky," 2012, by Cris Fulton, Bowman, North Dakota (see p. 110).

See Resources and Credits on pages 208–211.

Printed in the United States of America by JOSTENS PRESS

2716 Sailor Avenue, Ventura, California
www.NordskogPublishing.com

Dedication

Dedicated to the stalwart Norse immigrants to America
— men and women of faith and courage.

and

To my children and grandchildren who by God's grace
belong to The Kingdom of The Rings.

Reenactment of King Olaf II's army,
and the King being blessed by the Bishop (lower left side),
before the Battle of Stiklestad, AD 1030,
in which the King was killed
Photographed at the 950th Anniversary

Acknowledgments

I wish to acknowledge with gratitude the privilege I was given as a young pastor to study the religious, cultural, political, economic, and ethnic factors which have been formative in the development of American society.

Generous scholarships from the former American Lutheran Church and the former Lutheran Brotherhood Insurance Society made it possible to pursue a PhD in American Studies at the University of Minnesota.

It was an inspiration for me, after serving as a parish pastor for seven years, to digest these experiences in the context of my Biblical/Confessional Lutheran Theology and the perspectives of several other academic disciplines. I owe a special thanks to members of the American Studies faculty, especially to Professors Mary Turpie, Rudolph Vecoli, and David Noble, for their encouragement and guidance in my studies and research.

This guidance and help has continued to open for me a wide vista from which to view the dynamics of cultural retention as well as cultural assimilation. These are the forces which have been influencing and directing the formation and reformation of ethnic groups, churches, communities, families, and individuals in our society.

I want to express my appreciation to the many parishioners, fellow pastors, professors, librarians, and museum curators who have helped me in so many ways to grasp the material, ideational, historical, and spiritual realities of the American experience.

I am especially indebted to those who have read and given helpful suggestions to improve the manuscript. These include John Eidsmoe, David Noble, O. A. Gillebo, Art Lee, Dennis Sorheim, Jon Tehven, Dean and Carol Sorum, Robert Dennis, Phil Froiland, and Kaare Swang. And thank you to Lars Walker for his endorsement.

Then, not only in the writing of this saga, but also for innumerable hours of help and encouragement during my 50 years as a pastor, church organizer, denominational head, and teacher, I owe a debt of gratitude to my loving wife and helpmate, Mardell.

Appreciation is in order to our children, grandchildren, Marsha Klinefelter, and others for reading and providing helpful input when this writing was in process, and to Rev. Fr. Rodrigue Constantin of the Holy Family Maronite Catholic Church, St. Paul, Minnesota for commentary; also to Erik Anundsen for early cover draft art concepts.

With special thanks for photographic contributions to: Pastor Len Brokenshire; Dusty Emerick, Copyright PraiseBanners; Cris Fulton; Stan Haley, President, and Connie Knutson, Photo Enhancement, Arrow Printing, Inc.; Paul R. Herold, Mayor, Fort Atkinson, Iowa; Angela Hoover, Chicago History Museum; President Frank Lamb, Paul Bunyan Museum; Andrew Lindberg; Erik Lindberg; Dean and Carol Sorum and The Lutheran Church of Christ The King and The Hjemkomst Center; Martha Stone; Jessica Almonte, Lorraine Goonan, and Sarah-Maria Vischer-Masino, Researcher, The Image Works. And for publication permissions, thanks to Michael Moore, Augsburg Fortress Publishers; Jóhann Sigurdssðn, Leifur Eríkksson Publishing Ltd.; Lottie Fyfe, Penguin Books Ltd.-UK; Jeffrey Corrick, Penguin Group (USA) LLC; Kevin McGee, Music Sales Corp. for G. Schirmer Inc. (ASOAP).

A special thanks must be given to Erik Lindberg for being my computer consultant, and to Vicki Weiland for editing, Forge Toro for map design, Minette Siegel for photo research and coordination, Desta Garrett for design, typography, and production. Thanks to Jostens Press for excellent printing and binding.

I also want to thank Jerry Nordskog for his partnership in the Gospel, his encouragement, and his invaluable guidance in the publication of this book.

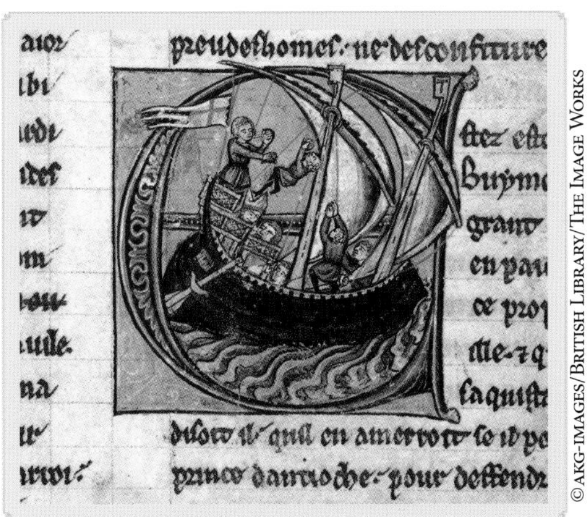

Bohemund I and Archbishop Dagobert sailing, (First Crusade, 1096–099)
Bohemond I, Prince of Taranto, and Prince of Antioch, c. 1058–1111
french illuminatation ca. 1250–59

Table of Contents

Lake Mjøsa, between Ringerike
and Ringsaker,
Hedmark County, Norway

Foreword

BY
JOHN A. EIDSMOE

Colonel (MS), Mississippi State Guard
Senior Counsel, Foundation for Moral Law
Pastor, Association of Free Lutheran Congregations
Author, *Christianity and the Constitution*, and
The Historical and Theological Foundations of Law (3 Vols.)

They came to a new land, but they brought much of the old land with them.

They wanted to become 100% American, but they wanted to preserve their Norse heritage.

They loved their new homeland, but still felt a longing for Norway.

And they wanted their children to be fully American without forgetting where they came from.

As they boarded the ship, they bade tearful farewells to loved ones whom in all probability they would never see again this side of heaven. They choked up with nostalgia as they watched the mountains of Norway recede into the eastern horizon. And they thrilled with anticipation as they approached the eastern seaboard harbors, traversed the Erie Canal, and traveled by covered wagon across the vast plains. Truly this was a land of unparalleled opportunity, but also a land of danger.

Their fears were not merely financial, physical, or even cultural. Besides being Norwegians, most of them were devout Lutheran Christians as well. Culture may be relative and negotiable; doctrine and worship are not. The faith must be preserved at all costs, and for these settlers the Lutheran faith was so enmeshed with Norse language and culture that, at least in their minds, it was virtually impossible to separate them.

Community interaction with Methodists, Presbyterians, and Catholics was one thing. Despite the differences in doctrine and liturgy, they at least shared a common Christian faith and morality. But secularism was another matter entirely. These Norse pioneers agonized over sending their children to the new and growing public school system which at first seemed to harbor traditional Protestant American values while being neutral about theology, but which seemed increasingly secular with succeeding generations. And the colleges and universities, which at times seemed increasingly hostile toward Christianity, posed an even greater dilemma: If these Norse immigrants' children were to become thoroughly successful Americans, but at the cost of their souls, would it be worth it? Is it possible to be both a red-blooded American and a true Norwegian Lutheran?

My good friend Dr. Duane Lindberg vividly portrays the Norse immigrants' dilemma in *The Kingdom of The Rings*. Combining the best of Tolkien's *Lord of the Rings,* Rolvaag's *Giants in the Earth*, and Moberg's *The Emigrants*, Lindberg's saga spans nearly a millennium beginning with the last of the Crusades, on through the nineteenth-century Norse immigrants to America, their cultural acclimatization to America, and their struggle to maintain their faith in an increasingly hostile climate of the twentieth century. A connecting thread throughout the saga is the set of three interlocking golden Rings, part of the treasure given to the Christ child by the Magi, revealed during the Crusades, separated in Cyprus, carried via the "Pilgrims' Way" to Trondheim, Norway, preserved at the Ringsaker and Hamar Churches, hidden for centuries, in different ways brought to America, always with the hope that finally they would be brought together. What do the Rings symbolize? What is the nature of their power? How do they become the possessions of Norse immigrants? How will those immigrants' lives be intertwined? And how will they and their Rings come together?

Through all of this, Lindberg weaves together a story of immigrants settling in Texas, Georgia, Iowa, and Minnesota. Although torn apart by the War Between the States, the love of Jesus Christ and a romantic love draw Reidunn Haraldson and Lars Hanson together. But first, they endure many hardships: Reidunn's siblings at an orphanage disciplined harshly for praying *I Jesu navn* instead of "American" prayers in the tradition of Walt Whitman's "Democratic Man," Reidunn's rigorous training at a music school in Chicago, Lars sent to Turkey as a journalist and held captive, the hard work and hard blizzards of homesteading in the Midwest, the founding of a small school that eventually becomes St. Olaf College, seminary training, founding new congregations on the Dakota plains, all amid the endless prairie wind that Midwesterners profess to hate but secretly love.

The Kingdom of The Rings speaks to me, because its story is the story of my family. My great-grandfather, Amund Eidsmoe, left Norway in 1852 and settled in Wisconsin. One of his sons, Chris Eidsmoe (my grandfather), homesteaded in South Dakota. One of his sons, Russell Eidsmoe (my father), taught in various schools and colleges in South Dakota and Iowa.

With my very limited Norwegian, I enjoy the letters Amund wrote from Wisconsin to Chris in South Dakota. Like Amund, Chris pursued various endeavors including construction, but throughout his life farming was his mainstay. He raised his children to be loyal, patriotic Americans. Dad spoke very little Norwegian, but he was always proud of his Norwegian heritage, and as a child in Sioux City I remember trips to South Dakota for church smorgasbords.

First and second generation immigrants from Norway were primarily concerned with making a living for their families and making sure their children were thoroughly Americanized so they could "make it" in this new kingdom. But once they had "made it," many of the third generation began to realize the richness of the Norwegian heritage they had left behind. As he gave so much of his life to public education, Dad believed he was serving the kingdom, but in his later years he became increasingly concerned that the public schools no longer taught the Christian values he believed in.

Of all the characters in *The Kingdom of The Rings*, I most identify with Arne Filkesager, the St. Olaf College professor who worried that the American "melting pot" was destroying the identity of Norse and other immigrants. I was a St. Olaf student, graduating in 1967. I loved St. Olaf, and I still love St. Olaf. But I saw then, and have seen even more since I graduated, that the struggle for Norwegian Lutherans was not only competing with other religions, denominations, and belief-systems, but also with the secular transformation of Lutheranism itself. I love my Church, I love America, and I love my Norse heritage. Putting them all together, and holding them together, is a lifelong challenge.

But *The Kingdom of The Rings* is not just for and about Norwegians,

Lutherans, and immigrants to America. All of us are the descendents of immigrants—even Native Americans, although their American ancestors go back thousands of years. Lindberg's book speaks to all who come to a new land and want to fit in to their new culture without abandoning their heritage, who try to distinguish between culture which is relative and faith which is not negotiable. And as we work to establish the kingdom in a strange land, may we remember that it is only a foretaste of the Kingdom which is to come.

And may we say with Reidunn, "Soon! The Kingdom is coming… soon!"

The Hopperstad Stave Church
(replica, 12th century church at Vik, Norway),
The Hjemkomst Center, Moorhead, Minnesota

King Olav II at Gudbrandsdal,
destroying the statue of the Norse god, Thor, ca. 1020

What Is a Saga?

A Word From the Author

As a student of American history and culture, it has been my desire to write a historical narrative in the style of the medieval saga. My focus in this effort has been to give expression to the hopes and dreams, the sacrifice, and faith of the millions of ordinary people who left their ancestral lands, carried forward by the tidal wave of European immigration to North American shores in the eighteenth, nineteenth, and twentieth centuries.

In writing this story, I have attempted to utilize the form of the ancient Icelandic saga. The word saga is difficult to translate, although words like story, tale, or history are approximations, or, perhaps even a combination of these three words would come closer to an English equivalent. This book is written as a "type of saga" to retain the flavor of the ancient Vikings and the culture of Norway... with some twenty-first-century adaptations for easier assimilation by readers.

According to Dr. Robert Kellogg in his "Introduction" to *The Complete Sagas of Icelanders* by Vidar Hreinsson, the "saga form" is characterized as follows:

> "The sagas... are... fictionalized accounts of events that took place during the time of the Vikings... from 874 to the year 1000.... They were written mainly in the thirteenth and fourteenth centuries.... All of the sagas in this collection are historical fictions of this type, the form known in Iceland as *'Islendinga sogur'* (sagas of the Icelanders)."

Professor Kellogg speaks of the saga as a blending of myth and historical tradition, which, he points out, is typical of the (saga) genre. In this story, *The Kingdom of The Rings*, I have employed both myth and historical tradition in keeping with the "saga form." Also in keeping with this genre, I have told the story from the standpoint of an omniscient narrator. Other elements of the "saga form" which I have employed in telling this story include minimal descriptions (if any at all) of persons and geographic places, and the use of numbering those paragraphs which constitute a shift in the story, and, in this book, are an indication of the location of the Rings. Furthermore, like *The Complete Sagas of Icelanders*, this story is not about kings and princes, presidents and powerful people, but about ordinary people and their day-to-day lives.

My attempt in using the saga-form is to combine historic and legendary figures and events in a modern heroic narrative which focuses on the lives and works of everyday people. These, like the mythical heroes of the past, represent the dynamic and spiritual forces which have formed and shaped this nation. They are our true "heroes."

I believe that the immigrants, inspired by their faith, were prepared to be Americans. Therefore, it has been my intention to portray America's connection with its roots in Europe and the Middle East by utilizing a religious metaphor. "*The Kingdom of The Rings*" suggests the dynamic influence of Christian hope in the lives of those who plowed the soil, established homes, schools, churches, and built the cities of our land.

As representative of those "heroes" who have sacrificed blood, sweat, and tears in reaching for their "American Dream," I have focused on emigrants from Norway. Approximately 850,000 Norwegians immigrated to North America between 1825 and 1925! They have contributed to many aspects of American life. Hence, in their victories and defeats, their commitment to hard work, education, rugged individualism, and a moral view of life, they bear the imprint of those forces which have molded America. They are, as it were, suggestive of the diverse elements in the "field" of American culture.

Whereas the characters and the story line are fictional, I have attempted to remain faithful to the historical record. Therefore, the story interfaces with actual events and historic characters from the thirteenth century through World War I.

The fictional aspect of the title of this narrative, *The Kingdom of the Rings,* is developed from the idea that three interlocking golden rings were a part of the Magi's gift of gold to the Christ Child.

The metaphor of the "Rings" is also drawn from the two regions of Norway from which the leading characters emigrate—Ringerike ("Kingdom of the Rings") and Ringsaker ("Field of Rings"). Hence, also, the metaphor of the three interlocking rings is a symbol of the Trinity—The Triune God—the Father, the Son, and the Holy Spirit.

By focusing on the Rings, I have emphasized the pervasive influence of Christian eschatological hope. This belief in "*The Kingdom of The Rings*" as expressed by the characters in the narrative is Christianity's "Second Coming of Christ," the "First Coming" having been at Bethlehem. This is the fulfillment of God's plan for mankind and all creation, as described in the New Testament Book of Revelation. This belief has had a powerful influence on the individual "heroes" who have shaped the "American Experience."

Welcome to an exciting adventure as we trace the journeys of the three interlocking golden rings through the changes and upheavals of seven centuries of Western history and the struggles of our immigrant ancestors, as we move inevitably toward the fulfillment of "The Kingdom of The Rings."

Duane R. Lindberg
July 29, 2014
The Anniversary of St. Olaf's death
in the Battle of Stiklestad,
the key event which won Norway
for the Christian faith.

The Historical Context of the Saga

AD 995–1000 – King Olaf I Tryggvesson attempts the conversion of Norway to Christianity.

1000 – Leif Eriksson discovers North America (Vinland).

1030 – King Olaf II Haraldsson of Norway is killed in the battle at Stiklestad. The conversion of Norway is advanced. Olaf is proclaimed a Christian martyr and canonized as a Saint of both the Western and Eastern Churches.

CA. 1050–1536 – The "Pilgrims' Way" to the Healing Spring at St. Olaf's grave in the Nidaros Cathedral, Trondheim, Norway was one of the four major pilgrim sites in Europe and the Mid-East.

1066 – Norman Conquest of England.

1099 – Crusaders capture Jerusalem.

1239–1263 – The expansion of the Kingdom of Norway during the reign of Haakon IV to include Iceland, Greenland, northern Scotland, Hebrides, Orkneys, Shetlands, and Isle of Man in the Irish Sea.

1248–1254 – The Seventh Crusade ("the last Crusade").

1267–1268 – The Siege of the Crusader Kingdom of Antioch by the Mameluke (Egyptian) Muslims.

1268 – Antioch falls to the Muslims.

1349–1350 – Outbreak of the Black Death in northern Europe.

1397 – Treaty of Kalmar uniting Norway, Denmark, and Sweden.

1453 – The Byzantine Emperor, Constantine XI calls for military reinforcements from Christian nations to help in the defense of Constantinople. The Emperor is killed in battle and the Muslims capture Constantinople.

1492 – Christopher Columbus discovers the West Indies and claims it for Spain.

1517 – Martin Luther posts the 95 Theses – The Reformation begins.

1529 – Muslim Turks attack Vienna, Austria, but they are defeated and turned back from central Europe.

1530 – The Lutheran princes of the Holy Roman Empire submit a statement of their beliefs supporting Martin Luther and his stand on Scripture to the Catholic Emperor Charles V at the Imperial Diet at Augsburg, Germany.

1536 – The King of Denmark / Norway / Sweden accepts the Lutheran Reformation and imposes it upon the people of his Realm. Norway is forced to submit to Danish domination in all aspects of national life: religious, social, economic, political.

1563–1570 – Northern Seven Years War between Denmark/Norway, and Sweden.

1618–1648—The Thirty Years War.

1648—The Peace of Westphalia (Prussia) determines the boundaries of Protestant and Roman Catholic areas in Europe.

1731—The Salzburgers are forced to flee from Austria and are invited by James Oglethorpe to settle in the newly established colony of Georgia.

1796—Hans Nielsen Hauge begins his preaching ministry in Norway, which flowers in a National Religious Revival.

1792–1814—The Napoleonic Wars in which Denmark-Norway was an ally of France.

1814—The Norwegian people write their Constitution, elect a King, and declare their independence from Denmark, but the European powers force Norway to accept a union with Sweden.

1825—The beginning of formal emigration from Norway to the United States.

1860–1865—The American Civil War (The War Between the States).

1862—"The Sioux Uprising" massacre of settlers in Minnesota.

1862—President Lincoln signs the "Homestead Act," offering free land to settlers.

1871—The "Great Fire" in Chicago.

1874—Founding of St. Olaf's School (College).

1893—Chicago World's Fair.

1898—Spanish/American War begins.

1901—Theodore Roosevelt becomes 26th President.

1905—Russo-Japanese War.

1905—Swedish-Norwegian Union ends without war.

1914—Archduke Francis Ferdinand of Austria assassinated.

1914—The First World War begins.

1914—Ottoman Empire (Turkey) allies with Germany and Austria-Hungary.

1915–1923—The Armenian Holocaust (genocide).

4-6-1917—The United States declares war on Germany.

11-11-1918—Armistice signed by Germany ending WWI.

4-1920—French Mandate over Syria/Lebanon.

8-10-1920—Treaty of Sevres cedes five provinces in eastern Turkey to the new Republic of Armenia.

9-1920—Turkish Nationalists attack and destroy the new Armenian Republic.

9-1920—French establish the state of Lebanon.

7-1925–27—Muslim uprising in Syria.

[Please Note: On pages 194–196, there is a "List of Historical Persons" who appear in each Part of the book, and on pages 198–200, there is a "Glossary of Religious and Theological Terms Used in the Saga."]

The Kingdom of The Rings

"Opening their treasures, they offered him gifts,
gold and frankincense and myrrh."
(Matthew 2:11)

Prelude

The boy stood, head bowed, beside the open grave. A brisk prairie wind dried his tears but left trails on his cheeks. When he heard the first spade-full of earth thump against the coffin, he squeezed his fist around the golden Ring which *Far* (father) had given him the day before he died.

> *Far* had told him the story of the Rings, a tale from thirteenth-century Norway. It was at the time when pilgrims from Europe and the Middle East followed the "Pilgrims' Way" (*pilegrimsleden*), to the "healing spring" at St. Olaf's grave in the Nidaros Cathedral at Trondheim. . . .

But *where* did the tale of the three interlocking golden Rings begin? *How* did the golden Rings get caught up in the great European migration of the nineteenth century? How did they find their way first to the "Land of the Midnight Sun" and then to the new "Promised Land" of America? What is the "Coptic Secret" which was hidden for centuries and was finally revealed in the light and shadows of the "City on the Hill?"

> *To find the answers to these questions, we must allow our minds to turn back to the beginning of the Christian era—to the time of the birth of the Christ Child. . . .*

When the Holy Family fled to Egypt to escape Herod's murderous wrath, they fled with the Magi's gifts. These included a chest of gold pieces among which were three interlocking golden rings. These "Gifts of the Magi" sustained the Holy Family during their sojourn in Egypt; so, the Treasure of Gold, including the Rings, remained in Alexandria. It was entrusted to the guardianship of a Jewish family who looked forward to the coming Messiah.

Tradition tells us that these gifts were later gathered up by Jesus' followers after his Resurrection.

It was St. Mark, the Evangelist, who brought the Gospel to Egypt, where many were won for Christ. Egyptian Christians (the Coptic Christian Church) revered St. Mark and often named their children and their churches in his honor.

St. Mark's Cathedral in Alexandria, Egypt eventually became the resting place for the Magi's gifts to the Christ Child. The three interlocking golden rings, symbolic of the Three Persons of the Godhead, pointed the faithful to the fulfillment of that Kingdom which is not of this world—The Kingdom of the Rings.

St. Mark's Cathedral, Alexandria, Egypt
Coptic Easter Ceremony

During the ensuing centuries, the Coptic leaders of Alexandria kept the golden rings in hiding. However, they were bold to share the saving message of the Rings—the good news of the presence and redeeming love of the Triune God—the Father, Son, and Holy Spirit. Many unbelievers were converted and many Christians were encouraged to faithful worship and service in the name of the Triune God.

So it was that the Rings remained the "Coptic Secret" until the time of the later Crusades in the thirteenth century.

And, thus, our Saga begins....

PART ONE

Alexandria, Egypt
to
"The Realm of St. Olaf,"
Norway

Thirteenth Century AD

Detail, Painting by Jean Victor Snetz, 1841; Bridgeman Art Gallery/London

Crusaders answer the Call to be Cross-Bearers.

"If any man would come after Me,
let him deny himself and take up his cross and follow Me."
(Matthew 16:24)

The Saga of The Rings

"Therefore, the Lord himself will give a sign."
(Isaiah 7:14)

1 In the year of our Lord 1267, the Mamelukes (the Muslim rulers of Egypt) were persecuting Coptic Christians and were also warring against the Crusader Kingdoms in Syria. In this unsettled and dangerous time, the Coptic Patriarch of Egypt sought his friend, an Alexandrian merchant, to carry the special treasure of the Alexandrian Church in person to the Syrian Orthodox Bishop in the besieged city of Antioch.

Marcarius of Alexandria, the scion of a wealthy and prominent Coptic Christian family, was preparing to sail with one of his merchant vessels to the nearby port of Tripolis. His "announced intention" was to unload his cargo and then to accompany his ship back to Acre and home to Alexandria.

However, his "secret plan" was to leave his ship and travel overland to Antioch, pass himself off as a soldier in the Egyptian Army, and smuggle himself through the Muslim lines into the beleaguered city.

This treasure from St. Mark's Cathedral in Alexandria was in a small chest, which tradition claimed contained the gold that the Magi brought to the Christ Child. It was believed to have been carried by the Holy Family to Egypt.

The Patriarch's instructions were to place this sacred treasure on the Altar of the Syrian Orthodox Church in Antioch as a reminder of Christ's presence and a source of encouragement to the Christians who were defending their city against the onslaught of the Muslim army.

The secret message, written in the Bohairic dialect of the ancient Egyptian language, was to be delivered to Bohemund VI, ruler of the Crusader Kingdom of Antioch, and translated for him by Marcarius.

2 The journey began in the early morning under a foreboding red sky. A Muslim customs officer cleared the ship after Marcarius paid the prescribed duty on his merchandise. The passage was uneventful and the cargo was unloaded without incident.

As the ship prepared to leave Tripolis, a passenger disembarked. He was carrying his personal belongings and a leather saddlebag, and he soon melted into the crowd. Since the Muslim recapture of Tripolis, no one paid special attention to a horseman who rode out from the city's defenses under the Muslim flag of Baybars I, King of Egypt.

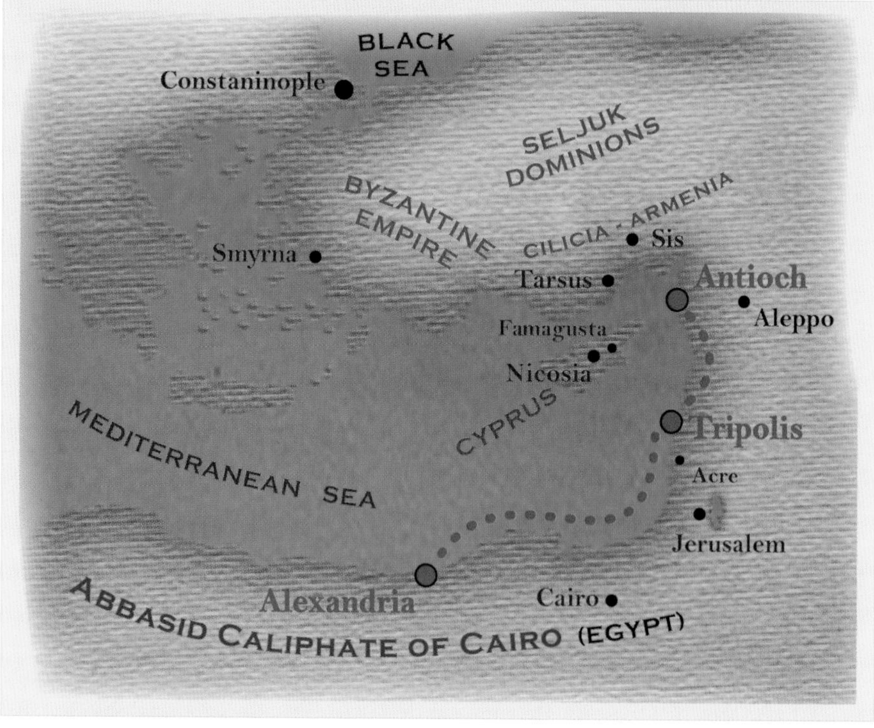

The Journey of Marcarius from Alexandria to Antioch

Marcarius stole through the battle lines and was welcomed by the Defenders. He accomplished his two-fold mission. He delivered the Patriarch's secret message to the Crusader King, Bohemund, who was defending the city.

Marcarius offered his services as a soldier. The Crusader King welcomed him and set him in charge of the defense of the West Gate. He fought bravely and led the effective repulse of many Muslim forays.

The word passed quickly that someone had smuggled the "Sacred Treasure of Alexandria" into the city and that it was secured within the sanctuary of the Orthodox Church. This good news renewed the spirit of the Defenders. They were emboldened to fight on for several months, in spite of being vastly outnumbered by the Muslim forces.

3 But Marcarius had a special reason of his own for coming to Antioch. Only the Patriarch knew Marcarius' full intention. Still, the regular run of a merchant ship was the perfect cover for this special mission. He had heard that the Fayumic family, who escaped the Muslim persecution of the Coptic Church, had fled to the protection of the Crusader Kingdom at Antioch.

Their daughter, Rachel, was also among the Coptic refugees. He had been in love with her from the first time they met. To Marcarius, she was beautiful, like Rachel of old. But they had not seen each other for three years, since the new Muslim pogrom against the Coptic Christian Church had begun.

Rachel's uncle, a Coptic Bishop in Alexandria, had been beheaded for sharing the Gospel and converting a Muslim to the Christian faith. The family had fled in the night and Marcarius had not seen her again.

In Antioch, Marcarius searched among the hastily built hovels of the refugees who had fled the Muslim attackers. Many lepers lived in the dusty squalor of this war ravaged city, but these were isolated in separate camps. Marcarius kept away.

Then, after many days of searching, he found the Fayumic family. They were overjoyed to see him. But he did not see Rachel, and no one spoke of her.

> Finally, in response to his inquiry, her father broke the tragic news to him, "Rachel is a leper! She was exposed to the disease as she helped the poor refugees who were flooding into the city. Rachel is in the leper encampment. No one can touch her!"
>
> "But can't I…see…just see her, even from a distance?" pleaded Marcarius.
>
> "I'm sorry," her father responded, "but Rachel won't see anyone. The disease has disfigured her face and she will allow no one to see her."

4 But Marcarius was determined to find her. The gate keeper at the leper camp refused to allow him entrance. He returned daily and left written messages for Rachel to come to the camp entrance to meet him, but she never came.

The only message from inside this forbidden world was a note from her which read: "My dearest Marcarius, because I love you, I will never see you. You must remember me as I was. This is my grave. *Kyrie eleison!* (Lord have mercy!)"

Marcarius was crushed, but he continued to return daily to the gate of the leper compound and left written notes for her. His final message written to her before the Muslim devastation of the city was:

> "My beloved Rachel, the bride of my heart, I shall always love you. And I know that we shall meet again in Christ's Eternal Kingdom —The Kingdom of The Rings."

The Mystery Revealed

"To them whom God chose
to make known the glory of this mystery."
(Colossians 1:27)

Several months later, when the Muslim forces broke through the Crusader defenses, terror reigned in the city. Pillage, rape, murder—shameless atrocities were inflicted on the populace. It is reported by historians that the sultan's army murdered 17,000 inhabitants and took 100,000 captives. As he learned of these atrocities, Marcarius was reminded that the Muslims again proved themselves to be even crueler than the Crusaders who captured Jerusalem in AD 1099.

The tragic difference, Marcarius thought to himself, is *not* that either the Muslims or Christians are the greater sinners. It is rather that payback is *not permitted* to Christians, but is *required* of Muslims.

Marcarius recalled that Christian Scripture declares:

> *"Beloved, never avenge yourselves, but leave it to the wrath of God; for it is written, 'Vengeance is mine, I will repay, says the Lord.'"* (Romans 12:19)

He knew all too well the teaching of the Muslim *Quran*, which commands payback and revenge, as in Sura 2:194:

> "A sacred month for a sacred month: sacred things, too, are subject to retaliation. If anyone attacks you, attack him as he attacked you."

Marcarius reflected that it seemed history was destined to repeat the bloody atrocities of the past so long as men can justify a spirit of revenge and retribution. It was obvious to him that neither Muslims nor Christians can achieve righteousness by their own efforts.

"Yes!" he exclaimed aloud with passion. Then Marcarius

became quiet once again. It was certain to him that *both* groups needed the message of The Rings—the "Good News" of the forgiveness and redemption, which Christ has won for *all* people...on the Cross.

5 Before the city fell in 1268, the Syrian Orthodox Bishop returned the "Treasure of the Magi" to Marcarius and bade him to carry it to safety in Cyprus. The Bishop instructed him to distribute the golden bounty among others in thankfulness for gifts of grace, which reflect the spirit of Christ Himself. Then the Defenders smuggled Marcarius out of the city with the "Treasure" and a letter of safe passage to Hugh III, the Crusader King of Cyprus.

6 Only then, in the safety of Cyprus and the castle of Hugh III, did Marcarius risk asking a priest to unbind the Treasure Chest of the Magi. He was awe-struck as the priest opened the Treasure—the golden pieces glistened in a beam of sunlight! The gold was formed in many different shapes and sizes, but prominent among them were Three Interlocking Golden Rings.

On the first was inscribed, in the ancient Persian language, the word, "AHURO," on the second the letters spelled, "ASHEM," and on the third was the word, "MAZDAO."

Marcarius remembered that the Coptic Patriarch in Alexandra had explained the secret of the Rings. The words were intended to be used together.

"The first Ring inscribed with the word, AHURO, is interpreted to mean *God,* or, *Lord of All,*" the Coptic Patriarch had told him.

"The second, ASHEM," he had continued, "is translated *Truth,* or, *The Incarnation of Truth.*

"And the third, MAZDAO," he concluded, "means *Wisdom,* or, *Spirit of Wisdom.*"

Marcarius explained these meanings to the priest in Cyprus and was flooded with wonderment.

He added, "How significant it is that these symbols were offered at the feet of the Christ Child! For He is The All-Wise

> God, The Lord of All, The Incarnation of Truth, and The Spirit of Wisdom!"

In response, the priest shared with him that the other gold pieces in the Treasure of the Magi were inscribed with other Persian inscriptions.

> "These can be translated as *Love, Goodness, Holiness, and Reverence*," he said. "Each is appropriate as a gift of *homage* to the King of Kings and Lord of Lords... the Christ!"

It was clear that the priest was in awe of the Treasure.

Marcarius went on to tell him that the instructions from the Syrian Orthodox Bishop were that the golden pieces of the "Magi's Treasure" could be given only as offerings of *thanksgiving* or as gifts of *grace*—freely given and undeserved—reflecting the Spirit of Christ.

Marcarius wanted to return the Treasure to Alexandria but he knew that he could not go home. The Muslim authorities would steal the Treasure, and also execute *him* as a traitor for his part in the defense of Antioch against the Muslim army.

7 Shortly after he arrived at the Crusader Court on Cyprus, a servant observed that Marcarius had a patch of very white skin on his otherwise tan countenance. At first he paid no attention to this spot but, soon, it became deathly pale and without feeling.

His worst fears were confirmed when a priest identified the condition as the first signs of leprosy. Leprosy! The word itself struck terror in the hearts of people of the thirteenth century! There was no known cure. Medicine was helpless to heal. The only hope was a miraculous healing from God Himself.

Statue of King Olaf II, Stiklestad, Norway

3

The Advent of The Rings in the Realm of St. Olaf

"Bless the Lord . . . who forgives all your iniquity,
who heals all your diseases." (Psalm 103:1, 3)

The Norman knights at the court of Hugh III heard of Marcarius' tragic fate and sought to console him. They told him of pilgrims who reported healings from leprosy at a "healing spring" which flowed from the grave of St. Olaf, Norway's Eternal King. This healing spring flowing from the martyred King's grave was now enshrined within a magnificent Cathedral.

The Cathedral at Nidaros and the spring which flowed from St. Olaf's grave were the goal of thousands of pilgrims who came from Europe and the Near East. Many Crusaders followed the "Pilgrims' Way" (*pilegrimsleden*), to receive the assurance of forgiveness or healing from wounds and illness.

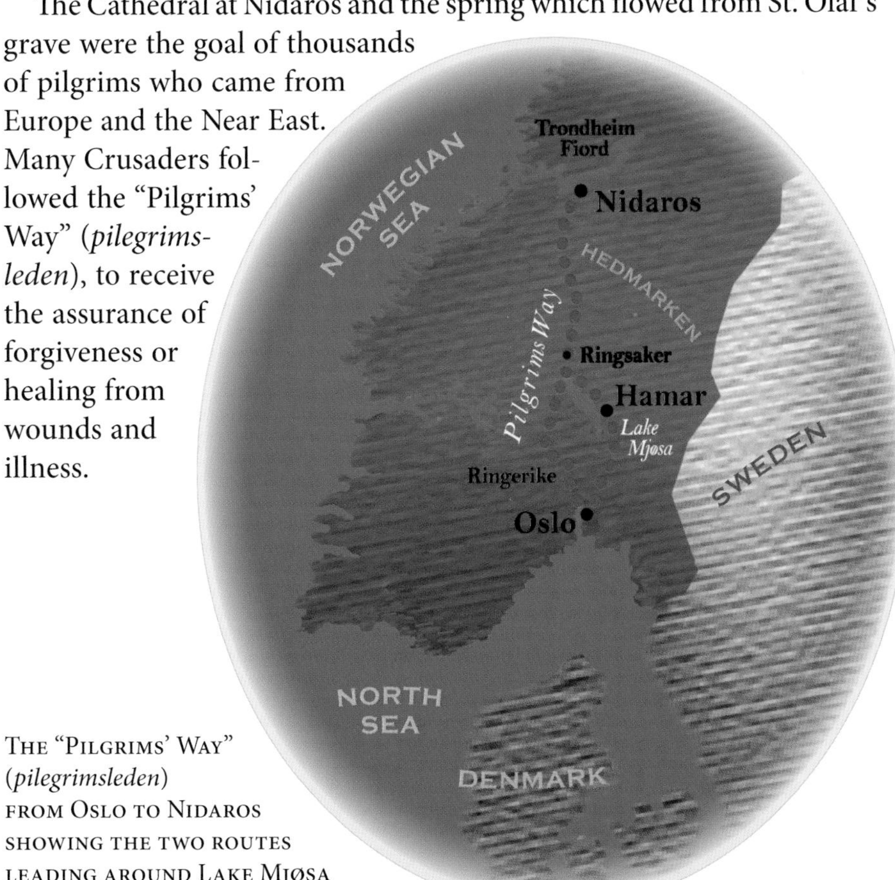

The "Pilgrims' Way" (*pilegrimsleden*) from Oslo to Nidaros showing the two routes leading around Lake Mjøsa

Marcarius was determined to join the pilgrimage to Nidaros in the spring of AD 1269. Because of his valiant service in the defense of Antioch, Hugh III offered Marcarius separate passage on one of his ships returning to Normandy in the spring.

8 As an expression of thanksgiving for his kindness, Marcarius asked the King's goldsmith to separate the Rings, and he gave King Hugh III the Second Golden Ring, which bore the inscription, "ASHEM" (*Truth*, or, *The Incarnation of Truth*).

9 From Normandy, Marcarius joined the pilgrimage to Nidaros. When the ship docked in the Oslo harbor, only one word was announced from the bow: "*Lepers!*" People scattered and vacated the quay. Only a Cistercian Monk remained to greet them. He spoke in French.

With a kindly voice he welcomed them. "Please follow me to Akers Church. There you will receive help for your journey to Nidaros." He continued. "Because people fear leprosy, you can't enter the Church, but you may receive the Holy Sacrament through a small window in the chancel wall."

Marcarius and the others welcomed the opportunity to receive the Sacrament and thanked the monk for securing supplies and horses, rules concerning lepers, and guidance concerning the Pilgrims' Way.

The route wound its way through Hamar and Ringsaker, the Gudbrandsdal Valley, and over the Dovre Mountains to Nidaros—to the Cathedral built over the burial place of Norway's sainted, martyr King, Olaf II, and to the healing spring which issued from his grave.

In fine weather, the pilgrimage from Oslo to Nidaros required 29 days, but in the spring of 1269, the late snows and heavy rains made this a difficult thirty-nine-day journey. Because of inclement weather, Marcarius needed to rest several days at the Ringsaker rectory.

Norwegian Directorate for Cultural Heritage Monument no. 85297

The Ringsaker Church

The priest at the Ringsaker Church was a very caring and compassionate man. He offered help to every pilgrim, regardless of station in life. He was, for those to whom he ministered, the very embodiment of Jesus himself.

10 So it was that Marcarius gave the First Golden Ring from the "Magi's Treasure" to the Ringsaker Church. He had met God here through the unselfish caring love of the Ringsaker priest. The word inscribed on this Ring was "AHURO" (*God*, or, *Lord of All*).

11 Marcarius' journey continued up the Gudbrandsdal Valley and across the Dovre Mountains. It was on June 6, 1269, that the group sighted the tall spire of St. Olaf's Church (Nidaros).

With tears they knelt to pray and give thanks to God for bringing them to this place of cleansing and healing.

The Nidaros Cathedral

Marcarius and the others then entered the city and found the area reserved for lepers. It would be several days before they and other lepers would be allowed to come near the well on the west side of the Cathedral's chancel. Here the healing waters were dipped up to sprinkle on their grievous sores and rotting flesh.

The time came for Marcarius to come forward to be sprinkled and to receive the prayers and the blessing. The priest seemed to be a very kindly man, but tired from many hours at the "well" and at his prayers.

Marcarius believed that the Lord could heal... even leprosy. Yet he also knew that, although there were testimonies of miraculous healings, not everyone who came was cured.

When the priest had completed the washing and made the sign of the Cross over him, Marcarius did not feel any physical change. But he continued to trust the words he had heard read by the priest:

> *"Confess your sins to one another and pray for one another that you may be healed. The prayer of a righteous man has great power in its effects."* (James 5:16)

He rose up from The Prayers and began his journey back on the Pilgrims' Way.

12 Then... it *happened*!

As he stopped at the Hamar Cathedral and knelt outside, near the "Lepers Window," he experienced a miracle. During the Mass, as he received the Body of Christ, he felt a surge of power within him. He lifted his hand and touched fresh, healthy skin on his face.

He was healed!

13 In thankfulness for the healing power of the Holy Spirit and the gift of the wisdom and knowledge of God, Marcarius offered the Third Golden Ring from the Magi's Treasure at the Hamar Cathedral. The word inscribed on this Ring was "MAZDAO" (*Wisdom*, or, *Spirit of Wisdom*).

THE FILKESAGER FARM IN RINGSAKER, HEDMARKEN, NORWAY

Under the large tree in the center, one can see the grave mound of an ancient king of Ringsaker, while the hills on the other side of Lake Mjøsa can be seen to the left.

4

The Rings of Hedmarken

"Hide Thy face from my sins, and blot out all my iniquities."
(Psalm 51:9)

The Rings of the Magi became the objects of veneration and the focus of penitential desires for many pilgrims who followed the *pilegrimsleden* (the Pilgrims' Way) to St. Olaf's Well at Nidaros.

Each Church kept its venerated Ring in the tabernacle on the altar with the consecrated host. As the faithful and the penitent stopped at the Bishop's Church at Hamar or the *Sokneprests* (Head Pastor) Church at Ringsaker, relics, including the Rings, could be viewed, confession made, the Rosary recited, and an offering given for the poor.

At Christmas, the two Rings would be displayed together in an ornate chest and carried in the Christmas pageants, first at the Hamar Cathedral and then at the Ringsaker Church. The bearers were "Wise Men" selected for this honor.

14 On one such occasion, in AD 1315, the King himself (Haakon V) was on his way from his castle at Stein to visit his daughter, Agnes, married to Knight Jorgen of Bye. He stopped to attend the Christmas Mass at Ringsaker Church and was asked to carry the Rings in the Christmas Pageant.

The King went on to celebrate the Christmas Feast at Bye. There the King's daughter accompanied the telling of the Nativity account and the coming of the Magi by playing beautiful music on her harp.

Throughout Ringsaker, in more humble homes where there was no harp music, the beautiful strains of children's voices singing the "Angelus" accompanied the retelling of the Nativity Story and the story of the Magi's Gifts. Grandparents told of the Egyptian Crusader who gave the Rings as offerings of *thanksgiving* to God for the Christ-like kindness which he had been shown on the Pilgrims' Way, and for the miracle of his healing from leprosy.

King Haakon V was very solicitous toward the churches of the Pilgrims' Way, and he had a genuine compassion for the pilgrims. The

King opened the Guild Hall at his castle, *Kongsgård*, to provide a resting place with food and lodging for the pilgrims. The Pilgrims' Way to Nidaros Cathedral was one of Europe's most traveled pilgrim routes during the age of Norway's greatness—the twelfth and thirteenth centuries.

15 However, this time of power and influence came to a sudden, tragic end in 1349. The terrible "Plague" or "Black Death" ravaged Europe, killing one-half to two-thirds of the population!

Norway was most grievously affected, where it is estimated that in parts of the country nearly *three-fourths* of the people died! In some areas there were few left to bury the dead or cultivate the fields.

In the Nidaros diocese, there were only 40 priests remaining, compared to 300 before the Plague. Bishop Jakob of Hamar was stricken with the Plague, but before he died, he confided the "Saga of The Rings" to one of the Canons, Olav of Ringsaker. He was the only clergy in his area to survive the Plague!

16 Olav entered this account in the parish registry on October 13, 1349:

> "Pilgrims and local people are crowding into the Hamar Cathedral and the Ringsaker Church to touch the golden Rings to receive assurance of forgiveness before they die. For all expect to be taken soon. This is the End of the World! God help us!"

But the *eschaton* (The End of the World and The Second Coming of Christ) did not happen, and in the continuing times of sorrow and joy, the two Rings were venerated by pilgrims and cherished by the churches in that region of Norway called the "Field of Rings" (Ringsaker).

Part Two

The Scattering
of
The Rings

Fourteenth, Fifteenth, and Sixteenth Centuries AD

The Ruins of the Hamar Cathedral

5

The Field of Turmoil and Truth

"When you hear of wars and rumors of wars . . . this must take place, but the end is not yet." (Mark 13:7)

It was spring in the year of our Lord 1536. Ominous rumblings had been rolling up from the south from Germany and from Denmark. Officials were uneasy.

17 The most prominent person in Norway at this time was the Catholic Archbishop of Trondheim (Nidaros), His Eminence Olav Engelbrektson.

His ecclesiastical domain was extensive, but had diminished since the height of Norway's power in the thirteenth century. At that time, the "See of Trondheim" (Kingdom of Norway) had included all of Norway and parts of Sweden, extended across the North Sea and the Atlantic Ocean, to the Isle of Man in the Irish Sea, to the northern counties of Scotland and the Scottish Isles, then, to Iceland, Greenland, and beyond to Vinland, the Viking name for North America.

However, as a result of the ravages of the Black Death and the vicissitudes of war, the See of Trondheim was greatly weakened. Still, the Archbishop had his own small army and fortress and was readying this force to meet the threat from Denmark. He sent a *Budstikke* (message) to all his Bishops to warn of this impending danger.

18 But the new Dano-Norwegian King, Frederick I, had moved quickly. After the Norwegian Council had elected Christian II as King of Norway in 1531, Frederick violated his own "safe conduct" pledge and ordered his troops to capture Christian II. He was brought in chains to Copenhagen and locked in the castle dungeons for the next twenty-six years. In his message, the Archbishop had warned:

> "The Danish King will not rest until he has subjugated Norway and instituted the Reformation throughout the Kingdom. This means removal of all Bishops and the seizing of church property. This is more than *reformation*. It is political revolution!"

The Expansion of the "Kingdom of Norway"
during the Reign of Haakon IV 1239–1263
included Iceland, Greenland, *Vinland*,

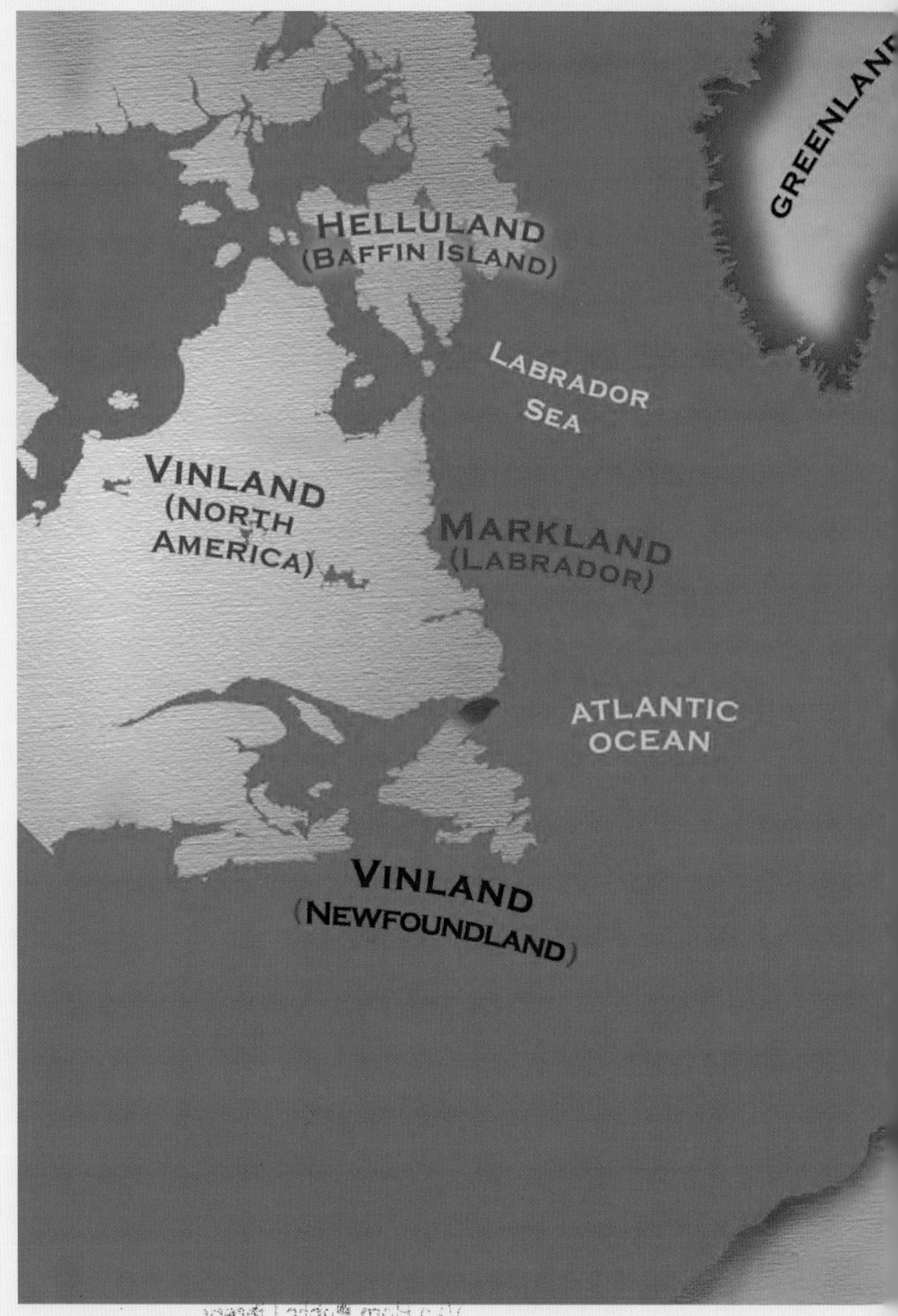

NORTHERN SCOTLAND, THE HEBRIDES, ORKNEYS, AND SHETLANDS, AND THE ISLE OF MAN IN THE IRISH SEA
(NOTE: Red dots indicate the *pilegrimsleden*.)

In the ensuing months, the Archbishop's small force disbanded and he fled into exile. The Danish army captured Trondheim, despoiled the Cathedral, removed St. Olaf's bones from the silver coffin under the high altar, and stole all the gold and silver with the intent of shipping it to Copenhagen.

19 However, when the ship, laden with booty, sailed into the Trondheim Fjord, a violent storm arose and sank the ship. Many believed that by Divine intervention, justice was done.

The violence continued to be carried out by the Danish forces throughout Norway against the existing churches. Bishops were driven out or imprisoned. Ecclesiastical lands were confiscated in the name of the "King of Denmark and Norway." There was much destruction of church property. Even where the churches were left intact, the Danish forces removed the gold and silver to enrich the treasury of the King.

But before the Danes came to the Ringsaker Church, the priest, Arnstein Johnson av Filkesager, hid the golden Ring. He placated the invaders' hunger for treasure by offering them the silver baptismal bowl and the silver candelabra.

20 So the First Ring of the Magi was hidden by the Filkesager family.

Arnstein became a Lutheran pastor, married, and entrusted the Ring to his eldest son, to be preserved in a secret hiding place known only to him. Thus the story of the Rings was passed on from generation to generation, but the *hiding place* of the First Golden Ring with the inscription, "AHURO" (*God*, or, *Lord of All*), was known only to the eldest son of the Filkesager family and his heir.

21 The tale of the Third Ring bearing the word, "MAZDAO" (*Wisdom*, or, *Spirit of Wisdom*), was even more dramatic. It was in May 1567, during the "Northern Seven Years War" between the Kingdom of Denmark-Norway and Sweden (1563–1570), when Harald, the Sexton of the Hamar Cathedral, heard some unsettling news. The Cathedral pastor announced:

> "The Swedish force was defeated at Oslo and is retreating. However, as the Swedes retreat, they are destroying towns,

> churches, and farms. Hurry! Hide The Ring and the sacramental vessels!"

Soon, Harald saw the smoke and heard the cannons as the Swedes attacked the City of Hamar. He ran to warn the Superintendent (Bishop) and his family of the danger. There was nothing to do but to flee by boat across Lake Mjøsa. The Superintendent and his family barely escaped as the first mercenaries attacked the Bishop's Palace and began carrying out the silver and gold from the Cathedral chancel.

This was the largest medieval church in all eastern Norway and had been the resting place of the Third Golden Ring since the thirteenth century. It was here that the Egyptian Crusader, Marcarius, experienced healing from leprosy. He had given the Ring to the Cathedral as a *thank-offering.*

22 But before the invaders reached the altar, where the Ring was kept, Harald had already removed it from its special place. He had hidden the Ring, and did not resist as the officer stole the chalice, paten, cruet, and candelabra. All were gold or silver, so the soldier was satisfied and let the Sexton go.

Harald ran to the shore of Lake Mjøsa. Once in a boat with his family, he looked back. His eyes were filled with tears and his heart was broken when he saw flames engulf the magnificent Cathedral. The *Dom* (Cathedral) of Hamar was destroyed.

Without a church building to tend and serve, Harald, the Sexton, decided to move his family to Ringerike, near his mother's people. He thought perhaps he could help at the Bønsnes Church, for he had heard that the Sexton there had died. Thus the Third Ring began its journey to Ringerike (the ancient "Kingdom of The Rings").

However, tragedy struck when their cart slid off the road on a steep mountain side. Harald was seriously injured but lived long enough to press the golden Ring into his oldest child's hand and tell her the story of the Rings.

With his final breath he whispered:

> "Karen, treasure the secret of the Rings and pass it on to your oldest daughter. It will be a blessing to your family and to many."

23 So the Ring with the inscription "MAZDAO" (*Wisdom*, or, *Spirit of Wisdom*) came to Ringerike, and was held in trust by the oldest daughter of the Haraldson family from generation to generation. They passed on the message that this was one of three interlocking golden rings offered by the Magi to the Christ Child.

6

The Mystery of The Second Ring

"By His wounds you have been healed."
(1 Peter 2:24)

In AD 1272 Marcarius had returned to the court of the King of Cyprus after being healed at the fountain of St. Olaf. He was ready to give his life as a Bearer of the Cross (Crusader), but was confronted with sad news as he arrived at Nicosia. King Hugh III had been killed in a battle at Tarsus. The Second Ring, inscribed with the letters "ASHEM" (*Truth*, or, *The Incarnation of Truth*) was now in the possession of Hugh's successor, Amalric de Lusignan, the new Crusader King of Cyprus.

Marcarius vowed his fealty to Amalric, who was preparing to lead a Crusader force to aid an ally, Cilicia, against the army of the Muslim Mamelukes of Egypt. Marcarius served his Lord faithfully as a Cross-Bearer in the King's army and as a servant of the poor and needy whom he met in this war-ravaged land.

On special occasions he was privileged to hold the Magi's Ring and share with others the message of the Second Ring: "Jesus is God and Lord, The Incarnation of Truth, the Savior of the World." Many believed in Him because of Marcarius' witness.

24 He was killed in 1303 by Muslim raiders as he was giving aid to the sick in Tarsus, the home city of the Apostle Paul. He is remembered by many for his witness to the message of the Rings.

The close tie between the Crusader Kingdom of Cyprus and the Armenian Kingdom of Cilicia was further strengthened by intermarriage and the Armenian openness to Norman/Frankish culture. This close tie eventually led to the marriage of the Armenian Queen to Guy de Lusignan of Cyprus (the son of Amalric), who was crowned King of Armenian-Cilicia in 1343. (See map on page 6.)

25 With his ascent to the throne, the royal treasury from Cyprus came to Cilicia. So the Second Ring was brought to Sis, the capital of Armenian-Cilicia. It was the most holy treasure of the

Armenian Kings until the city was captured by the Muslims in 1375.

At this time, the King was imprisoned and his treasury confiscated by the Mameluke General Farouk. He had heard that one Golden Ring from the Magi's Gifts was among the gold pieces in the Armenian royal treasury. Although as a Muslim, he refused to believe in the divinity of Jesus, His crucifixion or resurrection, yet he was drawn by a mysterious power to reach for the Ring and hold it in his hands.

As he did, he noticed the letters inscribed in the ancient Persian alphabet, "ASHEM."

He couldn't decipher the word, so he sent for the captured King and commanded him to explain the meaning: "Though I care little about this Jesus whom you Christians worship, I am interested in languages and wondered about the meaning of this word ASHEM, which is engraved on this Ring."

Farouk threatened the King with a knife to his throat, while two guards secured his arms and legs. But little did Farouk realize that the King did not need these inducements to bear witness to the meaning of the Ring and its cryptic message. He was in fact eager to tell.

The King answered Farouk, "This Ring is one of three golden rings offered by the Magi to the Christ Child. These were originally interlocked to one another. This is the Second Ring, and the word engraved on it is interpreted Truth, or, The Incarnation of Truth. It means that Jesus is...."

The King was interrupted by Farouk's shout:

"Stop! I won't hear your heresy! Take him away!"

With this terse rebuff and a curse, Farouk commanded that the captive King be thrown back in the dungeon.

But Farouk couldn't stop his mind from dwelling on the words of the King: Three Rings were given by the Magi, and this Ring had the imprint of the Persian word meaning "*Truth*, or, *The Incarnation of Truth.*"

Almost afraid of forming the words in the quiet of his mind, Farouk connected the dots.... "Could it be," he asked himself, "that, as the Christians teach, the Prophet Jesus, is in fact the very *incarnate* presence of God—that this Jesus is The Way, The Truth, and The Life?"

This thought so disturbed Farouk that he vowed to Allah that he would not look on this Ring again. It was too dangerous. Should he throw it into the sea? Should he grind it into powder?

But would this erase the image in his mind?

Much as he tried in the ensuing days and weeks, Farouk could not forget the message of the Ring. It haunted him day and night. He could talk to no one about this Ring and this blasphemous word, "ASHEM," which kept his mind focused on the forbidden thought that Jesus is truly the Incarnate God.

Perhaps a pilgrimage to Mecca would remove this heresy from his mind? Or, should he prove his loyalty to Allah by torturing and putting to death all Christians in Sis who refused to convert to Islam? Maybe he should undertake a personal jihad, by riding with sword in hand into the Crusader ranks to kill as many of the enemy as possible and die a martyr's death?

But the General's fear was that whatever he did, it would not be enough to erase this dangerous thought from his mind! Could it be that Jesus *is* the Son of God?

Farouk kept the Ring in a secret place, hidden from his own gaze. But the power of the Ring's message did not diminish. It kept returning to his conscious mind. This forbidden thought was with him and would not be silenced.

Silence did come, eventually. It was several years later, in 1383, that news leaked out of the Muslim Kingdom of Egypt – the story was that General Farouk had been stripped of his rank and beheaded for his apostasy to Islam! He had become a Christian.

The message of the Second Ring had won him for Eternity in Christ's Kingdom.

26 Before Farouk was executed, he secretly entrusted the Second Ring and its message to one of his wives. It was Fatima who passed on the secret and the Ring to her son, and so it was passed to each generation in Alexandria.

Many became believers because of the Ring which bore the inscription, "ASHEM" (*Truth*, or, *The Incarnation of Truth*) and the Holy Spirit's work.

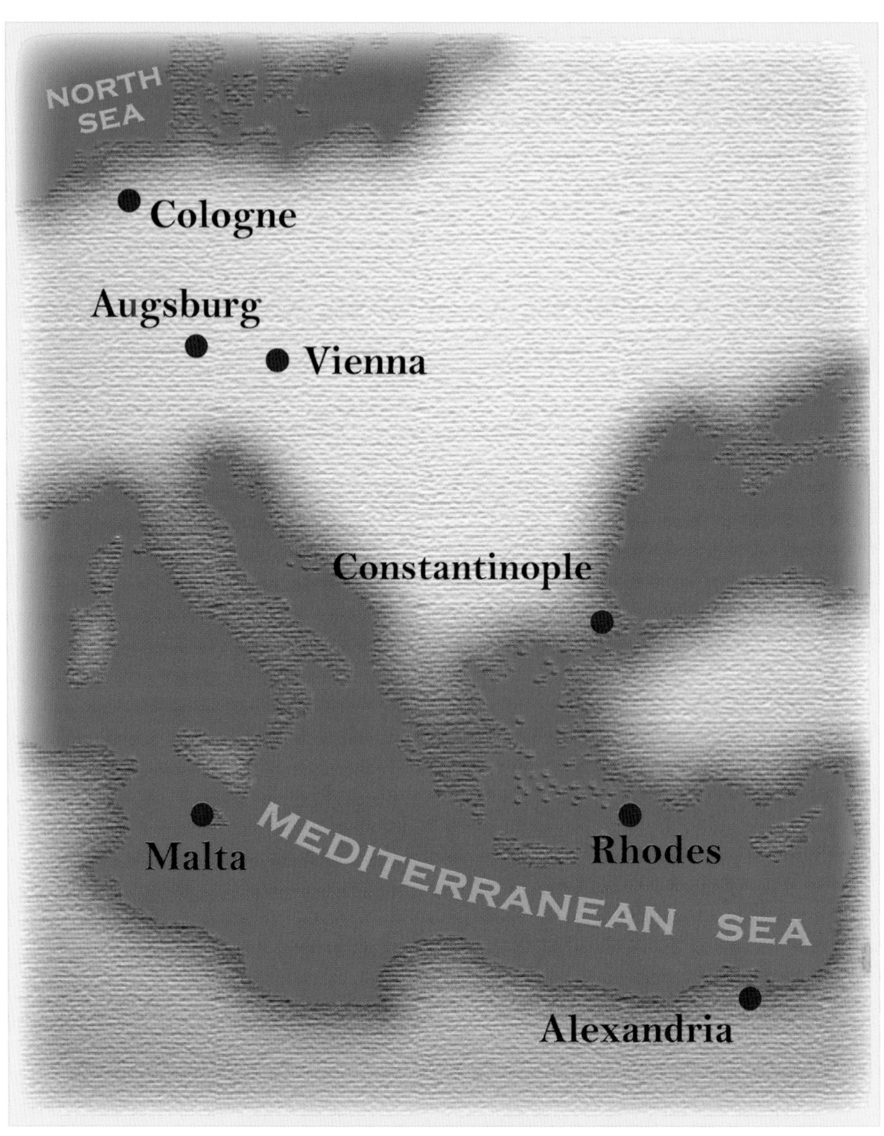

Journeys of the House of Anthony
in the Fifteenth-Sixteenth Centuries

7

The Coptic Secret

"The mystery hidden for ages and generations and now made manifest." (Colossians 1:26)

Egypt in the fifteenth century was still ruled by the Mameluke caliphs. However, because of their natural ability to handle the finances of the country and their intensive training in accounting, the Coptic Christians were employed by the caliphs to staff the Egyptian government administration.

By AD 1450 the increasing persecution and frequent Muslim mob attacks were making it very difficult for the Copts. The Caliph then gave in to the mob and dismissed all of the Coptic Christians from government service and confiscated their possessions.

27 It was at this time that the scion of the "House of Anthony," the *direct descendant of Farouk of Alexandria* and the keeper of the Second Ring, made secret contact with a spy for the "Knights of St. John," the Order of Crusaders based on the Island of Rhodes. (See map on page 32.)

The arrangement was made to smuggle Gregory F. Anthony and his family aboard a Venetian ship loaded with Egyptian cotton and bound for Rhodes. Only the Coptic Patriarch of Alexandria knew of their plan.

Patriarch Pachomius came under the cover of darkness. He blessed the Second Golden Ring and the Anthony family, exhorting them, saying:

> "You are the guardians of the Secret Treasure of the Coptic Church. Hold fast to the faith symbolized by this Ring."
>
> Then he lifted up the Ring and spoke these words of encouragement: "Let this Ring remind you of the Golden Number 7, which points us to the Paschal (Easter) Celebration—the Resurrection of Him who is ASHEM (*Truth*, or, *The Incarnation of Truth*). Give your life in commitment to Him and in service to those in need."

It was January 6, 1451, when the Venetian vessel set sail. The cold winter night was still and the stars were bright in the Mediterranean sky. As Gregory looked up from their hiding place, he thought of that first Christmas when the golden Ring which he held in his possession was laid at the feet of the Christ Child.

The Mediterranean crossing was cold but calm and the ship laid anchor in the harbor of the city of Rhodes without incident. Rhodes was a stronghold of the Knights Hospitaller of St. John since AD 1310. From there they continued their Crusader efforts against the Muslim Turks.

As their title suggests, the Knights were hospitable to the new refugees from Egypt. Gregory offered his services to the Knights, who were defending the sea lanes against the Turks. The Anthony's served the Knights with distinction during the fourteenth century.

Then, in 1452, the Anthony's again offered their services to the Knights, when they were preparing to answer the Byzantine Emperor's plea for reinforcements. He was asking for help in the defense of the city of Constantinople against the threat of the Ottoman Turks. Gregory F. Anthony II, the current scion of the Anthony family, along with other Copts, joined the Theban Legion of the Knights, and arrived at Constantinople in 1453.

The Muslim forces began massing for the attack in April. Their first attacks against the west wall were repelled by the Defenders, though the Byzantine forces were greatly outnumbered by the Turks.

The Defenders rallied again when the Muslims attacked on Easter Sunday. The Emperor himself, bearing the Greek cross on his armor and his standard, fought bravely and inspired his troops to hold the City.

The turning point came when the Turkish Navy was able to bypass the heavy blockade chain across the harbor entrance. Thus the Defenders were being attacked from both land and sea.

The Emperor was killed in the final battle and the City fell to the Muslim infidels on May 21, 1453. While the Turkish forces were engaged with pillage, looting, murder, and rape, a remnant of the Knights' forces succeeded in fighting their way back to their ships and returned to their fortress on Rhodes. The Theban Legion, like their namesake of old, had sustained heavy casualties.

28 Among the wounded was Gregory F. Anthony II, but the placement of the Ring had saved his life.

The House of Anthony continued to serve the Hospitallers as both civil servants and as soldiers. The Ring was passed from father to son. It was Gregory's grandson, Mark F. Anthony, who answered the Call of the Order when the Knights were asked by Emperor Charles V, the Holy Roman Emperor, to help with the defense of Vienna in AD 1529.

29 So the Second Golden Ring entered the Austrian Empire on the person of its keeper, Mark F. of the House of Anthony. Much to the relief of Charles V, as well as the Lutheran princes of Germany, the Muslims were defeated at the gates of Vienna.

In 1530, as an expression of his appreciation for their courage and commitment in their defense of Vienna, the Emperor gave the Island of Malta to the Knights for their new headquarters. They continued their Crusade against the Muslims and defeated a large Turkish force which attempted to capture Malta in 1565.

Mark F. of the House of Anthony received permission from the Grand Master of the Knights to move his family to Vienna in 1530. He was impressed by the beauty and culture of the city. He was also intrigued by rumors he had heard regarding the preaching of a certain German "heretic" named Martin Luther.

PAINTING BY ANTON VON WERNER (1843–1915)

MARTIN LUTHER AT THE DIET AT WORMS, 1521

"Unless I am convinced by Scripture and sound reason, I am held fast by the Scriptures and my conscience is taken captive by God's Word. I neither can, nor will, recant. God help me. Amen."

Mark had secretly secured a copy of Luther's *95 Theses*, and he found himself to be in agreement with several of the theses. Now he wanted to meet the man himself. But Luther was under the Papal Ban and the direct threat of death by the Emperor. It would not be wise to let his wishes be known, since he was among the Emperor's favorites and a defender of the Holy Catholic Church.

So he suggested to his wife Sarah that they should plan a pilgrimage to the Cologne Cathedral, where tradition maintains that the bones of the Magi are resting. Then, on the way, perhaps they could visit Augsburg when the Diet would be in progress.

It was AD 1530 and the German princes who supported Martin Luther had been invited by Charles V to present a statement of their beliefs to the Diet. As a member of the Knights Hospitaller of the Order of St. John, Mark was welcomed into the Diet Hall at Augsburg. He was disappointed that Luther was not there, but when the Princes' *Confession of Faith* was read, he recognized their statement as a well-articulated summary of the Christian faith. He believed that it was the faith which his spiritual ancestors at Alexandria had died to defend, and the faith to which the Rings gave testimony.

Mark said nothing to the Emperor's attendant who accompanied him. All he acknowledged was the earnest desire of his wife, Sarah, and himself, to continue their pilgrimage to the Cologne Cathedral and view the relics and bones of the Magi of Old, which had been brought by Frederick I Barbarossa, Holy Roman Emperor, to Cologne in AD 1162.

> Mark thought: Indeed, IF the bones of Gaspar, Melchior, and Balthasar are resting at Cologne, it is only right to touch them with the Ring in *thankfulness* for leading mankind to Bethlehem!

As he looked down at the golden Ring, his mind was flooded with questions:

- "*Where* are the other Rings?"
- "*Who* is charged with keeping them?"
- "*Will* they ever *meet*, or even come together again, before the Second Coming?"
- "What *good* has come to those who have kept them?" or, "What great *suffering* have they been Called to bear on behalf of the Cross?"

Mark understood that the golden Ring was a symbol of God's *Love*, and as he held this Ring which had been given to his family in trust, he was reminded that the *endless circle* of the Ring was a tangible reminder of God's *endless and eternal Love* for all mankind.

Mark wondered why his family had been chosen to be the guardians of the Second Ring.

The Cathedral of Cologne

Vista of "The Promised Land"

PART THREE

"The Promised Land" of America

Eighteenth and Nineteenth Centuries AD

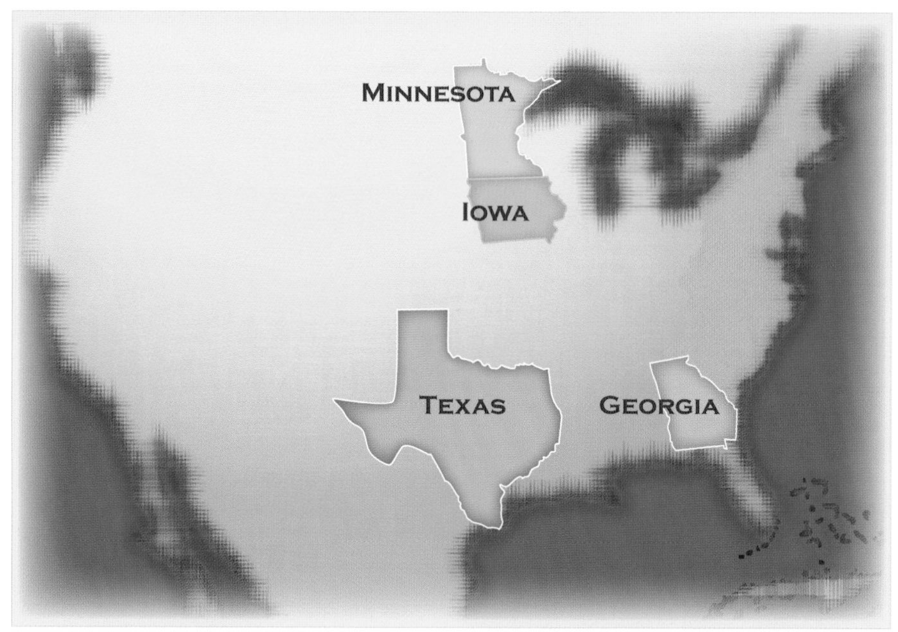

THE ADVENT OF THE RINGS IN AMERICA

MAP KEY:

LAVENDER: GEORGIA, 1734, John F. Anthony, "ASHEM" (*Truth*, or, *The Incarnation of Truth*)

BLUE: TEXAS, 1854, Eirik Filkesager, "AHURO" (*God*, or, *Lord of All*)

GREEN: IOWA, 1855; MINNESOTA, 1857, Ole Haraldson, "MAZDAO" (*Wisdom*, or, *Spirit of Wisdom*)

8

To "The Promised Land"

"Go from your country and your kindred
and your father's house
to the land I will show you."
(Genesis 12:1)

In 1530, on the journey from Cologne back to Vienna, Mark F. of the House of Anthony and his wife and company were attacked by robbers who stole all their possessions, except their clothes and their breviary (prayer book).

30 But the Second Ring was not discovered in its secret compartment within the cover of the breviary.

In Austria, the Anthonys were aided by peasants and burgers in the town of Salzburg. Thus began a close association between the House of Anthony and the people of Salzburg. Eventually, the Anthonys moved to the Salzburg area and joined the Reformation movement. They became a prominent Protestant family.

Following the Peace of Westphalia in AD 1648, it became very difficult for the Protestants in Austria.

Salzburg was ruled by a Roman Catholic Archbishop, whose attitude was clear when he stated: "I would rather have thorns and thistles in my fields than Protestants in my lands."

This statement was only the prelude to years of persecution, which finally culminated in an "Expulsion Order." On October 31, 1731, the Archbishop of Salzburg recognized the anniversary of the beginning of the Reformation (1517) by issuing his own version of the "95 *Theses*"—the Order for all Protestants to leave Salzburg!

Within a few months 30,000 refugees left their homes and walked north to Protestant Germany!

Although they had much of this world's goods, the Anthony family sold everything and followed in the train of refugees. As groups of them reached Protestant soil, they were received with great enthusiasm.

Leopold F. Anthony, who was the keeper of the Ring, made this entry in his journal on January 6, 1732:

"As the procession moved into the city, all joined in singing 'A Mighty Fortress Is Our God.' Townsmen broke ranks to lend a helping hand to the aged; children were kissed and embraced by welcoming townsfolk.

"On the following day, religious services were conducted for the honored guests, and when we departed, we were given money and personal apparel."

The plight of the Salzburgers had come to the attention of an English philanthropist, James Oglethorpe, who had received a Royal Charter to establish a new colony in the "Promised Land" of America. With financial aid from the "Society for the Promotion of Christian Knowledge," it was Oglethorpe's intent to establish a *refuge* for English debtors and for the distressed Salzburgers and other Protestants. The colony was named *Georgia*, in honor of George II of England.

The first group of Salzburgers to accept Oglethorpe's offer left from Rotterdam in the spring of 1734 and after a dangerous voyage arrived in Charleston, South Carolina. John F. Anthony (son of Leopold) and his family, together with two Lutheran ministers, were among this first contingent of Salzburgers.

As a businessman and a man of letters, John F. was instrumental in organizing the local government of the new colony and in building the first saw mill. He donated the lumber for the first church building in the colony, the "New Jerusalem Lutheran Church" in Ebenezer.

31 That day, as he held the Second Golden Ring, John Anthony breathed a quiet prayer of thanksgiving to God: "Holy God — Father, Son, and Holy Spirit — I thank You, Lord, for granting us safe passage and for establishing our colony in this New Land.

"Thank You for entrusting me with the Secret of the Coptic Church and help me to be a faithful steward of this golden Ring.

"May this Ring be a reminder of Your saving presence and of Your promised blessing to us and to our New Land. Amen!"

While he thanked the Lord for the privilege of being the steward of one of the Magi's Rings, John had often wondered about the other Rings. *Who* held them in trust? *Would* they come together in this Promised Land? What would the *message* of the Rings mean for an American nation about to be born? *Would* the Truth which they represent be received by a people on the frontier of civilization?

But the Rings kept their secret.

BY ADOLPH TIDEMAND, 1848 (1814–1876)

A HAUGEAN PRAYER MEETING

9

Awakening in "The Field of Rings"

"Repent, for the kingdom of heaven is at hand!"
(Matthew 3:2)

Meanwhile, for some 250 years between 1536 and the late 1700s, Norway was like a "sleeping giant," while Denmark infused its language and culture into the veins of this once proud nation. Then, in the late eighteenth century, the giant began to stir. Poets, storytellers, writers, composers, and preachers aroused her with images from her past and visions of the future.

They gave Norway a glimpse of her true identity and her future greatness.

It was in this time that the population of Norway began to outstrip the opportunities for young people to find employment and to maintain their accustomed standard of living. Many of the younger children of the *bonder* (farm owners) were losing their land-owning status and were reduced to *husmann* (cottar) status, with little hope for economic advancement.

The religious soul of the nation was also coming to life. In reaction to Rationalistic preaching, a prophetic voice was heard in the fields and towns. This was the voice of an articulate lay preacher and loyal son of the Lutheran Church.

Hans Nielsen Hauge (1771–1824) called the nation to repentance and recommitment to the Christian message, to true "wisdom." Although Hauge was not received by all, his revival was the event which finally brought the Reformation message to the common man:

> *Salvation* is not by works or by merit, but by *grace* (God's undeserved favor), through *faith* in Jesus.

Hauge's preaching communicated the essence of Luther's *faith* as stated in the *Small Catechism:*

> "I believe that I cannot by my own understanding or effort believe in Jesus Christ my Lord, or come to Him, but the Holy Ghost (Spirit) has called me through the Gospel,

> enlightened me with His gifts, and sanctified and preserved me in true faith."

But Hauge's life and preaching not only spurred a religious revival within the Norwegian Lutheran Church, it also catalyzed the efforts of the common man — the *bonde* — to political action…and to entrepreneurial adventures in trade and industry.

Hauge traveled the length and breadth of Norway, preaching to gatherings in homes and in the fields, by *fjord*, and in the forests. His preaching ministry lasted only seven years. However, in this time he walked more than 10,000 miles, preached to thousands, wrote books, established his own publishing house, and initiated several other businesses.

All the while, he was harassed by local officials and accused of violating the "Conventicle Act" ("lay preaching"), which the government of Dano-Norway declared to be illegal. In 1804, he was arrested and imprisoned at Akershus Castle. Hauge spent ten years in prison awaiting trial. The terrible prison conditions broke his health. When he was released in 1814, although he was no longer allowed to preach, he continued his writing, and through his friends continued to have an important influence on many in all levels of society.

This was a time of great turmoil in Europe — the French Revolution (1789–1799), the Reign of Terror in France (1792–1795), Napoleon's rise to power and the Napoleonic Wars (1795–1813).

It was also the birth pangs of a new, modern Norway that included: a time of blockades and near starvation, independence, at last, from Denmark, and hostilities with Sweden.

32 This was the *Kairos* (the special time) when the nation *needed* "The Blessing of the Rings." But there was a dilemma: What *had happened* to the Rings of the Magi? Had they been lost in the River Nid, or covered by the Jotunheim Glacier, or buried with the keepers of the Rings? No one seemed to know!

Then…at the right time, after 250 years, the two rings safeguarded in Norway were *revealed*. They came out from their two secret hiding places to become a part of the "Renewal of Norway" and "The Great Migration of the Norwegian People to America." The Rings were carried in that stream of 850,000 Norsemen who caught the "America Fever" and immigrated to North America.

33 The story of the two "Rings of Hedmarken" became an integral part of the American saga—Ring One ("AHURO," *God,* or, *Lord of All*) arriving with the Filkesager family from Ringsaker, and Ring Three ("MAZDAO," *Wisdom*, or, *Spirit of Wisdom*) arriving with the Haraldson family from Ringerike.

AHURO

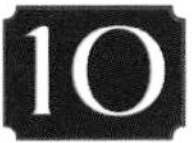

The Keepers of The Rings—AHURO

"As servants of Christ and stewards of the mysteries of God. . . ."
(1 Corinthians 4:1)

It was in the eighth generation after 1536 that Eirik of Filkesager and his wife, Cecilie, were blessed with a son. They named him Arne after his grandfather.

Eirik was a prominent *bonde* (farm owner) in Ringsaker and descended from Norwegian nobility on his mother's side. He carried three white wolf skins over his right arm when he attended the annual *Ting* (assembly). The *bonder* from the entire county of Ringsaker gathered each year at the Filkesager *gård* (farm). The *Ting* (assembly) was held in the open field beside the burial mounds of ancient kings of Ringsaker and near the Stave Church.

Eirik was respected as a wise, fair-minded man and was chosen by the Ting to serve as *Lensmann* (sheriff) of Ringsaker. When trying to settle a property dispute between Olger of Bye and Torsten of Kjoss, Eirik was fatally wounded. Before he died he summoned his son, Arne, privately, and gave him the sacred Ring, telling him the story of the three interlocking golden rings, their secret inscriptions, and how the two Rings came to Ringsaker in the thirteenth century.

It was 1777 when Eirik av Filkesager died. Arne, the only child, was seven and not old enough to manage the large farm. His mother, Cecilie, was accustomed to the finer things of life and was not trained in the business of agriculture. So Cecilie hired Martin of Bratvold, a distant relative of her family, to serve as farm manager.

Martin was capable enough—young, strong, and industrious—however, he needed frequent reassurance from the flask which he kept hidden in the *stabbur* (food storage shed). After his consultations with the flask, Martin revealed a quiet temper, but when he was far from the *stabbur*, he showed a mean, demanding nature. In these times between visits to the *stabbur*, Martin was hard on the *husmenn* (cottars) and hired hands but especially harsh with Arne. However, when Cecilie was within earshot, he could control his angry outbursts.

So it was that Cecilie didn't take seriously her son's reports of Martin's harsh, unfair treatment. Far from reprimanding her farm manager, Cecilie fell in love with Martin and in the course of time they were married. Arne was eleven when his first half-brother was born.

> "A little too soon after the wedding!" he heard the neighbors say, but he didn't understand, yet.

As she gave birth to another half-brother and then a half-sister, Arne and his mother grew apart. He was now seventeen and Martin had become harsher and more demanding, even when he had his consolation from the *stabbur*. Life was difficult for Arne, and quarrels with his step-father more frequent.

It was 1788 and the Dano-Norwegian Army was recruiting for service on the Continent as an ally of Napoleon. The Emperor of France was at his height of power. Arne confided in his mother that he had joined the King's army and would be gone for a long time. She wept when he told her, but given the circumstances at "Filkesager," she understood.

34 Before he left, he found a hiding place for the Ring. He left a sealed letter with the Pastor, with instructions to open it if he were to be killed or never return.

Napoleon's armies seemed to be invincible. Victory after victory was reported. Only Russia remained to be added to his trophies. But the vast expanse of the Russian plains and the consuming cold of the winter of 1812 were more than a match for Napoleon's army. Arne was one of the few who lived to tell and return home.

It was the Year of our Lord, AD 1813—twenty-five years since Arne had left home. His mother had died and Martin had convinced the court that Arne was dead and that Filkesager should be willed to Jakob, his own son. And so, in the year before Arne's return, the decision had been made and the judge had declared that Jakob Martinson was the rightful owner of Filkesager.

While Arne appealed the court's decision, there was no willingness to overturn the verdict. So the rightful heir of Filkesager became an unwelcome stranger on his own ancestral lands.

The only ray of light which broke through the gloom of Arne's homecoming was that the now-old Pastor, even in his retirement, had kept *unopened* the letter which Arne had entrusted to him. He had prayed often for Arne's safe return. He rejoiced that the Lord had answered his prayers. Arne, too, was thankful that the place of hiding had guarded well the Ring his father had given him so many years before.

Although the Martinsons shunned him, other friends came to his aid. They remembered his father, and Arne's promise as a youth. They offered to help set him up in a business in Hamar. He became successful in the mercantile business, married, and raised a family of one son and two daughters.

Arne also became a devout supporter of the Lutheran Church. His deep faith, honest piety, and desire to help those in need was formative in the life of his son. Thus it was no surprise to Arne that young Eirik sensed "the Call" from the Lord to become a pastor. With his father's financial help, Eirik graduated from the Theological Department of the University of Christiania. He was ready for a Call to serve a congregation.

Eirik and his fiancé, Elisabet, had been moved by the "American letters" and reports of the dire need for pastors to guide and comfort the *diaspora* of Norse immigrants.

It seemed to Eirik that the Lord was leading him to answer the Call to serve among the immigrants in America. So, in due time, after appropriate letters of introduction and recommendation from the Theological faculty of the University had been sent, a letter arrived from Decorah, Iowa, USA. It was an invitation from Rev. U. V. Koren, of the newly-formed Norwegian Synod, asking Eirik to make himself available for Call to serve as a pastor in the U.S.

Eirik was thrilled at the prospect of answering God's Call to this New Land, but Elisabet had some misgivings. Only after much prayer and the encouraging words from a cousin who had traveled to America, was Elisabet willing to leave her family, the familiar surroundings of her beautiful homeland, and accept Eirik's proposal of marriage.

> Yes, she thought, with God's help, I will go with Eirik to this strange, new Land.

So they were married in the Ringsaker Church and, soon after, bade farewell to family and friends.

35 But before their carriage swept them away to the port of Christiania, Arne Filkesager had a secret meeting with his son. The Ring with the inscription, "AHURO," would travel in Eirik's possession to America. And Eirik promised to keep the secret of the Rings locked in his heart until that appointed day when he would entrust the story, and the First Ring, to his own son.

When the young couple arrived at Decorah, Iowa, Rev. Koren himself met them at the Ellingson Store, and brought them to the log cabin of a kindly couple, Ole and Sena Bakken. Here, a bed in the loft and a shared kitchen would be the setting for their first home.

Soon, however, after the formalities of colloquy (Pastoral examination) were completed, Rev. Koren invited the young pastor and his wife to his office to meet someone from Texas. Henrik Werenskjold was a businessman from the Norwegian settlement east of Dallas.

> "I've been sent by our *Four-Mile Norsk Lutherske Kirke* (Norwegian Lutheran Church) at Prairieville, Kaufman County, Texas to secure a pastor," he told them. "Reverend Koren speaks very highly of you, Pastor Filkesager, so I've come to meet you and to answer any questions you may have regarding our church and community."
>
> He paused, and then said with feeling, "The folks in Prairieville are in prayer that you will accept the Call to serve our church."

It was 1854 and Texas was "Slave Territory." Prairieville was a dusty Texas town where Norsemen and Anglos met and drank, argued politics, and debated the slavery issue.

> It is a *strange new world*, thought Eirik, but certainly a world that needs the Gospel of Reconciliation.
>
> Eirik confessed to himself, that he was not in favor of slavery, but he was wise enough to refrain from suggesting to Mr. Werenskjold that he would make this a major issue of his ministry.

So, after prayerful consideration together with Elisabet, he determined that he would be willing to accept the Call from the Four Mile Lutheran Congregation. Thus, within a few days, after they had expressed their appreciation to Rev. Koren and the Bakkens, Pastor Eirik and his bride set out on the long, arduous journey by coach, river boat, and buggy from Decorah, Iowa to Prairieville, Texas.

The Texas folk were generous and demonstrated "Southern hospitality" toward their new Pastor and his beautiful wife. They were especially generous with praise and with extra food when the parsonage family added their first child! Eirik and Elisabet named their son Arne, after Eirik's father. He was destined to be the bearer of the Ring, but Eirik told no one.

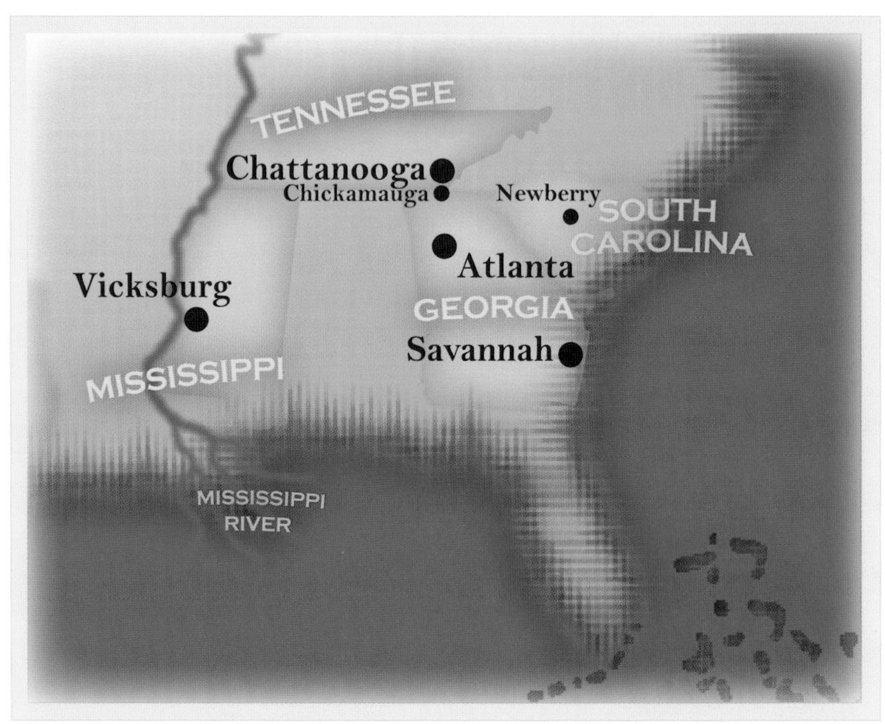

The "Western Campaign" of the Civil War

When the Time Is Right

"There is a time for all things under the sun . . . a time to be born and a time to die . . . a time for war and a time for peace."
(Ecclesiastes 3:1, 8)

Pastor Eirik Filkesager was making his morning walk back from the post office when the Dallas stagecoach flew by him in a cloud of dust, threw off a bundle of the *Dallas Times* newspaper in front of the general store, and was off to the next town on its circuit. He paid his 5¢ for a copy and went back to his office.

The *Dallas Times* proclaimed with jubilation that the "Dred Scott Decision" of the U. S. Supreme Court had been announced on March 6, 1857:

> "A Democrat-dominated Court," reported the paper, "declared that Dred Scott, a slave, was *not* a citizen, either of Missouri or of the United States, and therefore, had no right to sue for his freedom."
>
> "The seven Democrats had voted for this decision, but the two Republicans on the bench opposed this decision," the paper lamented.
>
> The paper went on to report that: "The majority of the High Court at this time also recorded their opinion on a matter which was not officially before the Court (a matter of *obiter dictum*). This issue concerned the anti-slavery clause in the *Missouri Compromise*."
>
> The Democrat majority seized this opportunity to record their opinion that the Missouri Compromise was unconstitutional. They maintained that slavery could *not* be excluded from the territories. "This is great news for the majority of Southerners," the paper concluded.

However, Pastor Filkesager and a few others in his Parish were saddened by the Dred Scott Decision. In private conversations, he reminded his friends that Dred Scott, the Negro slave, was a human being, a person created in the "image of God" and should not be denied his rights.

> "These rights," said Eirik, "are also assumed by the Declaration of Independence as self-evident—that all men are created equal, that they are endowed by their Creator with certain unalienable rights, and that among these are life, liberty, and the pursuit of happiness."

But the Democrats were too powerful and too vocal in Texas for an open and fair public discussion of the matter. So Eirik and other Southerners who opposed the Dred Scott Decision and supported the *freeing* of the slaves, were carried along like bobbing corks on a flowing river, to the seemingly inevitable tragedy of a civil war.

Eirik made this entry in his diary on December 2, 1859 (the day that John Brown was hanged at Harpers Ferry, West Virginia):

> "Perhaps the Abolitionists are correct—that the issue at stake in the Dred Scott case is the full *personhood* of a slave. He is not simply a *thing* to be bought and sold and used, but he is the bearer of the Creator's image and therefore is a *person*. I believe this, but to speak thus in public, I find myself to be too much the coward. Still, in my secret heart, I yearn for the courage of a John Brown."

Although Eirik Filkesager could not push back the tide of a civil war, he did not forget the image and the message of John Brown, the fiery Abolitionist.

Life must go on, and regardless of one's politics or philosophy, there's always birth and death, joy and sorrow, labor and rest. He reflected that, as a pastor, his days were tied to the universal events of life. He was there when a young father announced with pride that his wife was to give birth to their first child, he was there to administer the mystery of Baptism and welcome the child into the family of God, and he was there at the bedside when death hovered close over a family's dear one.

> He was the one, the "Parson" (the person), who had the privilege of being a part of each family's inner sanctum. He had been Called to that special office, where time and

events touched the souls of his people. It is such an awesome privilege! he thought.

But his reverie on the privilege of the pastoral office ended suddenly with the sound of heavy boots on the wooden porch outside, and an urgent knock at the door.

It was David Nelson. A look of fear was on his countenance and his voice shook as he entered the room, "*Kari dør!* (Kari is dying!)" he said with despair. "Our baby is stuck, and she needs help! Pastor! Come quickly!"

When Eirik arrived with the midwife, Kari and her baby (with its buttocks protruding from her womb) were both dying. The long birth labor had taken its toll. Their energies were spent.

Kari looked at Pastor Eirik, and spoke one word, "*Døp!*" (Baptize!) Out of her anguish, she was appealing to Pastor Eirik, "Please baptize my child!"

Even though the baby was not yet fully birthed, Pastor Filkesager knew what God would have him do. He nodded to the midwife, and together they were able to turn the dying baby in the womb so that he could be born. Kari's deep sigh of relief, and the child's faint whimper, announced that a new life had been born.

But the birth trauma had been so severe. It seemed evident to Eirik that both mother and baby would die.

With a little water from the bedside pitcher and David's one word, "Johan!" Pastor Eirik quickly sprinkled water three times and spoke the ancient words of entrance into the Kingdom of The Rings: "I baptize thee, Johan Nelson, in the name of the Father, and of the Son, and of the Holy Spirit. Amen!"

After the *Far Vår* (The Lord's Prayer), Eirik made the sign of the Cross over both mother and child. It was done!

Kari may have heard the prayer, because, as she died, a look of peace came over her countenance. David and the mid-wife sobbed. Eirik was fighting back his tears as he took The Ring from its chain around his neck and touched it to the baby's head. The gesture was *a sign without words* of the Lord's welcome to His Eternal Kingdom.

The Ring, with the inscription, "AHURO" (*God*, or *Lord of All*), which had welcomed the "Earth-coming" of the Savior, now signaled the "Heaven home-coming" of baby Johan.

As Eirik sat at his desk that evening, he wrote these words in his diary, for that day, December 2, 1859:

> "Today I have witnessed a profound miracle with the birth of Johan Nelson. But I have also come to the realization that the unborn child is a person for whom Christ died and a soul who has the right to life. Not only Dred Scott, but also the unborn child, is a person who, some day, I pray, will be granted the legal right of personhood."

Thus it was that a humble country parson on the Texas frontier, at the beginning of the Advent season, expressed a profound hope which would find fulfillment through the vicissitudes of political battles, national trauma, and approaching civil war. But he knew that the realization of the hope regarding the rights of the weakest of the human race would await another time—another *kairos*—when the time was right.

Ministry in the South became an increasingly difficult Calling during the mounting disruptions and destructions of the "War Between the States." Eirik volunteered to serve as a chaplain with the Lone Star Brigade. He was with his men at Vicksburg during the Union bombardment. He risked his own life to minister to the fearful, the injured, and the dying.

On one occasion, he was called to minister to a captured Union Soldier who could speak only Norwegian. The man was dying. He asked for the Sacrament and requested that the Pastor write to inform his family of his death. The soldier's name was Niels Sørenson. His sister in Minnesota was named Petra Sørensdatter Hustad Haraldson.

36 Eirik could not know that she was the lady who held the secret of the Third Ring!

But the mystery was not ready to be revealed.

Eirik continued his ministry through the Civil War years. He and his family often endured hardships, but he ministered to the sick and dying in season and out of season.

By 1863 the Civil War had turned against the South, but Eirik, though tried and tested, never gave up his commitment to be a faithful servant of Jesus Christ. This was his first duty. He spent himself in his pastoral work. He often went with very little sleep. When the flu epidemic struck in 1866, Pastor Eirik fell to the illness, contracted pneumonia, and died. He was only 40 years old.

37 But before he died he gave the golden Ring and its secret to his son, Arne.

MAZDAO

12

The Ring of Wisdom — MAZDAO

"But where shall wisdom be found?"
(Job 28:12)

Ole Haraldson was Sexton of the Bønsnes Church in Ringerike, Norway. He farmed a small place called Bakkerud near the church, and had a growing family. But there seemed to be no positive possibilities for his children's future, so when he read immigrant letters from cousins who had emigrated from Norway to the American frontier, he set his eyes to the "West."

It was 1855 when Ole and his wife, Petra, bade farewell to friends and their beloved pastor. Pastor Mohn knew them well, and he wrote in the church record that he had given permission to Ole Haraldson, his wife Petra, and their children to emigrate. The eldest son was only seven. All had been baptized. Their first daughter was christened Reidunn.

38 She had a special place in the family, but her mother did not reveal the secret. Reidunn would one day be the keeper of the Third Golden Ring.

Pastor Mohn also made note in the church record that the Haraldson family had no outstanding debts and no communicable diseases. Thus they met the requirements of Norwegian emigration law and were ready to sail for America!

Members of the congregation and other friends of the Haugean persuasion accompanied them to the port at Drammen. The Haraldson family was sent off with prayers and tears. The unspoken reality was, as everyone knew, that this would be their final meeting until the Day they met again in The Kingdom of The Rings.

Their destination, written on the family trunk, was "Bjørn Bjørnsen, Ossian, Iowa, Amerika." The year was Anno Domini 1855. Four of Petra's brothers accompanied the Haraldson family on the trans-Atlantic journey. They were young and strong and eager to make their mark in the New World. They dreamt of taking land on the Iowa frontier. But the noise of an impending Civil War was loud enough to distract their dreaming.

Petra had another concern. She worried that if they were lost at sea, the Ring would be lost forever. She shuddered to think of it, and clutched the leather strap which secured the Ring in a money belt around her waist. It was going to be a long journey!

After six weeks on the North Atlantic, the ship "Baltic" put into port at Quebec, Canada. Their overland route to Detroit by wagon was painfully slow. However, the next leg of their journey from Detroit to Chicago by rail was an exciting experience for the elder Haraldsons and their children. They were experiencing the new age of speed.

> "Twenty miles per hour!" the conductor exclaimed, with a strong suggestion of bragging in his demeanor.

The seemingly almost insurmountable barrier between Chicago and their destination in northeast Iowa was the mighty, flooded Mississippi River. Petra believed it was the blessing of the Ring which brought an old French fur trader and river man to their aid. Nothing was lost when Felipe Cariveau ferried them to the Iowa shore.

All of their earthly belongings were loaded on a buckboard wagon and the Haraldson family walked alongside. The drayman guided his team along an invisible course through ravines and across prairies to Fort Atkinson.

Before their old neighbor Bjørn Bjørnsen (Ben Benson) arrived from his farm along the Turkey River, Reidunn and her siblings were making friends with the Indian children who still lived near the abandoned Fort. They had read stories about the American frontier and the forts that were built to protect the settlers from the Indians. But here in northeast Iowa was a fort that was built by the United States government to *protect the Winnebago Indians* from *other* Indians!

During the time Ole Haraldson spent working for Ben Benson to pay off his debt of passage, Petra was busy caring for her children, teaching them their daily tasks and instructing them in Scripture and the *Forklaring* (the "Explanation" to Luther's *Small Catechism*). Elling Eielsen, the pastor from the Norwegian settlement in northeast Illinois, had walked the 230 miles from the Fox River to organize the "First Lutheran Church." It was located in the country south of Ossian near the Benson farm. Pastor Eielsen had given each family a copy of the

Fort Atkinson

Forklaring so that they could continue the Christian education of their children and prepare them for Confirmation.

Eventually, the time came when Ole Haraldson had completed his obligation to Mr. Benson and he was ready to establish his own farm and home on the prairies. It was a slow and laborious journey. Everyone walked, as they followed their wagon pulled by a team of one-speed oxen. It took five weeks before they arrived at the Upper Sioux Agency on the Minnesota River.

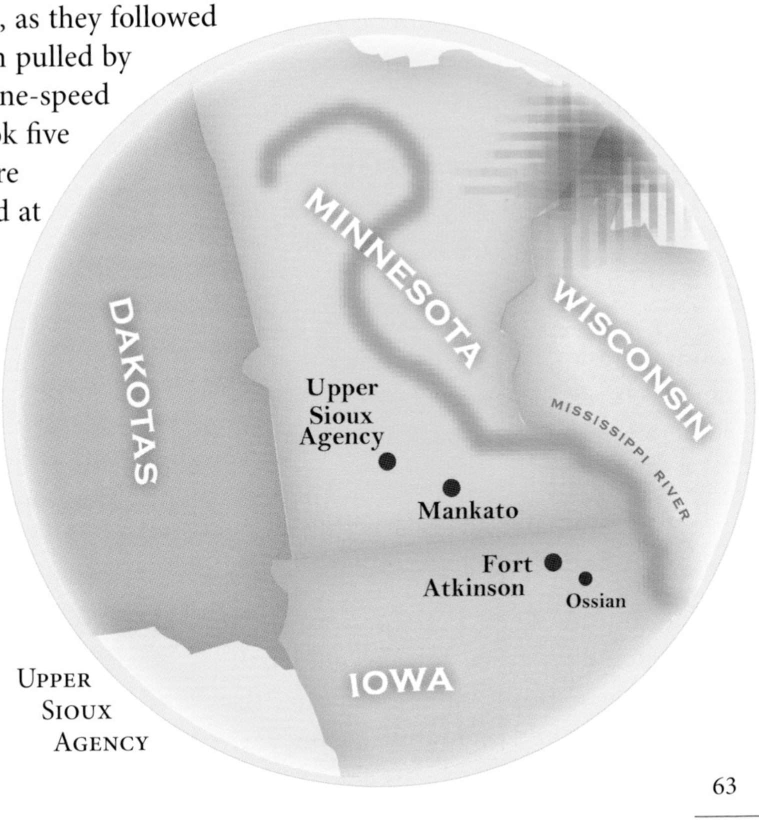

MINNESOTA
WISCONSIN
DAKOTAS
MISSISSIPPI RIVER
Upper Sioux Agency
Mankato
Fort Atkinson
Ossian
IOWA

Upper Sioux Agency

Reidunn and her siblings were a big help on the journey. They herded three young calves and cared for the chickens, but they also wondered if they would ever find their new home. Perhaps *Far* had lost his way? There were many things for the children to think about. However, reassurance came when they met an old Indian who pointed in the direction they were going and spoke the word "*Mankato*." The children knew that this town was along the route to the Upper Sioux Agency.

The tall prairie grass on a flat plain above the Minnesota River Valley was fun for the children to play in, but it was dangerous because of the threat of prairie fires. So, as soon as *Far* could hitch his breaking plough to the ox team, he plowed many large circular furrows around the wagon and the place where they would build their sod house.

The Indians seemed to be friendly enough, so long as *Mor* (mother) had some food for them. But this summer was hot and dry. It was now 1862 and the country was in the middle of a Civil War. Petra's four brothers had already joined the Union Army.

During the next two years she would receive the sad news that the great cost of victory for the Union forces would claim the lives of three of her brothers. One would be killed in Arkansas, one at Chattanooga, and her oldest brother, Niels Sørenson, would die in the battle at Vicksburg, Mississippi.

39 She received a very comforting letter written in Norwegian by a Confederate chaplain who had administered the Holy Sacrament to her brother before he died. The letter was written by a chaplain named *Eirik Filkesager*.

Meanwhile, Petra and her wonderful husband, Ole, were facing the arduous task of planting their home in a strange and unpredictable land. Petra felt the deep fear of helplessness when two wagonloads of settlers were heading back East past their claim.

> One of the men stopped and told Ole the rumor he had heard: "The Indians are real restless. There seems to be trouble brewing at the Upper Agency."

She did not share her worries with the children, but she did find a secret hiding place for the golden Ring inscribed with the word "MAZDAO." If *only* she knew what that word meant and where the other Rings could be found! Then she would feel safe and secure.

13

A Kingdom That Cannot Be Shaken

"Therefore let us be grateful for receiving a Kingdom that cannot be shaken."
(Hebrews 12:28)

Reidunn *clutched* the golden Ring. She stood in the dry summer heat.

40 Reidunn's tears made little puffs as they fell on the dusty ground beside the grave. The pastor's voice seemed distant as the words of the *Far Vår* echoed from the open grave. She squeezed her eyelids tight as she heard the first spade-full of dirt thump on the wooden casket.

She stood in the dry summer heat with her siblings and a few neighbors. The prairie cemetery was already marked by several wooden crosses. Reidunn's father, Ole, had been killed in the Sioux Uprising (1862). Her mother never recovered from the shock.

Now, both her father's and her mother's bones would lie in an unconsecrated plot of ground on the prairie plains of the Promised Land, far from the ancestral graveyard surrounding the Bønsnes Church in Ringerike ("The Kingdom of the Rings"), Norway.

Reidunn was overcome by the thought that her mother, Petra Sørensdatter Hustad Haraldson, should be buried so far from her homeland. The Bønsnes cemetery had been the resting place of her ancestors' bones for centuries, even as early as the thirteenth century. But the golden Ring, which her mother had given her before she died, was a tangible reminder that she and her siblings were not alone. The Ring reminded her that they belonged to something *greater* than this moment of sadness.

> As she gazed at the golden Ring, she remembered the question that had been on her mind for a long time, "Why did you give me such an old fashioned name? No one else has this name, Reidunn!"
>
> On the day before her mother died, she asked this question. *Mor* was weak but she answered without hesitation, "My

> child, you were born to be the bearer of this Ring, which is a blessing to those who possess it."
>
> Then, as she placed the golden Ring in her hand, *Mor* explained, "Your name dates back to the Middle Ages in Norway at the time when this Ring was given to the Hamar Cathedral by an Egyptian Crusader. He was healed of leprosy, and in thankfulness to God he offered this Ring. It was one of three interlocking golden rings in the treasure of gold which had been given by the Magi to the Christ Child, and one day, when the Rings are re-joined, the world will be blessed as well."
>
> How awesome, thought Reidunn, that I should be the guardian of such a treasure, which will bring a great blessing when the companion Rings come together!

She longed to know the saga of the other two Rings! Perhaps the letters inscribed in her Ring held the secret—"MAZDAO." She prayed for the time when the other golden Rings would be found and the secret revealed.

41 *Arne stood* at the open grave of his father. In his clenched fist, he held the golden Ring which *Far* had given him before he died. As the eldest son, *Far* said it was his responsibility to pass the Ring with the inscription "AHURO" to the next generation.

Far told him the story of the Rings—a tale from thirteenth century Norway. It was at the time when pilgrims from many Christian lands in Europe and the Mid-East followed the Pilgrims' Way to the healing spring at St. Olaf's grave in Nidaros.

> *Far* had spoken softly when he said, "Keep the Ring and its story secret until you pass it on to your own son. Thus it will be handed from generation to generation until the other interlocking Rings are revealed."

While Arne could still hear the words of the committal service, his mind was drifting back to what his father had revealed about the Ring. *Far* had emigrated from an area in Norway called Ringsaker, which means "Field of Rings." Here, an ancestor of his Filkesager family, who was the Pastor at the Ringsaker Church, came into possession of the Ring.

Far had revealed the meaning of the secret writings on the Rings and explained that two of the interlocking companion Rings had been lost.

> "There would be a great blessing when the three Rings came together!" *Far* promised.

Arne's imagination distracted him. "*Who* had the other Rings?" "*Where* were they?" "*How* would he find them?"

The Pastor's voice summoned him back to reality: "Earth to earth, ashes to ashes, dust to dust…."

Arne heard the words of the graveside service. It was the Church's reminder that death is real. Life on this Earth will come to an end.

> But he found comfort in the words of Scripture which *Far* often shared with his family and with the congregations he served. He believed the promise of Jesus: *"I am the resurrection and the life; he who believes in Me, though he die, yet shall he live."* (John 11:25)

42 Magnus Olson was standing, gazing into an open grave, a hollow, distant look on his face. He shed no tears, and showed no emotion. His was the countenance of a man whose dream had died.

He had been depressed even before his devoted wife, Gyda, had become sick with typhoid fever. It seemed that his American dream had died after three years of backbreaking toil on his homestead and three years of crop failure. As his dream passed away, it seemed that his own identity had died.

Magnus no longer knew who he was or why he should continue.

His fears began to consume him. He was sinking in deep mire. Nothing could reach him. No one could rescue him.

> He felt like the Psalmist: *"I sink in deep mire, where there is no foothold; I have come into deep waters, and the flood sweeps over me."* (Psalm 69:2)

He was accusing himself for his failure, and for the death of his dear wife. He had come to America to prove something to his father-in-law, Haldan of Pilerveien. But all he had proven was what Haldan had already articulated in such a cruel and overbearing way—Magnus was a *failure*!

The Pilerveiens were an upper-class *bonde* (farm owner) family. They had inherited a large, productive farm in Ringsaker, which had its roots in the pre-Viking age. They were "somebody" and he, Magnus Olson, was a "nobody." They had opposed his marriage to Gyda, even though he had shown much promise when he attended Latin School. The Pastor at the Veldre Church had recommended Magnus for further study. Still, Haldan refused to give his daughter's hand in marriage.

But Gyda chose to follow her beloved to the "Promised Land" and forfeit her inheritance at Pilerveien. Now, he had lost everything—his wife, his homestead, and his dream!

14

The Promise of The Rings

"I will not fail you or forsake you."
(Joshua 1:5)

When the last spade full of dirt was mounted on the grave of Petra Sørensdatter Hustad Haraldson, Reidunn and her siblings knew they were alone. The kindly pastor loaded them in his own wagon and brought them to the sod house which had been their home for these past six years.

He secured the help of a friendly neighbor, Ruth Bjork, who helped the Haraldson children make final preparations for leaving the homestead. As a farewell gift, Ruth had knitted each child a pair of warm mittens for next winter.

The older brothers would go back to Iowa to live with Bjørn (Ben) Benson, who needed help with the farm work. Reidunn and her younger sister and brother would travel by covered wagon to New Richland, Minnesota, to their mother's brother. Knut and Astrid Rice had many children, but were willing to adopt the two youngest. However, Reidunn was too old.

At fifteen she was old enough to be employed as a kitchen maid and governess, so she agreed to employment at a large farm in the Northfield, Minnesota area. Reidunn was still close enough to the Rice farm to visit her younger siblings on special occasions.

Then tragedy struck during the cholera epidemic. Knut and Astrid both died. The Rice children were left as orphans. So they, as well as the younger Haraldson children, were brought to the orphanage at St. Peter, Minnesota. Reidunn could not bear to see them sent away alone! She asked permission to be hired as a helper in the orphanage kitchen, so she could watch over them.

The orphanage director, Catherine Buxton, was a strict disciplinarian who ruled the orphanage with an iron will and a big stick. "Dr. B," as she was called behind her back, had come from New Hampshire with the zeal of a Congregational missionary. She had vowed to make "100% Americans" out of these orphans, many of them children of recent immigrants from Norway, Sweden, or Germany. She was committed to shaping her charges in the image of Whitman's "democratic man." Her zeal was etched in her countenance. As one studied the profile of Dr. B's face, one sensed that Nathaniel Hawthorne could have been inspired by her visage when he wrote *The Great Stone Face*.

It was apparent to all that Dr. B was unbending in her opposition to any hint of "un-American activity." She would institute the "Melting Pot" ideology in her own private "kingdom!" The orphanage would become an island of "100% Americanism" in the midst of this sea of the mongrelized American West—no foreign words, and no foreign customs, and no foreign religions! All would attend the Congregational Sunday School, sing "American" hymns, and pray "American" prayers!

Reidunn had warned her younger siblings not to speak Norwegian, but little brother, Niels, soon forgot her admonitions. He unconsciously spoke out loud the "*I Jesu navn*" ("In Jesus' name") prayer as he bowed his head before the evening meal. His words were overheard by an "American orphan" and his infraction of the "Rule" was reported to Dr. B. After giving her "English only" lecture, she laid her ruler on Niels with stinging emphasis, and sent him to bed without supper.

Reidunn, from her post in the kitchen, witnessed this administration of "orphanage justice." She wanted to run to her brother's defense, but she could only watch, lest she lose her job. She clutched the bag in her waist band, which held the Golden Ring, and prayed that Mr. Benson would soon come from Iowa to *rescue them* from this "Melting Pot." But, sadly, he didn't come. Perhaps her letter had been lost or worse, tragedy had struck again!

Every day at the orphanage was becoming more like a prison sentence for the Haraldson children and for all who were so unfortunate as to be German or Scandinavian. But Reidunn, like a guardian angel, kept watch over Niels and Grace. When she was alone, she clutched the golden Ring and prayed that the Lord would send help.

> She remembered her mother's words, and encouraged Grace and Niels with Jesus' promise, *"I am with you always!"*

Encouragement they needed! The "crack" of Dr. B's ruler on the knuckles or the "behind" was a daily reminder that they had broken the “English only” rule. There was no room in Dr. B’s America for those who spoke a different language.

When the state inspector visited the orphanage in June, Reidunn asked for permission to speak to him. Would he allow them to leave the orphanage and live with Mr. Benson in Ossian, Iowa? Bjørn (Ben) had promised their mother that he would make a home for them. The inspector listened, but was uncertain what he could do.

Weeks passed and there was still no word. Reidunn was very sad and thought perhaps the promise of the golden Ring had no power in this “Promised Land.” Maybe the “blessing” would never come.

She still had many questions, yet she held on in hope. Then, in answer to her prayers, suddenly their “purgatory” came to an end! It was just before Christmas in 1868 Bjørn Benson arrived at the orphanage to take them “home.” They were overjoyed to meet his bride of three months. The children felt a close bond with this beautiful lady, especially when they learned that her first husband had been killed in the Indian Uprising at the same time as their own father.

They sensed that Martha Benson was a kindly person. Reidunn believed she would be good to them.

She touched the Ring, and remembered the promise of blessing that it would bring, and now, it was clear, even on the American frontier!

Bjørn Bjørnsen
27 June 1855

A Typical Norwegian Bride, circa 1855

15

Wedding Banns

"Therefore a man leaves father and mother and cleaves to his wife." (Genesis 2:24)

Reidunn and her siblings were happy at the Benson home. Martha Benson proved to be a caring mother-figure for the Haraldson children. They all pitched in with the chores, and Bjørn was pleased that he and Martha had made a home for them.

Sunday was special because they all rode together in the large buggy or in the sleigh to the "Stone Church." At worship, the boys sat with Bjørn on the men's side and the girls with Martha on the women's side.

Reidunn loved to hear the pastor chant the liturgy. The "Ære Være Gud!" ("Glory Be to God!") resounding from the chancel seemed to her like the voice of God Himself. It gave her a secure feeling that the God of the Rings was very close.

She loved to sing the hymns which were intoned by the *klokker* (sexton). In many Norwegian churches a layman opened the service with prayer and led the singing. Martha noticed that Reidunn had a beautiful voice and encouraged her to sing at home and at church.

Bjørn made arrangements for all the children to attend parochial (church) school. He drove them to the school, which was held in the building across the road from the Stone Church. They studied both religious and secular subjects. The Bible, the *Forklaring*, and Bible history were standard text books.

Religious instruction was in Norwegian and general subjects were taught in English. Their teacher, Mr. M.O. Wangsness was a good musician. He accompanied the school singing with his violin, and encouraged Reidunn to use her beautiful voice to praise God.

It was following the School Christmas Program that the pastor and the teacher spoke with Mr. Benson, encouraging him to purchase a piano for Reidunn.

> The Pastor began the matter. "Reidunn has a real talent for music. She should have the opportunity to learn to play the piano."

> "*Ja!*" chimed in Mr. Wangsness. "She's been picking out tunes on the piano here at school. When she hears a tune, she can play it!"
>
> Bjørn agreed. "She's been singing to the cows when she's milking. And Martha tells me she sings a lot around the house, too."

Reidunn was thrilled when, a few weeks later, Bjørn drove into the yard with an upright piano in the buckboard wagon! She was so pleased that Mr. Wangsness gave piano lessons after school. Soon it was apparent that Reidunn was indeed very talented. Before the first year of lessons was over, Reidunn had even composed several pieces—including a *sonatina* dedicated to her favorite cow!

On her twenty-first birthday in 1872, Bjørn and Martha surprised Reidunn with the suggestion that she should receive professional voice training. This meant she would need to go away to study at a music conservatory in Chicago. She was humbled by their willingness to sacrifice for her, because the Chicago Conservatory was very expensive.

She just couldn't accept their offer. "It would cost too much!" she protested.

There was, however, another reason why she wasn't as eager as they thought she might be, but Reidunn didn't say anything more. She needed time to think and to pray.

What would the Lord want her to do?

It seems that Reidunn was enjoying the attention she had been receiving from Lars Hanson, the Pastor's son. He was a handsome, kind, and hard-working young man who had shared with her his dream of becoming a newspaper reporter. She liked him and was tempted to share her secret of the golden Ring.

They enjoyed being together... but, Chicago? It was so far away!

> There were so many questions! "*Would* she ever see him again?" "*Would* he remember her?" "*Would* he find someone else when she was away?" "*What* would Bjørn and Martha say if she refused their offer?" "*What* should she *do*?"

If Lars promised to come to Chicago to visit her, the time of separation would go faster. They talked about this whenever they met, so Bjørn and Martha were not surprised when Reidunn told them of her struggle. Her attraction to Lars was urging her to stay in Iowa, but something was drawing her to Chicago, too.

> Could it be, thought Reidunn, that the promise of the golden Ring is leading her there?

Her decision was made when she learned that Lars was going to Chicago to work for his father's cousin, Victor Lawson, who owned and published the *Skandinaven*, a large Norwegian language newspaper.

Bjørn and Martha warned of the many temptations and dangers in the big city, but, nevertheless, they felt good that Reidunn would stay with Martha's sister and her family while she attended the Conservatory.

Reidunn received a letter from Lars before she boarded the train for Chicago. He was enjoying his new job in the typesetting department. Also, he had attended a Norwegian Lutheran church where he felt right at home because the pastor had gone to school with his father! It was close enough to the Conservatory so they could go to services together on Sundays.

Reidunn clutched the golden Ring and thanked the Lord for answering her prayers again.

In Chicago, her mentors at the Conservatory were impressed with Reidunn's natural ability and that she was no stranger to disciplined hard work. It would mean four years of study, long practice sessions, and little time for leisure. She and Lars would be able to see each other only on Sundays. He was disappointed with this, but when she sang for him or he attended one of her concerts, he was warmed and thrilled by her beautiful soprano voice. He was reassured that Reidunn was in *her* Calling. She was created to sing.

But Reidunn had more on her mind.

Although she loved being part of a concert choir and she dreamt of being a soprano soloist with the Chicago Metropolitan Chorale, she knew that her greatest joy would be found elsewhere. She knew that she would find her fulfillment in marriage with the man who loved her, and with their children whom she would hold in her arms.

> Yes, thought Reidunn, I believe that the family of father, mother, and children is the pattern of the three interlocking rings, which holds the secret to fulfillment for me, and for others.

Reidunn and Lars set their wedding date for June 6, 1878, but Lawson, who had recently purchased the *Chicago Daily News*, promoted Lars to the status of "Foreign Correspondent" for the newspaper. He would have to leave from New York on January 6 in order to cover the Balkan Conflict between Russia and Turkey. His journey would take him to Bulgaria and Greece and other points in the Balkans.

Reidunn sent him off with a warm embrace and a prayer. It was a real opportunity for Lars to "scoop" other newspapers and bring credit to the *Chicago Daily News*.

Lars wanted to be in the middle of the conflict…and get both exciting news and a bonus to help with wedding expenses. However, after several weeks in the war zone, he was captured along with some Russian troops at Solonika. They were imprisoned in the Fortress of Istanbul (Constantinople). He tried to get word out to his newspaper, but the Turks were suspicious.

No one knew whether he was alive or dead. Reidunn held on in faith that her beloved Lars would be found alive.

Finally, on May 15, 1878, the U.S. State Department was notified that an American newsman was reported being held as a prisoner of war in Istanbul. However, Turkish authorities were willing to exchange him for Turkish prisoners.

Within one week, a telegram from the State Department gave Reidunn the wonderful good news that her Lars was well and would be home in time for their scheduled wedding.

43 One of the U.S. State Department's staff who negotiated for Lar's freedom was *Gregory F. Anthony* from Savannah, Georgia. When he met with the Ottoman officials to negotiate for the American reporter's release, he had in his vest pocket over his heart the golden Ring which *his* father had given him before he died. It was one of the three interlocking golden rings, his father had told him, which had been offered by the Magi to the Christ Child on that first Christmas.

It warmed his heart, when he heard Lars' story of capture and imprisonment, to know that he was an instrument of good news for this young reporter and his anxious bride. Gregory felt a bond of friendship for this man. It was a *strange* sensation, like they were bound together from long ago.

On the day of her wedding, Reidunn's prayers were answered. As she entered the sanctuary escorted on Mr. Benson's arm, she knew her mother would be proud of her. She was wearing the silver wedding crown which was handed down from generation to generation in her family.

She held tightly to Lars' arm as they stepped up to the altar of the Stone Church. When she placed the wedding ring on Lars' hand, she thought of the golden Ring and of God's Blessing on their marriage.

It was a day to remember!

The Red River Lumber Company Sawmill,
Akeley, Minnesota

16

The Vision of The Rings

"Here am I, send me!"
(Isaiah 6:8)

Magnus Olson was still grieving the death of his beautiful wife, Gyda. As he turned from her grave at the Evanger Church Cemetery, Magnus was aware that he had no place to go. He was homeless and defeated.

Then a friend took him under his wing. Kristian Johnson was a logger. He encouraged Magnus to join him working for the Eau Claire Lumber Co. cutting white and Norway pine in Wisconsin. Magnus worked on farms in the summer between logging seasons. He was well-liked for his kind demeanor and his uncomplaining commitment to hard work. In the farm home after supper, when the chores were done, he would entertain the children with nostalgic tunes on his mouth organ.

Often tears would well up in his eyes as he played tunes which reminded him of his homeland: *"Kan Du Glemme Gamle Norge?"* ("Can You Forget Old Norway?") and *"Hils Fra Meg Der Hjemme"* ("Greetings from Me to Those at Home").

In 1877, Magnus and Kristian found work with the Camp and Walker Lumber Co. in Minnesota. They continued working for T. B. Walker when he started his own company, the Red River Lumber Company. The logs they cut were floated down rivers or hauled by rail to the sawmill.

Eventually, Walker built the largest sawmill in the world at Akeley, Minnesota. The mill ran 300 days a year, and shipped 32 railroad carloads of lumber every 24 hours. During the four months of logging (December through March), each camp of 100 men were pushed to cut 800,000 board feet of logs! They could accomplish this Herculean task only because they were well equipped, well organized, and well fed.

The key to their success was due largely to the industry of the loggers, and the fact that the owner, T. B. Walker, insisted on camp discipline — no alcohol, no gambling, no fighting, no women in the bunkhouse, and no talking at meals except to ask for food.

Though the camp was well disciplined under the watchful eye of the "Push" (foreman) who ruled with an iron hand, the logging camp wasn't exactly a "Sunday School picnic." The mixture of French, Norse, Swedes, Germans, and Irish always held the potential for heated tempers, lying, cheating, and fist fights when the "Bullcook" and the "Push" weren't looking.

"Paul Bunyan"

The "tall tales" of the lumberjacks were both entertainment and a contest. Magnus recalled hearing that a "character" the loggers called "Paul Bunyan" was created to be the bearer of that collection of "logging tales" which were boasted by the French, Irish, Germans, and even the Scandinavians.

> "The story has it," related Magnus, "that this big lumberjack, Paul, and his Blue Ox, Babe, made their entrance into history at the Red River Lumber Camp No. 5, north of Akeley, Minnesota.

"Ja!" exclaimed Kristian, with a smile. "I can swear to it!"

The Loggers of "Camp No. 5"

On the Way . . . with Logs Piled High!

Magnus was an ideal logger — strong, capable, quiet, hard-working, and even-tempered. The "Push" liked him, and soon Magnus was the leader of the log loading team. Though Magnus was making good money ($30 a month), he was quite sure that this was not to be his life's work.

One day he shared with Kristian a strange and somewhat frightening experience:

> "It was either a vision or a dream," Magnus explained. "I saw three interlocking golden rings, and an audible voice called to me, saying, 'Magnus, I am the Triune God, come follow me!' "

Since meeting his friend Kristian, Magnus had "come back" to his faith, but he had no experience with "visions."

> He asked his friend: "What does all this mean? What do you think God is telling me? What should I do?"

These questions were rising from deep inside the guarded inner sanctum of his soul. It wasn't easy for Magnus to give words to personal, spiritual matters, but he trusted his friend to guard his secret.

After Kristian had thought and prayed about Magnus' "vision" for some days, he ventured his opinion:

> "I'm not smart enough to give a full answer to your questions, but I know from the Bible that God Calls all Christians to serve him through their work. Also, He Calls some men to serve in special ways such as pastors. It seems to me that you are being Called by God to something special."

> After a long, thoughtful silence, Magnus asked, "But how can I *know* what He wants me to do? How can I know for *sure?*"

> Kristian didn't look up from his work on the horse harness. His words came slowly. "I sure can't tell you what to do! But my uncle, Pastor Laugaland, told me that he always needed time for prayer and study before he knew what God wanted him to do."

It seemed to Magnus that this was wise counsel. Yes! He would continue his education as his pastor at the Veldre Church in his homeland had encouraged him to do.

In the spring of 1882, when the logging season was over, Magnus applied for admission to the Hauges Synod School in Red Wing, Minnesota. He was accepted. Here he had the opportunity to test his Calling under the wise and caring oversight of men of faith and learning.

Because he was older than most of the students and had experienced many of the joys and sorrows of life, Magnus took time to reflect on the deeper meaning of his studies. In the quiet of his own contemplation, he would revisit his "vision" and the voice which called to him out of the three interlocking golden rings.

He began asking himself questions regarding the deeper implications of the vision of the Rings…for both individual human life and for the society of his adopted country.

As he studied the story of America, he understood that commitment to the "unalienable rights" of the individual was prominent in the thinking of the Founding Fathers. Also, he saw how important the spirit of brotherhood and working together were for a community and the nation.

Then there were the prized commitments to fairness, justice, and equality. But it seemed to Magnus that these national ideals were in *conflict*. They were like ideas wrestling with each other for control of the public mind.

> Magnus wondered how these commitments could be held together without destroying the nation. "What would happen," Magnus spoke out loud, "if each of these ideas were pushed to the extreme? Could a democratic society exist if the principle of unrestricted individual freedom was to dominate in public life? How would this affect the strong desire for conformity and community?"
>
> Kristian knew that Magnus was really talking to himself, but as he listened, he scratched his head and smiled as he responded, "*Uff da!* (an expression of frustration). You're getting too smart for me. You'd better roll those big 'logs' out to me one at a time. I don't follow you. My only answer is '*Ja,* sure! (If you say so, then.)"

Realizing that he was talking over his friend's head but not sure just how to translate his questions, Magnus turned the conversation back to his vision of the Rings, which was their "common ground."

> "I have been thinking that locked in the vision of the Rings may lay the key to understanding the mystery of relating individual freedoms and community responsibilities," he

> said. "But it seems to me that this mystery will not be solved by man's efforts, and that the final answer locked in the three golden Rings will be given by revelation only from *outside* human reason and human effort." He paused. "I believe that we must wait for the right time for this mystery to be revealed."
>
> "How will we know when that time has come?" queried Kristian.
>
> "Now you've stumped me!" admitted Magnus. "All I can say is *Ja,* sure! We'll have to wait and see, then."

Still, it is in the nature of inquiring minds to reach beyond what has been revealed and to grasp at meanings which are just beyond the veil. So it was with *expectancy* that Magnus and Kristian continued to probe with questions and to share their mutual excitement of learning what had been revealed regarding the "Triune" nature of God.

They knew that they had touched on profound mysteries, but sensed the limits of their understanding. To speak of these sacred things was to them like treading unwashed into a holy place.

Nevertheless, they held on in faith to the mystery.

A Signet in the South — ASHEM

"Proclaim liberty throughout the land to all its inhabitants."
(Leviticus 25:10)

Gregory F. Anthony III stood below the dome of what had been the largest church in all Christendom.

44 He took the golden Ring from its place next to his heart and held it in his hand. He had been part of the delegation which met with Turkish officials in Istanbul to negotiate the release of an American news correspondent. Now he was visiting the *Basilica Sancta Sophia* (*Hagia Sophia*), which the Islamic Turks had desecrated by plastering over the magnificent Christian mosaics.

Basilica Sancta Sophia (Hagia Sophia)

He recalled that he had received this Ring from his father, John F. Anthony III, on that sad day when he lay dying from a wound he had received in the defense of the city of Savannah, Georgia. His father told him the saga of the Ring which he held. It was inscribed with the cryptic word, "ASHEM," meaning *Truth*, or, *The Incarnation of Truth*.

Gregory thought back to the story his father had told him. This Ring had been here, in Constantinople, in AD 1453 when his ancestor-namesake, Gregory F. Anthony II, fought under Emperor Constantine XI to defend the city from the onslaught of the Ottoman Muslim Turks.

The golden Ring reminded him of those in his family who had sacrificed their lives in the cause of the Cross.

He thought back to what he knew about his family's early days in the "Promised Land." By 1741, there were 1,200 Salzburgers in "Oglethorpe's Colony" in Georgia. They were industrious people, and, like the Anthony family, took their faith very seriously.

When Methodist Pastors John and Charles Wesley and Evangelist George Whitefield visited Ebenezer, they were, as John F. had written, "deeply impressed by the faith and piety of the Salzburgers."

From their ranks came many early leaders of Georgia. John Adam Treuitlen, a Salzburger, became the first governor of Georgia. Prominent among the early leaders were members of the Anthony family. Some were clergymen, others were business leaders and soldiers. Following the Revolutionary War, several were prominent in state and federal government. During the Civil War, John F. Anthony III distinguished himself in the Battle of Savannah. He sustained a severe wound from which he never fully recovered.

45 After the War Between the States, the Anthony family helped with the rebuilding of the war-devastated South. They gave generously to the rebuilding of the Lutheran college in Newberry, South Carolina. Gregory, as the scion of the Anthony family, had matriculated there in 1868. He was carrying the Second Golden Ring next to his heart when he arrived at Newberry College. (See map on page 54.) He treasured the Ring his father had given him, and often pondered the mystery of the three interlocking golden rings.

Upon graduation he became active in politics, and in 1876 was appointed to the U.S. State Department, representing his country on the staff of the United States Legation to the Ottoman Empire in Istanbul (Constantinople), which allowed him to visit this holy place where he was now standing.

He looked again at his golden Ring and wondered when all Three Rings would come together. *Would it be in his lifetime? Would he ever meet the keepers of the other Rings?*

It was awesome for Gregory to realize that this Ring held within its endless golden circle the "Coptic Secret" which his ancestors had pledged to protect. Gregory recalled that this Ring was part of the Gift which had been offered by the Magi at the feet of the Christ Child.

When he held it, he was reminded of the very presence of Christ Himself.

It spoke to him of the indelible stamp of God's Triune nature, which is mirrored in God's creation of church, state, and family. Also, he saw this imprint of the three interlocking rings in the U.S. form of government.

It is no accident, thought Gregory, that the Founding Fathers of this nation were led to structure a *tri-partite* (three-part) government in which each part has its own unique function and serves as a check and balance to each of the other branches.

They understood, Gregory believed, that only when this design is maintained can the nation experience balance between liberty and equality, individual freedom and community responsibility, minority rights and majority rule, and enjoy national unity in the midst of diversity.

Though he was young in government service, Gregory was beginning to understand that whenever one branch of government usurps the prerogatives of the others, the balance is destroyed and the nation suffers.

What is needed to heal this nation, from the residue of the Civil War, he thought, is the empowering image of the three interlocking rings functioning together in the spirit of unselfish love.

PHOTO 24 / EXACTOSTOCK

Storm Clouds Gathering

PART FOUR

Conflicts — And The Great Divides

18

Beyond the Realm of The Rings

"He who blasphemes against the Holy Spirit will not be forgiven."
(Luke 12:10)

Four years of prayer, study, and reflection at Red Wing Seminary had come to an end for Magnus, and he was recommended for a Call to pastoral ministry by the Seminary faculty.

His first Call was to a six-point (4 churches and 2 preaching places) parish on the prairie-plains of Dakota Territory. In several counties of eastern and northern North Dakota, the Norse settlers were beginning to constitute a majority of up to 69% of the total population! To serve this massive migration, many pastors were needed.

Magnus was excited to be Called by God to be part of this adventure in Kingdom building. As a former lumberjack, Magnus knew the foibles of man—the reality of "The Fall" of Adam and Eve, and the impossibility of human beings to perfect themselves or their culture. He would not be crushed or embittered by the reality of this imperfect world.

> But, he *vowed*, by the *grace* of God, he would be faithful to the Triune God who had Called him and given him the vision of the three interlocking golden rings.

As he stepped off the morning milk train, Pastor Magnus Olson looked past the station to view the main street of the town, which was to be the focus of his Calling. This was Dakota Territory in 1886. Homesteaders were already pushing west beyond the Red River Valley.

Settlement followed Jim Hill's Great Northern Railway westward into Indian country. Echoes of Custer's defeat at Little Big Horn were still in the air, but the relentless tide of land-seeking settlers could not be stopped.

Magnus had been sent by the Hauges Synod to minister to the spiritual needs of the Norse settlers. It would not be easy, the "Fathers" had advised him. And Magnus knew that every day would give him more opportunities to experience the limits of his own abilities and his need for the promise of the Rings. The church leaders had selected Magnus because he had already been "baptized with fire" as a homesteader and a lumberjack! Although he had a soft heart for suffering humanity, his "hide" had been toughened by the trials and troubles of life.

As he surveyed the new storefronts on Main Street, he observed that half were saloons.

> "*Ja!*" he thought, "I'll have work to do in this place."

> Just then, a red-bearded young man driving a team hitched to a buckboard pulled to a stop at the station. He called out to Magnus in Norwegian, "*Er du Presten, den?*" ("Are you the Pastor?") "*Velkommen*!" (Welcome!")

This was the welcome committee from *Ringerike Kirke* (Ringerike Church). Like many Norsemen, he was a man of few words, but there was obvious joy in the tone of Knut Sole's welcome. He and the others in the Congregation had been praying for a pastor and had been notified by the Synod that Magnus was on his way.

Though the church building was recently completed, there was as yet no parsonage. So Knut explained that Pastor Magnus would have room and board at the Thorseth farm. They had lost their three children in a diphtheria epidemic the previous winter. There was an extra bedroom and a place for the pastor's books.

The Thorseths were a devout Christian couple who welcomed Magnus in the familiar Norwegian tradition with lots of good food. Though they were still mourning the loss of their children, they were not defeated. They had not given in to despair.

> The message of the Rings is evident in their lives, thought Magnus. I believe that they can be a source of great encouragement to me.

Andrew Thorseth knew the region well and offered to accompany Pastor Magnus as they traveled by buggy to each of the other three churches and two preaching places. Two were in nearby towns and the rest were in the country. As they journeyed, he shared information about the people in the parish. Magnus was pleased that his comments were kindly and could not be taken as gossip.

Most of the parishioners had been scarred by the harshness of the homesteading experience. There was something inhospitable about this land without the covering of clouds or trees…or traditions. Some had given up and left their claims. A few had tried to assuage their sorrows in alcohol, but most held fast to their faith and to their "American Dream."

But there was one tragic exception to Andrew's rather positive picture of the folks in the parish. This man lived alone on the fringe of the community in a one-room homestead shack.

> "Down that trail," Thorseth pointed, and began in a near whisper….
>
> Then, after a second thought, he reined his horse and the buggy turned away. "We won't visit him, but I think that you should know about him…." Thorseth waited for Magnus to look up as a sign he wanted to know more.
>
> He nodded, and Andrew continued: "La Barge came out West from New England when the country was just opening up. He was a preacher of the Congregational Church who was sent to gather us newcomers into Sunday Schools, so we could learn English and become good Americans. But I guess we didn't do as well as La Barge had hoped. So he got real discouraged. Then, worst of all, his wife died when she was having their first baby, and he lost them both."

As Andrew related the tragic story, Pastor Magnus learned that La Barge had become a bitter man, blaming God for his misfortunes, and that he was unwilling to be comforted. As his anger hardened into hatred, La Barge rejected his Calling as a pastor, and he turned away from his Christian faith.

Now, he took pleasure in ridiculing people of faith and making blasphemous remarks about the Bible. He rejected Christian teachings. He denied the existence of "Absolute Truth," and had become a "free thinker" (agnostic). He championed Charles Darwin's hypothesis of evolution.

Andrew related that La Barge could see *no hope* of Eternal Life.

> To emphasize his denial of God, and of Christian tradition, La Barge had said, "When I die, I don't want a funeral or any burial service. I want to be cremated and have my ashes spread on the Red River."

> The thought of cremation brought a shudder over Magnus. The cremation fire reminded the Pastor of the "Fires of Hell" which are the promised reality (Matthew 18:9 and 25:41) for La Barge and all who reject God's gracious offer of forgiveness and eternal life through Jesus Christ. However, Magnus reminded himself that the most important issue in La Barge's case is not body burial or cremation, but the attitude of the person's heart.

It became apparent to Pastor Magnus that La Barge, in his rejection of the Christian faith, put himself beyond help from God or from his fellowman.

> This, thought Magnus, seemed to be the "unforgiveable sin"—the hardening of one's heart against God. But his rejection was not only a spurning of God, church, and community, it was also a denial of the foundation of America. As Magnus reflected on La Barge's blasphemy, he saw it as a sign of the growing secularization of American society.
>
> *Could* this rebellion against Christianity isolate the nation beyond the realm of the Rings? *Would* this mean that the United States, by rejecting the message of the Rings, could condemn itself to sow the seeds of its own destruction?
>
> The *power* of the Rings, thought Magnus, is the needed *grace* to press on, even when we have failed, or fallen, and to know that the Triune God has *forgiven* us and is *carrying* us in His arms.
>
> That night as he sat at his study table, the Pastor prayed: "Lord, if there is any help for La Barge, free him from the prison of his own presumption. Preserve us all from the idolatry of our own rightness. Give us the humility to seek your gracious help in all circumstances. Liberate us from the prideful desire to live beyond the power of the Rings. *Amen!*"

Magnus was deeply grieved. He realized that the man had slipped beyond the grasp of his theology. It seemed to the new Pastor that Andrew had witnessed the ravings of a damned soul.

19

Kingdoms in Conflict

"Now war arose in heaven, Michael and his angels fighting against the dragon."
(Revelation 12:7)

In the Fall of 1875, Arne Filkesager and the other pre-seminarians at St. Olaf's School in Northfield, Minnesota were walking across town to study Latin and *koine* Greek at St. Walden's College. This was a time not only of secular versus religious conflict in the United States, but also of theological conflicts within the Norwegian churches in America. These conflicts were portended, even in the classroom at St. Walden's.

As they moved through the semester, it became apparent that Professor A. K. H. Tranne was intent on utilizing his own debating prowess to *demolish* their defense of the Biblical accounts of Jesus' birth, miracles, Crucifixion, and Resurrection.

Yes, mused Arnie, Andreas Tranne was an "interesting" choice as a professor of New Testament Greek.

Born into one of the "better" families in Norway, his grandfather had been a *Sokneprest* (head pastor) and his family had its crest on the wall of the *våpenhus* (the vestibule of the church where weapons were left behind, before entering the sanctuary). In short, the Tranne family had status, and Andreas knew he was "somebody."

Upon graduating from the Theological Department of the University of Copenhagen in Denmark, he presented himself to the *Sokneprest* at the Tunsberg *prestegard* (parsonage), K. M. P. Reishus. The faculty at the University was strongly committed to Rationalism and was especially opposed to Pietism.

Presten Reishus, who was the "Head Pastor" of Andreas' home church, was also a Rationalist and was adamantly opposed to the Haugean revival. He spent considerable effort in his sermons pointing out the *improbabilities* in the Biblical accounts of the Virgin Birth of Christ, the visit of the Magi, the miracles of Jesus, the accounts of Jesus' death, and his resurrection from the dead.

He looked at Andreas with a fatherly sort of smile, expecting to hear his protégé echo his own sentiments. But as they spoke the Pastor became quite disturbed that Andreas, though still a "Rationalist," had become a "Social Idealist." Andreas talked of helping the poor and the unjustly treated. He asked his Pastor for a reference to serve in an inner-mission group among the miners in Røros or Kongsberg.

> After an uncomfortable pause, the *Sokneprest* thrust his face out, and proceeded to give Andreas a piece of his mind regarding Social Idealists: "I consider them in the same camp as those simpletons who believe everything recorded in the Bible. Certainly you are not that naïve!"
>
> Andreas hastened to defend himself. "Of course, I don't take the Bible *literally!* I *don't believe* the miracle stories of Jesus. Yet, I do accept the moral imperatives which these illustrate —I want to save people from poverty, disease, and poor working conditions in the mines and factories."

But the *Sokneprest* was unrelenting in his criticism of idealism and of Andreas. So the young man left without a letter of reference. He remembered the sting of that verbal thrashing for a long time. It was the first brush his idealism had with the cold reality of life outside the protective walls of academia.

But he did not give up his idealism. He thought that the poor, starving miners in Røros would surely appreciate his charitable efforts. So he volunteered to serve with an inner mission group working with the copper miners at Røros. Andreas soon learned that if a person bases his commitment to unselfish service on the *thanks* he will receive from those he helps, he will soon become disappointed, bitter, and even resentful toward the needy. After two years, he had enough.

Yet he did not surrender his idealism even when his application for appointment as a parish clerk (assistant to the pastor) was rejected. Andreas became angry with those who sat in positions of power in his homeland.

Soon, however, his anger was transmuted into a strong case of "America Fever." He resolved to follow the flood tide of *husmenn* (cottars) and small farmers who believed that America held the secret to their happiness and success.

> Yes, he thought, in *Amerika* his idealism would be appreciated. This was the land of Walt Whitman's new "democratic man." Here, as St. John de Crevecoeur had observed, the old world immigrants *forget* their past and are *remade* into new men. Certainly this was a nation of idealists!

The filth and squalor which greeted Andreas as he disembarked in lower Manhattan, New York, was disturbing, yet he believed this was only a temporary phase in the metamorphosis of America. However, his fellow Scandinavian immigrants didn't share his dream of an ideal, utopian society. They didn't seem to have time to listen to him!

Furthermore, in his mind, most of them were "hopelessly conservative" in their religious and social views. They seemed to believe that humanity, even in America, was tainted by "The Fall" and could not be expected to bring about the perfect society.

Andreas learned that many immigrants had brought the Bible, *Psalmebok* (hymnbook), and *Huspostill* (Book of Sermons) with them to this New Land. It was obvious to him that his own people would have much to *unlearn* if they were to become "real Americans."

Andreas believed that he had caught the "real vision" of this new land. It was to be a "Melting Pot" where all differences among nationalities, races, classes, and religions would be *melted together* into one undifferentiated mass of humanity.

Driven by his idealism, Andreas sought out kindred spirits. He was repelled by the "naïve faith" of the Norwegian and Swedish immigrants and by their Lutheran churches which actually believed and taught the Bible's orthodox Christian message.

But he believed they were "not beyond hope" and that they could be *changed*!

In his search for a platform, Andreas answered an ad in the Norwegian newspaper, "*Frimand*." The ad was for a "liberal" theologian who had the requisite educational background and who could speak the Norwegian language. It seemed that every "American" religious denomination was trying to reach the new immigrants who were flooding the frontier.

The Unitarians had established a church in the Minnesota frontier town of Hanska. They were trying to reach the Scandinavians with their idealistic "gospel," which emphasized the "Fatherhood of God" and the "Brotherhood of Man."

This was just what Andreas was looking for! He had good credentials from the Theological Faculty at Copenhagen. Furthermore, the Call from the Unitarians included a part-time position to teach classical languages at St. Walden's College in Northfield, Minnesota.

So in the fall of 1875, Rev. Andreas K. H. Tranne, newly ordained and installed clergyman at the Unitarian Church in Hanska, Minnesota, was hired to teach Latin and *koine* Greek at St. Walden's. Along with the St. Walden's students, in his first Greek class there were a few from the new Lutheran Academy across town called St. Olaf's School. These men were preparing to enter the Lutheran ministry and were required to have ability in Latin and Greek. St. Walden's had opened its doors to them until such time as their own faculty was appointed.

Among the St. Olaf students was a young man from Texas by the name of Arne Filkesager. Reverend Tranne thought that this was his golden opportunity to *transform* these St. Olaf students into "real Americans." Arne seemed to be the leader of the group. Andreas would start with him.

The primary text for studying *koine* Greek is the Greek New Testament. Professor Tranne assigned the study of grammar as well as the reading of passages from this text. He assigned the first chapters of both Matthew's Gospel and the Book of Luke as the primary readings, because he wanted his students to "get" his teaching on the *mythology* of the Christmas Story and the miracles of Jesus.

He introduced his students to the ideas of Leibniz, Hegel, and Semler in an attempt to *undermine* the orthodox teachings of the Christian Church. Professor Tranne was a very astute debater and became particularly eloquent just before the Christmas Holiday in his attempts to *discredit* the Biblical teachings regarding the Virgin Birth, the Nativity, and the visit of the Wise Men.

Arne and his friends didn't swallow the Professor's rationalism, and defended their faith with Scripture.

> Tranne ridiculed the account of the Wise Men and their gifts. "Certainly you aren't so *naïve* as to believe that three Persian astrologers were guided by a bright star to the place of Jesus' birth and brought him gifts of gold, frankincense, and myrrh!"

Arne wanted to trump Tranne's argument by holding up the golden Ring.

> But he remembered *Far's* instructions: "Keep the story of the Rings in your heart until you tell your own son, or meet those who possess the other Rings."

Arne held his tongue. He would say nothing!

> But the arguments of the Professor were disturbing. Arne struggled with the questions: "*Is* the Biblical account *accurate?* Is the story of the Wise Men and their Gifts to the Christ Child really *true?* If only he could talk to *Far!*"

Each day Arne and his fellow classmates walked from Manitou Heights (the hill on which St. Olaf's School was to be built) to Professor Tranne's classes. Every trip was like advancing into enemy territory. After each skirmish with Professor Tranne, they returned to their own fortress bruised and bloodied, but not beaten.

The next day they would sally forth with more ammunition for the defense of the faith. But throughout the semester they had a growing conviction that their own power of reason was not the final bastion of defense for the faith. Scripture alone would be their ultimate fortress.

AHURO ASHEM

MAZDAO

20

The Wisdom of the Rings vs. The Wisdom of the World

"The way of the fool is right in his own eyes: but a wise man listens to advice."
(Proverbs 12:15)

Arne's struggle continued for the entire semester. But finally, he understood that the Ring which his father had passed on to him was not what *proved* the Bible.

> Arne reminded himself: "It is the Scriptures which testify to the truth of the message of the three interlocking rings. The Bible tells us of the tri-personal nature of God. The inscriptions on the Rings simply *point to* this truth:
>
> "He is AHURO (*God*, or, *Lord of All*)."
>
> "He is ASHEM (*Truth*, or, *The Incarnation of Truth*)."
>
> "He is MAZDAO (*Wisdom*, or, *Spirit of Wisdom*)."
>
> Arne prayed that his teacher would come to know the truth of Scripture—the Message of the Rings!

One evening, as he carefully removed the Ring from its hiding place, Arne yearned for the time when the Three Golden Rings would be brought together.

> "*Who* were the keepers of the *other* Rings?" he asked himself. Yet a deeper question was crowding into his consciousness: "*What* would happen to the individual, the family, or the *nation* that rejected the Wisdom of the Rings?"

It seemed like a breath of fresh air for Arne and his fellow students to return to their own campus and be encouraged in their faith by

President of the Board and Founder of the College, the Reverend B. J. Muus, and the faculty. (See photo on page 130.) Their lectures were solidly anchored in the Bible as the ground of Absolute Truth.

It seemed to Arne that the most *critical issue* for Western civilization and for the New Land of America was the issue of *Truth*.

He felt himself on the "horns of this dilemma" when he walked between Professor Tranne's classes and those taught by the St. Olaf's faculty. One of his favorite professors emphasized that ultimate Truth could not be discovered by Hegelian reason or by science. It must be revealed by the Triune God Himself. He made this point in a lecture entitled, "America — A *Pilgrimage* To Destiny."

Arne had notes on that lecture. Now, he read them again:

> "America is on a *pilgrimage* to its ultimate destiny. It is yet in the *process* of becoming. Whether or not it will reach its God-appointed *destiny* depends on whether this process is guided by a commitment to *absolute* Truth or to *relative* truth."
>
> "But *where* are we to find this Absolute Truth?" Arne asked himself. "Surely not by human reason or intellect, not by philosophy or politics, and not by science or medicine. Truth is revealed for all to see through the Word of God — the Bible."
>
> The Triune God is the Truth for all men. *He* is the central Truth of Scripture. In Him all things *hold together*."

Arne sat back in his chair, looked at the golden Ring, and continued his reflection regarding the Kingdom of The Rings—the Truth of the Triune God. He paused as he read his notes, struck again by this reminder of the *three* interlocking rings, and he wondered *when* they would come together.... Perhaps this would happen only at the Second Coming.

Suddenly, his thoughts were interrupted by shouting.

> Someone was running in the hallway: "Jesse James and his gang just robbed a bank in downtown Northfield! Jesse and Frank have escaped! They took Sonja Melby hostage!"

Arne was stunned! Sonja was very special to him. He thought a lot about her and she always smiled when he spoke to her at the bank. Now, she had been captured by robbers!

What would happen to her? *How* could he help?

His immediate reaction was to join the posse and try to rescue her. But the posse was already on the trail of the outlaws.

Before Arne and the other St. Olaf's students could catch up, the posse had surrounded the James brothers and their hostage at the Bakken Farm, west of Northfield. There was a firefight, but Jesse and Frank escaped on fresh horses. All was quiet as the posse cautiously approached the barn.

Then someone heard a moan. It was Sonja, who had been struck by one of the posse's bullets.

When the posse arrived at Doctor Sandquist's office in Northfield, Sonja was still breathing but unconscious. The bullet had lodged in her brain. She was bleeding through the ears and nose. Arne was near her when she breathed her last.

He touched her hand with the Ring and remembered God's word of promise from his father's funeral:

> *"Even though I walk through the valley of the shadow of death, I will fear no evil for thou art with me."* (Psalm 23:4)

He tried to comfort Sonja's mother with these words of Scripture, but like Rachel of old, weeping for her children, she sobbed and would not be comforted.

On the day of the funeral at St. John's Church, no easy words were spoken, no pious platitudes, no Darwinian explanations, no Hegelian reasons were voiced.

> "Thankfully, it is not Professor Tranne's arguments which accompany us as we walk through the Valley of the Shadow of Death," Arne said softly to a classmate, as tears welled up in his eyes. "Even philosophy seems like tinkling brass or the noise of broken glass in the face of untimely death."

Faced with the reality of Sonja's tragic death, Arne knew that the only source of refuge and strength was the Word of Him who has already conquered death.

The text for Pastor Muus' funeral sermon was Jesus' promise recorded in John 11:25:

> *"I am the Resurrection and the Life, he who believes in me, though he die, yet shall he live."*

Arne looked over at Sonja's grieving mother and saw her countenance lifted. He saw that *this* Word alone was able to comfort her broken heart.

It is this promise of Jesus, guaranteed by the Cross and Resurrection, which defines the boundaries of the Kingdom of the Rings, thought Arne. All who are received by the Triune God in baptism and who respond to his grace in faith and repentance belong to His Kingdom.

As he stood at Sonja's open grave, clutching the Ring which *Far* had given him, he knew that his life must be given to *sharing* the message of hope — the Message of The Rings!

He *would* become a pastor!

21

To the End of the Earth

"You shall receive power . . .
and you shall be my witnesses
to the end of the earth."
(Acts 1:8)

Arne did not feel like a pioneer, but he was in the first graduating class from St. Olaf's School. He had five classmates. All were young men, though the school was open to women as well.

He was good friends with Emilie Brandt, who started two years after him. She was studying to be a parochial school teacher. Her father and mother were also immigrants from Hedmarken. Because their dialects were very similar, Arne loved to hear Emilie speak. Her poetic Norse language reminded him of home. They had much in common to talk about. Both had been friends of Sonja.

Emilie's father, too, had served in the Civil War ("War Between The States"). He had joined Colonel Heg's 15th Wisconsin "Scandinavian" Regiment and was killed in the Battle of Chickamauga. Now that her father was dead, her younger brothers and mother were operating the farm.

They spoke often of the Civil War and of their fathers, who had served on opposite sides. Arne's father was a Confederate chaplain and Emilie's father was a Lieutenant in the Union Army. Both had served in the Western Campaign. In spite of their fathers' conflicting loyalties, Arne and Emilie were becoming more than just "good friends." However, Arne didn't allow himself to get too serious, because he still had four years of Seminary training ahead of him.

The Synod Seminary was located at Madison, Wisconsin. For the next four years, this was to be Arne's home during the school year. After his father's death they had moved from Texas to Stoughton, Wisconsin. During Seminary he would be close to his mother and younger siblings.

It would be good, he thought, to get home more often.

46 It was in June of 1882 that Arne graduated from Seminary and received his first Call. He was to serve at Northby Parish, Dakota Territory. At his ordination, Pastor Muus preached on the "Great Commission" text. This message encouraged the young pastor to consider his Calling to be like that of a missionary. He was being sent to new country, new communities, and new congregations which had been planted in the wake of the recent upsurge of Norse immigration to Dakota Territory.

It was now over seventeen years since the end of the Civil War, and the settlement of the plains was proceeding apace. Thousands of Norwegians and Norwegian-Americans were heading to Dakota to "prove up" their claim to a quarter-section (160 acres) of this virgin land.

However, in the midst of all this newness, Arne knew that he was still Called to proclaim the "old, old Story"—the tested and true message of The Kingdom of the Rings.

Most of Arne's flock would be young. The typical Norse immigrant was 18–28 years old. Yet they were breaking the sod and establishing farms, homes, churches, schools, and towns on an expanding frontier which flanked the Great Northern Railroad as it moved west across the prairie-plains. Most of the towns were too new to be on a map!

This was missionary work! As he thought about the "Dakota frontier," it almost seemed to Arne that he was being Called by the Triune God to go to "the end of the earth!"

A feeling of fear came over him.

He thought, *This work is impossible for someone like me!*

But when Arne touched his golden Ring, it reminded him that he was not *alone* as he answered the Call. He felt humbled by the awesome task to which the Living God was Calling him. He knew that he did not compare with the faithful, committed, and strong men of the cloth who had gone before him.

In closing, when Reverend Muus read a tribute to pioneer pastors, Arne thought of his own father, who had sacrificed so much as a pastor and chaplain during "The War Between The States." Reverend Muus prefaced his reading of the poem by pointing out that the Norwegian immigrants had a great respect for their pastors.

"Northby Parish" –
"Dakota Territory"

"They stand," he said, "as *heroes* among their people, even as the poet J. J. Skordalsvold pictures them:

"It brings relief in such an age as ours,
An age of 'can't' and mock-heroic deeds,

To look around for *heroes* worthy of the name,
Nor far we need to go to find them.
The *Norseland preachers* in our western wilds
Have left a saga more bright and fair to see,
Than Minnesota's Indian-summer skies.

Some were at home in Greece and Rome of old,
While the others knew but little of the world
Save Canaan and their native mountains,
With their vales and fjords.
But all went out with this in mind:

To serve their Master
and to help their fellow man."

It was an awesome responsibility to follow in their steps. But in that moment, the golden Ring next to his heart reminded Arne of his father's favorite Bible passage:

"I can do all things in Christ who strengthens me."
(Philippians 4:13)

As he said his farewells to his mother, brothers, sisters, and Emilie Brandt, the words stuck in his throat and he had to bite his lip to hold back his emotions. He spoke only a few words as he hugged his family.

> Then, holding Emilie's hand, he struggled with his farewell:
> *"Jeg elsker dere! Be for meg! Ha det bra!"*
> ("I love you all! Pray for me! Take care of yourselves!")

His books, robe, *prestekrage* (pastor's collar), and his clothes fit into two small handbags. It would be a long trip to Grand Forks, Dakota Territory, and then southwest beyond the railroad tracks to Buffalo Trails County.

(See map on page 107.)

The Prairie Winds

22

Apostles on the Prairie

"As the Father has sent Me, even so I send you."
(John 20:21)

This was *new country!* The first homesteaders had come only ten years earlier, in 1872.

Arne, like most new pastors in Dakota, was Called to serve several congregations. His Call was to six congregations and "preaching places" in the Buffalo River Valley. But this was no surprise. Before he had arrived in Northby Parish, Arne had heard of the "church-planting exploits" of several pastors who were well known in that region.

Folks told him of Reverend B. A. Harstad of the Norwegian Synod who had founded sixteen congregations during the first two years of his ministry in Prairie County! He also had a strong commitment to parochial schools and had organized two boarding schools and an academy.

The young pastor had also heard of the good work of other Norwegian Lutheran pastors, like Reverend C. T. Saugstad of the Konferents, who served seventeen congregations as a new pastor just out of Seminary and, then, led a wagon train of settlers to Canada. The Hauges Synod Pastor, Reverend B. Anderson, was another "hero" who served fourteen congregations on both sides of the Red River and was a strong advocate of *afholdsforenninger* (temperance societies).

When he thought of these pastors, his own charge of six congregations and preaching places didn't seem so formidable.

But first he wanted to meet the people in his own parish. The members of *Trefoldigheds* (Trinity) Congregation had planned a special welcome for him at the home of Lars Rockne. He was given a real Norwegian welcome, with lots of food and coffee. It was encouraging for Arne, since their words and faces beamed of *thanksgiving to God* for sending them a pastor.

As he visited with his people, they spoke of both their joys and sorrows. There were children to be baptized, couples to be married, young people to be confirmed, the sorrowing and grieving among them to be comforted, the sick to be visited and communed, false teachers to be corrected, and churches to be built.

Arne was thankful that a deacon from each congregation would take him by buckboard or buggy to each of his preaching places and to the neighboring towns. Only the Highland Congregation had completed its church building. All the others were still meeting in homes, barns, and in the open air on nice days. As the new pastor looked across the treeless prairie, he realized that there was no lack of open space for services and gatherings.

The only contender that seemed jealous of this open space and eager to keep it for itself was the wind.

Summer or winter, day or night, seedtime or harvest, the wind kept pushing on homesteaders, their animals, houses, churches, and schools as if to say: *"This is my country—go back to where you came from!"*

And in the face of the relentless pressure of the wind, some people did give up and went back East, but most faced it down and conquered. Arne heard of people who became depressed by the open space and the relentless wind. His problems with the wind—blowing pages in his books, sweeping his sermon notes into a mud puddle or watering trough, or teasing him as he chased his cap across the field—these were trivial matters when compared to the burdens that some were called to bear.

Most of his parishioners were thankful for his ministry and his visits, but not everyone! One day he ventured out on his own to visit settlers near Frog Point, on the Red River.

> He greeted a fellow who answered him with, "Ministers and machine agents ought to be driven out of the country!"

In that embarrassing moment, he remembered the counsel of Pastor Muus, who reminded him that the ministry is not a popularity contest. More important than his own hurt feelings; was the Word and promise of Jesus: *"He who hears you hears me and he who rejects you rejects Me."* (Luke 10:16)

There were a few other times when his ministry was rejected, but most often, the people were thankful for his presence. Arne knew that it was not him, but *Him* whom he represented. It was a humbling and awesome thought that the Triune God came to these people through his preaching of the Word, the administration of the Sacraments, and through his prayers and care of their souls.

Six months after Arne arrived in the Buffalo River settlement, the *klokker* (sexton) at *St. Johannes Lutherske Menighet* (St. John's Lutheran Congregation) lost both his wife and two children to cholera.

Johan Styrk Salmonson was broken-hearted! He shared with his pastor his pain and loneliness in a moving poem which Arne read at the graveside:

"*When life's storms sweep*

And darkness breaks in,
And sorrow follows me
Like waves in the wind,
When deeds and faults
Stand side by side,
And all my works are broken
Like spoiled leaves and straw,

Then in my lonely heart
Tears and sorrow burn,
And in all its pain
I don't know where to turn."

But life must go on. Johan built a wooden coffin for each of them and with the help of his neighbors dug the graves. It was only Pastor Arne's third funeral, but one of the most difficult he would have in his entire ministry.

However, for Johan and the many neighbors who gathered in the new cemetery to share in his sorrow, there was the Word of Hope: Christ has won the Victory over death and has promised Life in His Kingdom to all who believe and are baptized. Arne was thankful that the Lord used his voice to speak the Word of faith and hope to the people as well as to himself, the Pastor.

"Rescue those who are being taken away to death."
(Proverbs 24:11)

23

In Season and Out of Season

"Rejoice with those who rejoice,
weep with those who weep."
(Romans 12:15)

For Pastor Arne Filkesager, the next two years were very busy — ministering in six places plus building two church structures. He had a great admiration for Reverend Harstad, who was an inspiring leader and visionary. Like many in the Synod, Harstad was committed to building parochial schools in order to teach the faith in its truth and purity, and to help maintain the identity of the Norwegian Lutheran people and "rescue" them from the "Melting Pot."

This was a real challenge in a culture which was trying to melt together all Norwegians, Irish, Swedes, Danes, Germans, Scots, French, Italians, and Poles into a bland mass of humanity in which everyone had forgotten his past and lost his own identity. Harstad taught that the parochial school was a bastion against the "dissolving" effects of the public school. Arne resonated to this philosophy.

Later, when Reverend Harstad asked if he would teach at the Gran Academy, Pastor Arne was eager to accept. He was pleased when his congregations gave their approval. This was exciting news to share with Emilie, for she was preparing to teach in a parochial school and was eager to secure a position.

Perhaps she could teach music and art at the Academy and serve as "house-mother" for the girls. Thus, she would have her room and board taken care of... *and* be close to Arne.

The School Board agreed with this plan. So Emilie arrived at Gran Academy in September 1884. During the school year, she and Arne made plans to be married the next summer, when the Trinity parsonage was finished.

There were dark clouds on the horizon in the summer of 1885 after their wedding. A split in the Norwegian Synod was looming over God's "election" of those who are saved. Arne favored the teaching which was summarized as "God's election in view of *faith*." The lay leaders of five of Pastor Filkesager's congregations agreed with him.

Arne felt comfortable that if *Far* were alive he would also, like him, join the "Brotherhood," who were opposed to slavery and who favored God's "election" in view of *faith*. But it was very painful to share his decision with Reverend Harstad, for it meant that he would lose a friend and could no longer teach at the Academy.

While he anguished over this loss of friends and the fellowship of his church body, he was drawn to a new circle of support. These were the Norwegian pastors who served the Konferents and Hauges Synods. They welcomed the young couple and included them in their "Pastors' Circles."

Among those who reached out the hand of fellowship to Arne and Emilie was a Hauges pastor who had lost his wife at the same time that Arne's father had died. His name was *Magnus Olson*. He also served several congregations and preaching places and was very active in the *afholds* (temperance) movement.

He spoke to Arne of the great evil of the American saloon. It was alcohol that held the common man down. He saw it in Norway and he saw the evil effect on his own parishioners. Alcohol captured the minds and the wills, as well as the money, of the settlers and turned them into slaves of the saloon keepers, the liquor industry, and unscrupulous politicians.

> Magnus shared with Arne, "One of the worst *Drinking Towns* in the whole region is River Bend on the Minnesota side. This small town boasts over *seventy* saloons with gambling joints and houses of ill repute! This is where some of our young men from West Forks, Buffalo Trails, and West Bend Counties are *wasting* their money… and their lives."

Pastor Olson confided to Arne that it was a fellow Norwegian who was backing the saloon keepers!

> "The politician whom the saloon industry supports and who secures big legislative favors for them is a Norwegian named Ivar Ondestad. The only way to defeat politicians like Ondestad is to organize *afholdsforenninger* (temperance societies) in all the churches! These will be centers for rallying voters and distributing literature to the public."

This, he believed, was the only way to defeat the evil of the "American Saloon."

It was apparent to Arne that the saloon issue and the public school issue were major points of disagreement between the various Norwegian groups. Perhaps there would be no resolution of these and other issues in this "Promised Land," until the golden Rings came together. Arne held on in hope to the promise of Christ recorded in Revelation 22:20:

> *"He who testifies to these things says,*
> *Surely I am coming soon. Amen.*
> *Come, Lord Jesus!"*

By the fall of 1889, five of Pastor Arne's congregations had completed their church buildings. He had now served seven years in the Northby Parish, and the Lord had used these good people to teach their young pastor that it was not them or their pastor who would build the Kingdom. Only the Triune God Himself is the builder.

> Thankfully, thought Arne, we have the privilege of being His hands and feet and voices as He builds.

The Filkesagers were now the proud parents of two beautiful children. The eldest was named Rolf Eirik, in honor of Arne's father, and the younger was christened Kari, a name which had been in the Brandt family for several generations.

There were tears when Arne, Emilie, Rolf, and Kari bade farewell to their friends among whom they had ministered for the past seven years.

> "It's hard to leave! You have been so kind to us. We'll really miss you!" Emilie was sobbing as she said her goodbyes.

Kari, too, was crying as she hugged her kittens and handed them one-by-one to her friends to keep and care for.

> The pain of leaving is also a part of ministry, thought Arne, as he consoled his wife and children.

It had been a difficult decision. They were leaving their wonderful parish—where folks loved them and where they had invested so much of themselves—to answer the Call to a new type of ministry. Arne was Called to serve as College Pastor, and instructor in Church and

American History, at the new Seminary which was just opening at St. Olaf College in Northfield, Minnesota in 1890.

As they boarded the "Great Northern" and waved *"Farvel!"* to the many who had come to the station, they felt they were leaving part of themselves behind. The wind-swept prairies of Dakota had become their home.

> As he looked into the faces of his people, Arne was reminded of those times of joy and sorrow when he had felt the *closeness* of The Kingdom of The Rings.

Part Five

All Roads Lead to Chicago!

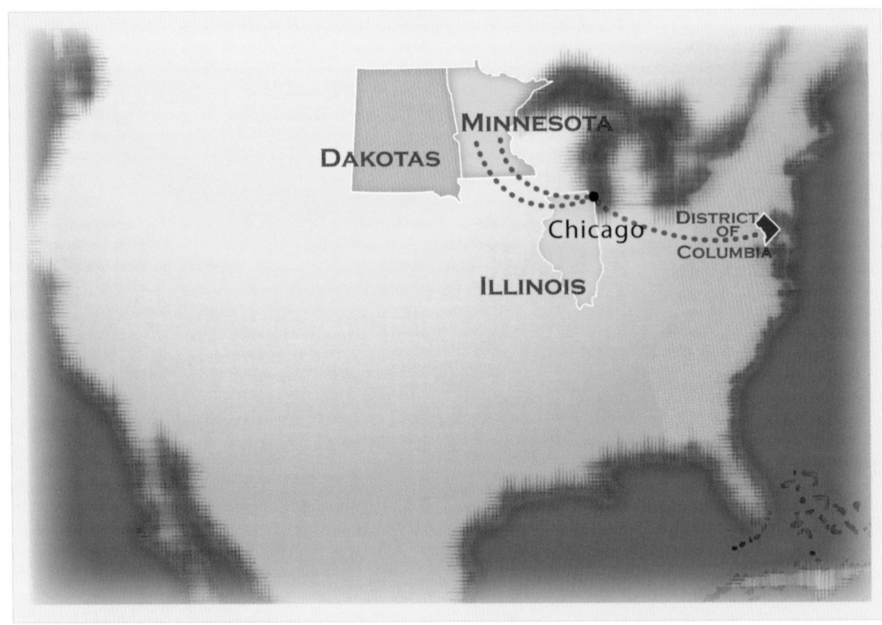

THE JOURNEYS OF THE RINGS TO CHICAGO

MAP KEY:

GREEN: (Northfield, Minnesota) "AHURO" (*God*, or, *Lord of All*), Pastor Arne Filkesager, also (Northwest Minnesota) Per Ondestad.

VIOLET: (Washington, DC), "ASHEM" (*Truth*, or, *The Incarnation of Truth*), Gregory F. Anthony III.
(Note: Washington, DC has been enlarged for easy viewing.)

ORANGE: (Illinois and Chicago), "MAZDAO" (*Wisdom*, or, *Spirit of Wisdom*), Reidunn Haraldson Hanson (and husband Lars Hanson).

24

In the City of Destiny

"He looked forward to the city
which has foundations,
whose builder and maker is God."
(Hebrews 11:10)

Chicago had risen like the fabled Phoenix from its own ashes. The "Great Fire" of 1871 had leveled most of the city, caused $200 million in property damage, and left many of its 300,000 inhabitants homeless.

But the "Great Fire" seemed to be an event of purgation—a cleansing of the city. From its ashes, Chicago grew to new prominence as the second largest city in America. As the city spread its new wings, it appeared to be the substance of the "American Dream" taking shape in tangible form.

The Publisher and the Editors of Chicago's greatest newspapers—the *Chicago Daily News*, the *Chicago Record*, and the *Times-Herald*—had become key leaders in the effort to rebuild Chicago as the industrial, transportation, and cultural center of America. Among these leaders was Victor Lawson, owner and publisher of the *Chicago Daily News*. He was a first-generation American, born of Norwegian immigrant parents. However, like many others, he had anglicized his name from Larson to Lawson.

His father, Ivar Larson, had helped organize the large Norwegian language newspaper in Chicago, the *Skandinaven*, and he also edited the *Amerika*. Ivar served as both a Chicago alderman and an Illinois State Representative.

When his father died in 1872, Victor had been called home from Harvard University to manage the family's Norwegian newspapers. Then, in 1875, he had bought the English language newspaper, the *Chicago Daily News*, and in a few years, the *Evening Post*. Lawson started the *Chicago Record* and took over the *Times-Herald*. He was also one of the founders of the Associated Press.

As a young reporter, Lars Hanson had been proud to be a part of the *Chicago Daily News* staff. He learned that Lawson was credited with making his newspaper into one of the greatest newspapers in the world, and keeping it an outstanding exponent of clean, enterprising journalism.

Furthermore, Lars knew firsthand that his boss was a vigorous and fearless advocate of all that was best in public and private life. Though he was only a news reporter, Lars had told Reidunn that he felt good that, through "his" paper, he had at least a small part in shaping the destiny of Chicago.

Reidunn prayed that the three golden Rings would come together to fulfill Lars' hopes for his family and for Chicago.

When Reidunn and Lars returned to Chicago in 1878, following his release from the Turkish prison and their subsequent wedding and honeymoon, Lars received a promotion, as well as a personal greeting and congratulations, from Victor Lawson. This was a testimony to Lawson's personal concern for the welfare of his workers and their families.

It was demonstrated again when Lawson and his wife, Jessie, attended the Conservatory Recital. When they heard Reidunn's solo in the recital, they were so impressed that they recommended her to the Director of the Chicago Metropolitan Chorale as a soprano soloist.

> When this honor was announced, Reidunn demurred with characteristic Norwegian modesty: "I'm just a poor immigrant girl who loves to sing. I don't deserve this honor. You've been too kind to me."

It was almost impossible for her to believe that she had been selected to be a soprano soloist with the Metropolitan Chorale! As tears of joy streamed from her eyes, Reidunn thought of her mother and father and how proud they would be. She touched the Ring, which she wore on a golden chain concealed in her bosom, in thanksgiving to God.

It was exciting for the young couple to be at the "nerve center" of this great city, which was striving to become the incarnation of the "American Dream."

One day she told her husband the story of the golden Ring which her mother had entrusted into her keeping.

47 *Could Chicago be the place where the three Rings would again come together?*

They wondered, but told no one.

Chicago History Museum. Color reproduction of Broadside; ICHi-14835; Broadside for Chicago Day at the World's Columbian Exposition; World's Columbian Exposition; Chicago (Ill); 1893; Lithographer: Goes

25

The American Dream—Destiny or Defeat?

"Your old men shall dream dreams
and your young men shall see visions."
(Joel 2:28)

Reidunn continued her singing with the Metropolitan Chorale until their first child was expected. They named her Brita Petra in honor of Reidunn's mother.

Lars was smitten by his daughter. She had fine dark hair and large blue eyes. But she was so tiny! When he held her, he was almost breathless, afraid that she might break. It was plain to see that Brita had her father twisted around her little fingers. Yes! Indeed, she held both parents in her tiny grip. Night and day they were her willing slaves.

> One day, Lars came home with a worried look on his face. He spoke in a hushed tone, trying to sound calm, lest he frighten his wife: "A diphtheria epidemic has broken out in the city. The reports say it's very serious. Many children are dying!"
>
> Reidunn's face mirrored her anxiety. "How can we keep Brita safe? Should we leave the city, and bring her to the Bensons in Iowa?"

But before they could make plans to send Reidunn and Brita away, fever and swelling struck. Brita had difficulty breathing. She was very sick.

> Reidunn pleaded with the Lord for her child's life:
> "Lord! Help us! Save our daughter!"

As she reached down and touched the golden Ring, she was *comforted*, knowing that the Triune God was *always* with her and ready to *help*. However, after two days and nights of prayer and minute-by-minute attention to their daughter, it seemed there was no improvement.

Then, in the third night, Reidunn was awakened by a loud cry. The fever had broken! Brita was crying for her mother. She had been saved, thought Reidunn, to be the keeper of the golden Ring!

In the next few years Lars and Reidunn were blessed with three more children. The next were named Tove and Grace. The youngest was named Karl Victor. He was only three in 1893, when Chicago staged its extravagant "coming of age" party—"The Chicago World's Columbian Exposition." It celebrated the 400 years since Columbus rediscovered America.

More than 27 million people from all over America and from distant corners of the world came to see and experience the birth of a new age of power and enlightenment. Most impressive was the turreted Palace of electric power, with its gigantic dynamos turning out electricity to fill every corner! With its soaring domes and miles of Grecian columns and Venetian canals, the "Chicago World's Fair" was a grand facade dedicated to the "American Dream" and the presumed victory of materialism and the machine.

Crowds with "Palm Sunday" enthusiasm could have imagined that God had prepared such a grand setting for the return of the three Rings to usher in the eschaton.

> Reidunn again wondered, *Could* this be the *kairos* (the right *time*), and the *place* which God had chosen?

Only the Maker of the Rings could know.

26

Where Fools Rush In

"Visiting the iniquity of the fathers upon the children to the third and fourth generation."
(Exodus 20:5)

Torstein Ondestad was the owner (*bonde*) of a large farm in the Glomma River Valley in eastern Norway. He was a drinking buddy and friend of the *Lensmann* (sheriff). When the sheriff reported that one of the Haugeans was preaching at a farm near the Grue Church, Torstein was adamant to *"stop this crazy man!"*

The preacher was calling people to repentance and to a life-style which reflected the true Christian faith. For many, this meant no more drunkenness and no more gambling. Torstein encouraged his son, Ivar, and his buddies, to ride over to the Grue Church and disrupt the Haugean prayer meeting. The *Lensmann* nodded his approval.

Ivar and his buddies did their best to harass the Haugeans' meeting. However, the *unforeseen* result of this encounter was that one of Ivar's gang—Amund Overgaard—was convicted of his sin...and became a *changed* man!

Both Ivar and Amund were *younger* sons of large farm owners. Since Confirmation they had become hellions—drunkenness, wild parties, and wild women had become their "badge of distinction." It was rumored that they had both fathered illegitimate children. They were well on their way to Hell when the Haugean preached at Grue.

It is a *testimony* to the strange moving of the Spirit that one rascal was converted and one was not.

> In the months that followed, Amund would pray for his friend and often ask the Lord, "*Why* did you rescue me and not Ivar? Why should *I* have been set free from my slavery to the flask and not Ivar?"

Try as he may, he could not reach Ivar, who was unwilling to be changed!

> Amund soon became the butt of Ivar's jokes: "Amund the pious!" and "Amund the Haugean!" Ivar would taunt.
>
> The final parting came in April 1868, when Ivar quarreled with his father and declared his hatred for his home. He vowed that he would "go to America" and "never write" and "never return."

His mother wept, but old Torstein sent his son on his way with a curse and a threat.

Ivar consoled himself with *akevitt* (liquor) and bought his passage to New York. As long as his money held out, Ivar was a popular fellow. But when he was down and out, none of his friends remembered him. He wanted to go West, but since he had wasted his inheritance, he had to work his way on the Erie Canal and up the Great Lakes.

He finally arrived in the "Windy City" of Chicago. During a drinking party, he learned that land was opening up for settlement in northwestern Minnesota, as a result of the signing of the Old Crossing Treaty with the Chippewa Indians. He determined to go and take land for himself.

In St. Paul, Minnesota, he bargained with the *Metis* (French-Indian) wagoners who were just beginning their trek back to Pembina and Winnipeg. He joined them as an oxcart teamster. It was a slow, noisy ride in the Red River Carts. When the oxcart train finally arrived at the Beaver River crossing in Clay County, Ivar bade farewell to the Metis and went on his way, alone, to the town of Prairie City and the Federal Land Office. He was told that an ideal quarter section along the Sioux Creek had not been taken. It was located in Skandia Township, so he filed on the southeast quarter, section 15, and proceeded to walk the fifteen miles to his claim.

When he was sober, Ivar was a capable farmer. He "proved up his claim to 160 acres" and added an 80 acre tree claim. His natural ability as a speaker made him a capable leader among his countrymen. As the community grew with many more Norsemen, Swedes, and Irish, Ivar was elected to positions of responsibility in the county, and eventually as a representative in the Minnesota State Legislature.

He was a real "deal-maker," and good at bringing rival nationality groups together, and in this way he secured his seat in the Legislature. Ivar was known for his ability to get political favors for his friends. He was loved by his constituents, but despised by his family.

His children were intelligent and gifted like their father, and also irreligious and unruly. Their mother tried to bring them up right, but the example that Ivar had set was indelibly inscribed upon the minds and hearts of his children.

Abuse of alcohol put its mark on the entire family.

Thus "the saga of the Ondestad family" was replete with stories of drunken excesses, abuse, illegitimacy, family feuds, and scrapes with the law. Ivar's daughter died of syphilis; one son became an alcoholic; and the other (Oscar) lived with a common-law wife. Her name was Rosie. She was a Gypsy—a kindly person—but not accepted by the community.

They lived together without the benefit of marriage. This, in a rural Scandinavian community, was unacceptable. Folks were nice, but cool. Their unspoken judgment was a barrier too difficult to cross! Rosie became depressed and found her consolation in the bottle.

Her son, Per, tried to overcome the hurdle of being a *"bastard."*

He sought to gain community acceptance by trying to get attention in whatever way he could. He became the local clown and buffoon, but it didn't work to his advantage. When he grew to manhood, he was determined to move away to find a part of America that would appreciate him—where he could begin *again*.

But... could he escape the chains of his inheritance and training in the Ondestad family?

On his own, by the wisdom of the world, he could do no better than to repeat the sins of his father and grandfather. But, his grandmother prayed that Per would be found by a power *beyond himself*—by the *transforming power of The Kingdom of God.*

St. Olaf's School (St. Olaf College),
Northfield, Minnesota, Board of Trustees, July 13, 1866.
Founder, Rev. B. J. Muus, is center, in the foreground,
holding a pipe.

27

A Pilgrimage to Ultimate Destiny

"I am the Way, the Truth, and the Life,
no one comes to the Father, but by Me."
(John 14:6)

Arne and Emilie Filkesager's new home at the foot of Manitou Heights was close to St. Olaf College where he was welcomed as the College Pastor and one of the faculty at the new seminary. It had been a challenging first two years, but the Filkesagers were making many new friends and were getting used to the tempo of the college community.

As he rode the train from Northfield to Chicago, Arne was reflecting on the lecture that one of his professors had given at St. Olaf's School. A few phrases continued to stick in his mind:

> "America is in the process of becoming…
> America is on its way to ultimate destiny…
> America itself is a pilgrimage to destiny."

Perhaps, he thought, the Chicago World's Fair would reveal the direction of this pilgrimage?

As an instructor in Church and American History at the new Lutheran Seminary in Northfield, Arne was excited for the opportunity to attend this "World Columbian Exposition." He was looking forward to hearing Professor Frederick Jackson Turner present his thesis on the effect of the *diminishing frontier* of free land on the future of America.

He also hoped to hear a lecture by Thorstein Veblen of the University of Chicago, who had launched the *Journal of Political Economy* in 1892.

It was October 9, 1893, the beginning of the much publicized "Grand Celebration" of Chicago's coming of age. This was the victory festival of its resurrection from the ashes of the "Great Fire" which happened on this date in 1871.

In spite of the shaky economic climate and the growing unemployment, it seemed that the Chicago World's Fair had mesmerized America into believing that Utopia — the fulfillment of the American Dream — was near. Here, at the World's Columbian Exposition, there was hope and starry-eyed optimism. Arne had read about the glitter of the thousands of electric light bulbs which lighted and framed the "Electric Building" at the Exposition grounds. This spectacle seemed to promote a feeling of transcendence beyond the real world.

"True Believers" were flocking to the Chicago Exposition. Twenty-seven million of them from all parts of the civilized world had come to see and experience the creation of this neo-cosmos which paid tribute to the American Dream and the supposed victory of materialism and the machine.

No one, it seemed, was really willing to see the poor, the unemployed, the homeless, and the powerless who were hovering at the edges of the World's Fair and the American Dream. Not many were willing to hear the pessimistic economic prophecies of Thorstein Veblen.

Few wanted to admit Turner's proclaiming that the frontier of free land or the vast white and Norway pine forests were coming to an end.

In the light of this atmosphere of imagined "Utopia," it seemed to Arne that America was on a pilgrimage, but indeed, a pilgrimage to disappointment.

> More than anything, he thought, America needed the *coming together* of the three golden Rings to point her beyond the gods of materialism and human reason.

The Rings testified to the Triune God who brings a *peace* which the world cannot give, *hope* which is anchored beyond the powers of men, and *love* guaranteed by the Cross and the victory of Easter.

48 *"Could this be the time when the Three Rings would come together for the mending of the nation and the broken world?"*

Arne's hope was not set on the glitter of the Exposition, but in the promise of the Rings.

> He looked at the golden Ring which he kept close to his heart and remembered the promise that *Far* had passed on to him, "When the three interlocking rings are *joined*

together, there will be a great blessing for the keepers and for the nation." Arne wondered, *"Was this the time?"*

He was startled out of his thoughts by a sudden jolt and the conductor's loud announcement:

"Chicago Station!"

"He is coming with the clouds, and every eye will see Him."
(Revelation 1:7)

28

In God's Plan

"I know the plans I have for you, plans for good and not for evil, plans to give you a future and a hope."
(Jeremiah 29:11)

Newly elected President Grover Cleveland was on his way to make his debut at the World Columbian Exposition in Chicago. On the Presidential Train was a contingent of government officials representing the Chiefs of Staff, the Congress, and the State Department.

Among those from the State Department was the newly appointed United States Ambassador to Egypt, *Gregory F. Anthony*, of Savannah, Georgia. Gregory was excited to be a part of the Presidential party on this special occasion. They would be in Chicago on October 9, 1893, just twenty-two years after the devastating fire which nearly destroyed the city. It was the right time to celebrate the great progress which the World's Fair portended for Chicago and America!

However, Ambassador Anthony believed that America needed more than material success. It needed an infusion of spirit—something bigger, and beyond the ken of men. As he reflected, he took out the golden Ring which he always carried next to his heart.

49 As he gazed on it, he asked himself: *"Is this the time when the three interlocking rings will come together?* Could it be that the Coptic Mystery would be *revealed* in this year? Is this the *kairos* which the world has been waiting for? *Is* this the prelude to the *eschaton* which Christians in every age have been hoping for?"

As the keeper of the Ring inscribed with the word "ASHEM" (*Truth*, or, *The Incarnation of Truth*), Gregory was looking forward to the Triune God's answer. Perhaps "the time of fulfillment" had come.

The knock on his compartment door meant that the President was asking for his morning briefing...and the President expected a prompt response from everyone!

Gregory returned the Ring to its secure place over his heart, and he was off—on his way to destiny.

Reidunn was hurrying to get her children ready for this big day. Lars had led them in their morning devotions before he ran off to join the other newspaper reporters at the President's briefing. *The Chicago Daily News* did not want to be scooped by any other paper!

With the President's visit and the Great Celebration, including the Grand Chorus Concert this evening, Reidunn and her family had much to be excited about.

> She had thought of leaving her youngest, Karl Victor, at home with the maid, but the boy pleaded: "Mommy! Please! Me go with!"
>
> The older children sided with their brother. "We'll mind him when you're singing in the Grand Chorus! We'll help! Please *Mor*, please!"

Finally, Reidunn relented and the three-year-old got his way. So it was decided.

> Reidunn glanced at the clock and hurried them along. "Everyone take your jackets! This is October. The wind is brisk this morning. We'll need to hurry to catch the street car!"
>
> As Reidunn looked for her music folder, she puzzled about the selections for the Concert. *Why* had the Metro Director chosen to end the Grand Chorus Concert with Handel's Oratorio, *Messiah?* They had sung it at both Christmas and Easter, but *why* on this patriotic and secular occasion?
>
> Still, she was pleased that she had been chosen to sing the soprano arias and prayed that she would do them justice.

The children were ready. She checked her music portfolio. As she glanced in the mirror, her eyes caught a glimpse of the golden Ring on the chain about her neck. She felt a quickened pulse of renewed confidence. Then she and the children trooped out the door and were on their way!

It was only 9:00 a.m. but the City was already bustling when they boarded the streetcar for the World's Fair. The car was full, so Reidunn grasped the strap and the hand of Karl Victor as the trolley jerked to start.

29

Blessed Are the Poor in Spirit

"Blessed are the poor in spirit, for theirs is
the Kingdom of Heaven."
(Matthew 5:3)

In 1893, as Chicago prepared for its grand debut as the "Great White City" of America, the nation was teetering on the edge of a major economic depression. But, for a short time, the bands played and the "Chicago World's Fair" distracted national attention from the poverty, unemployment, economic distress, and urban misery which plagued America.

Into this cauldron came homeless and unemployed men, some from the dregs of society and others the innocent victims of accelerating change. Some came to find work in the building of Chicago's new wonderland — The World's Columbian Exposition of 1893. Some came to pray for help; others came to prey on the benefactors of progress.

50 Among the transients who were drawn to the glitter of Chicago was a young man named *Per Ondestad*, the *grandson* of Representative Ivar Ondestad. He was a bitter man when he arrived in Chicago. Per was angry that he was different from most of the other people in his home settlement — the only "dark skin" in a community of "pale faces."

He resented his mother, Rosie, for being a Gypsy. He resented his father, Oscar, for never marrying her. Per was angry at his rural community for not accepting him. He was angry at God for treating him so unfairly. He had tried to be accepted, but whatever he did seemed to backfire. People laughed at his humorous antics, and purposely got him drunk so he could make a bigger fool of himself.

> Like his parents, he turned to the bottle to try to escape that judging voice from within, "You are just a buffoon, a fool! You have no self-respect and no one respects you! Nobody cares about you! No one loves you! You're just a 'no-good *bastard!*' "

Per was not sure why he had jumped on the box car and had come to Chicago. Maybe he wanted to get lost? Perhaps he wanted to find himself?

The Vast Crowd at the Chicago World's Fair

It was October 9 when the box car came to a jolting stop in the Chicago rail yards. He quickly followed the other bums as they jumped from the car and ran for cover to escape the clubs of the railroad switchmen and guards. There were many people in the rail station and along the tracks. It appeared that they were all moving toward a common destination. It was the anniversary of the Great Chicago Fire.

The World's Fair was celebrating "Chicago Day" with spectacular fireworks which was billed as the "most gorgeous display ever seen in America." There were marching bands, speakers, and a Grand Chorus scheduled to sing patriotic songs and conclude with the great "Oratorio" by George Frideric Handel.

Per wasn't a singer but he did enjoy good music. He remembered an old lumber jack who would play beautiful songs on his mouth organ. Old Ralph had told him the names of these tunes, but he couldn't remember them. Per knew he wanted to hear this concert, but he had only 50 cents—just enough to get into the Fairgrounds.

He was awestruck by the 254-foot-high wheel with swinging glass compartments built by G. W. Ferris to hold more than 2,000 people at one time (the original Ferris Wheel). There were the acrobats and the trained animal shows. Most of all he wanted to watch the trick horses, the 40-horse hitch, and the wagon races.

But there was danger all around: pick pockets, pan-handlers, and runaway horses.

As he moved through the crowd toward the area where the Grand Concert was to be given, he heard the sound of stampeding hoofs and a mother's cry for help. He immediately saw that her young child, a toddler, was running away from her straight into the path of a runaway team!

Per lunged in front of the horses to push the child out of their path.

51 He saved the child, but Per's chest was crushed by the horses' hoofs.

"I was sick and you visited me."
"As you did it to one of the least of these
my brethren, you did it to me."
(Matthew 25:36, 40)

30

The Kingdom of God Is Near

"The Kingdom of God has come near to you."
(Luke 10:9)

People rushed to help but Per's lungs were crushed and he couldn't breathe. As he lay on the pavement, he heard the sobs of thankfulness from the mother as she hugged her child to her breast.

The three-year-old was *Karl Victor Hanson.*

52 His mother, Reidunn, knelt by the man who had saved her son's life. Amid her sobs, she thanked him for his bravery. Though Per was not able to respond, Reidunn saw a faint smile when her tears fell on his face and the Ring which was on the chain about her neck touched his forehead.

Per died on the way to the hospital, but before he passed on, he remembered that there was one person who believed in him, who had prayed for him every day, and who believed that God would help him do the right thing when he was given the chance.

> In his mind's eye he saw the smile on his Grandma's face. She is proud of me, he thought, and in that moment he knew that the Lord was with him. He was "somebody."
>
> His soul could rest in peace.

As the medics carried Per's limp body to the ambulance, Reidunn tried to pick herself up from the pavement, still clutching her son. Two men rushed to help her, one was a *pastor* and *the other had a strong Southern accent.*

> "I am with the President's party," he said.

53 *One* took *her* arm and the *other* carried Karl Victor. When they had brought Reidunn and her children safely to a ladies' rest station, the men paused for a moment as if *some power* had come over

them. But, then, they parted with kindly wishes for the safety of her children and herself, and went their separate ways.

Reidunn spoke a polite "Thank you!" and wanted to say more. But words would not come…her son had been saved! She somehow *felt* like the Three Golden Rings had come together, as though she were surrounded by "The Kingdom of The Rings!"

The words of the "Hallelujah Chorus" from Handel's *Messiah* rushed into her mind:

"The kingdom of this world is become
the Kingdom of our Lord and of His Christ.
And He shall reign forever and ever,
King of kings, and Lord of lords,
Forever and ever!
Hallelujah!
Hallelujah!
Hallelujah!"

31

The Kingdom Tarries

"A little while, and you will not see Me,
and again a little while, and you will see Me."
(John 16:17)

As Gregory rejoined the President's entourage and boarded the train, the words of the "Hallelujah Chorus" were still ringing in his ears. He had attended the Grand Concert at the Chicago World's Fair and thrilled to the music and the words of the *Messiah* sung by the massive chorus of 2,400 voices.

At the time, it seemed that the *kairos* moment had arrived—that moment when the Three Golden Rings would *join* together and the "Message of the Kingdom" would be fulfilled.

But the Lord was not ready. He would tarry a while longer.

As the Presidential train moved slowly out of the Chicago station, Gregory began to see the other side of Chicago—the throngs of homeless, jobless men, the crowded tenements with thousands of recent immigrants huddled together. They and their children were working in factories and sweat shops, living from hand-to-mouth. Yet most still held on to their "American Dream."

> How appropriate, Gregory thought, that George Frideric Handel did not conclude the *Messiah* with the "Hallelujah Chorus," which focuses on the fulfillment of the Kingdom of God. But, he chose to close on those verses which direct our *hope* to the Redeemer, who is Living, and who will come again on the Last Day.

54 Gregory had felt the nearness of that Day when the *soprano soloist* sang the air, "I Know That My Redeemer Liveth." It seemed to Gregory that the whole assembly was surrounded by the golden Rings, that they had come together to bless the people and the nation.

However, as Gregory looked out his Pullman window at the reality of Chicago behind the World's Fair facade, he knew the *kairos* (the right time) was not yet. The fulfillment of "The Kingdom of The Rings" had not yet broken into history. This was still the time of "limited things." Government would still be necessary, even though politics could never usher in the *eschaton*, or even the secular dreamers' "Perfect Society."

> "Yes!" he sighed and mumbled into his newspaper. "I guess elections and politicians and politics will still be necessary. Fallible as the democratic process is, it seems far superior to the 'solutions' of the anarchists, or those of the secular or religious totalitarians."
>
> In this light, Gregory was content to continue his State Department service, in spite of his own beliefs about the imperfections of his country and its leaders. "I will do my best," he confided to himself.
>
> "I am looking forward to that Day when *the Kingdom of this world* is become the *Kingdom of our Lord and of His Christ*, as the words of Handel's *Messiah* declare."

Before he turned away from his compartment window to catch a brief nap, Gregory F. felt the golden Ring in the pocket over his heart, and looked forward to the day when the three golden Rings *would* join together.

55 As Arne returned to his family and his teaching duties at the Seminary in Northfield, he reflected on the Chicago World Columbian Exposition. He remembered that on two occasions he had felt as though the three golden Rings were coming together to bless the people and the nation.

The first was when he had helped a mother and her three-year-old son who had narrowly escaped a tragic accident. He hadn't caught the woman's name but it sounded distinctly Scandinavian. Also, out the corner of his eye, he had glimpsed something that looked like a *gold ring* around her neck, when she had knelt beside the dying man.

> *Could* it be that *she* held the secret to the other Ring—the one that had been offered by the Egyptian Crusader at the Hamar Cathedral so many years ago? It was an intriguing thought, but *how* could he find a Norwegian mother of three in a city with more than 60,000 Norsemen?

> 56 The second time this feeling had come upon him was when he assembled with thousands of listeners at the Grand Concert. It happened during the singing of the *Messiah*, as the audience stood for the "Hallelujah Chorus." It seemed that "the time of fulfillment had come." Arne remembered feeling as though the three golden Rings had come together. The Grand Concert was for Arne the capstone of the Chicago World's Fair. It gave the Exposition its "soul." For, amidst the appearance of the material fulfillment of the American Dream, the concert pointed the nation to the *spiritual* dimension of life and the ultimate fulfillment of history.

Arne sensed that the three golden Rings were there!

He could not know that *never before* in the past six centuries had they come so close together. He sensed the nearness of the mystery.

The *eschaton* would tarry, awaiting the *kairos* known only to Him who rules The Kingdom of The Rings.

Like Gregory F., Arne's reverie on the nearness of the Rings was interrupted by the visage of squalor, which was only partially hidden by the facade of the Chicago Exposition. It was sad to see how many had not realized their "American Dream."

Perhaps the key to this reality was to be found in Frederick Jackson Turner's suggestion that the disappearance of the frontier of free land must be taken seriously, if America is to solve its social and economic ills. Another factor responsible for the growing poverty and failure of the "American Dream" was identified by Thorsten Veblen as the insatiable appetites of middle and upper classes for material things in their quest for status.

> He admitted to himself, "Perhaps Turner and Veblen are right."

His reflections were interrupted as his eye caught the stack of papers on his lap. It was time to begin his preparation for his lecture on American religious and political history. The poverty he had seen had caused him to question the splendor of the "Fair." He noted the tension between cherished elements of American democracy. There was a potential for *conflict* among "hallowed" American ideals, which, if pushed to the *extreme* in *either* direction, could be destructive of society, and ultimately of the nation. These ideals, which had inspired

America from its birth, were often spoken of in pairs, without recognizing the tension between them:

Freedom and Justice...
Faith and Reason...
Individual and Community...
Majority rule and Minority rights.

Professor Filkesager would remind his students that through the democratic process this nation attempts to resolve the tensions which are inherent in our treasured ideals. However, he would point out that the ultimate resolution of these natural, predictable, and inescapable tensions will not be accomplished by the plans and efforts of *men*. The ultimate resolution of these dichotomies has been accomplished by *Jesus Christ on the Cross.*

> Arne wrote in his notes: "The final solution is in the hands of Him who rules The Kingdom of The Rings, who is the source of freedom, justice, and love. He has paid the price on the Cross for all injustices of this world. He is the King of kings and Lord of lords, who promises, *'I will make all things new. I am the Alpha and the Omega, the beginning and the end.'* (Revelation 21:5,6)"

As he finished up his lectures, Arne's mind flashed back to the words and music of the soprano aria in Handel's *Messiah*:

> "I know that my Redeemer liveth, and that He shall stand at the latter day upon the earth."

He remembered vividly the response by the entire 2,400 voice chorus when it sang:

> "Worthy is the Lamb that was slain, and hath redeemed us to God by his blood, to receive power, and riches, and wisdom, and strength, and honor, and glory, and blessing.... Blessing and honor, glory and power, be unto Him that sitteth upon the throne, and unto the Lamb, forever and ever. Amen!"

As he reflected on his experience at the Chicago Exposition, Arne reminded himself that the Advent of the Three Golden Rings, the Day of the Second Coming, may be... *very soon.*

Part Six

A Joining . . .
and
A Separation

32

Seeing As Through The Rings

"One thing I know, that though I was blind, now I see."
(John 9:25)

Reidunn had returned from the Grand Concert tired but overjoyed. She had much to be thankful for. Her son's life had been saved and the Grand Chorus sang the *Messiah* as under the inspiration of the Holy Spirit. She was thankful, too, that this same inspiring spirit seemed to carry her as she *sang* the soprano arias.

The following Sunday, as Reidunn sat with her husband Lars and their four children in the family pew at *Trefoldeghets Kirke* (Trinity Church), she knew it could not be just an "ordinary Sunday." The spirit of *thanksgiving* which rose up in her soul was deeply passionate, even in her silence.

57 When they had entered the sanctuary, she sensed that there was something different. The new paraments (cloth hangings) on the altar and the pulpit caught the children's attention. The central symbol was *three interlocking rings!*

Since children believe it is their prerogative to speak out, even in church, Karl Victor pointed to the altar and exclaimed, "Mommy! See the three circles!"

As a dutiful Norwegian mother, sensitive to other worshipers around her, she admonished, "*Shhhhhh!* You must be quiet in church!"

But Reidunn did not forget her son's question. After services, on the way home, she mentioned it to her husband. As they walked, Lars saw this as a "teachable moment" in his children's lives. He began by complimenting his son for noticing the new altar hangings. Then he proceeded to explain that the three interlocking rings are an ancient symbol of the Triune God who is One, yet shows Himself in Three personal natures—Father, Son, and Holy Spirit.

> Lars admitted, "This is too difficult for you to understand, and I must say that I don't know all that the symbol of

the three rings means either. But I do know that each ring represents the truth about God. When these are interlocked, they remind us that the Triune (three in one) God is present with us.

"Today at worship, the interlocking rings on the altar and the pulpit cloths were telling us that God — Father, Son, and Holy Spirit — is really present with us through God's Word and the sacraments of Baptism and the Lord's Supper."

Tove interrupted with her question, "Was the Triune God *really present* when the baby was baptized at church today?"

"Yes!" responded Lars. "In the Bible, God gives a command and promise for all people, including the tiny ones. Do you kids remember the Bible verse we learned last Sunday, Matthew 28:19-20?"

Grace responded eagerly, "Can I say it, *Far?*"

"Yes, Grace. In fact, let's all recite it together," suggested Lars.

"Go therefore and make disciples of all nations [all peoples], *baptizing them in the name of the Father, and of the Son, and of the Holy Spirit, teaching them to observe all that I have commanded you; and Lo, I am with you always, to the close of the age."*

Reidunn was pleased that her husband had answered the children so well. It seemed to her that God had planned it this way: that Karl Victor should ask about the interlocking rings at this very time when *she* had sensed the presence and power of the Three Golden Rings.

Oh, how much Reidunn wanted to tell all her children that she, herself, carried one of the golden Rings which had been offered by the Magi! But she and Lars had agreed that the mystery of the Ring would not be revealed until it was given in secret to their eldest daughter.

Yes, thought Reidunn. The Ring would shape Brita's life even as it has mine.

33

In God's Field

"Earth to earth, ashes to ashes, dust to dust!"

It was common knowledge that Per Ondestad had followed the wayward path of his father and grandfather. However, his grandmother, old Mrs. Ondestad, confided in the Pastor that she had *prayed daily* for her grandson and believed her prayers were answered. Though she was not proud of how he had *lived*, now she was proud of how he had *died*. She had been told that he had thrown himself in the path of a runaway team in order to save the life of a little child!

In her eyes, Per was a hero, someone she could be proud of.

But there was no hero's honor guard at the Ringsaker Church Cemetery in Minnesota that day. Besides the grave diggers, only a few gathered for the morning graveside service – *Pastor Magnus Olson,* Mrs. Ondestad, Per's mother Rosie, and his father Oscar, who had fortified himself for this religious occasion with a generous draft of spirits.

Though Magnus had officiated at many funerals, both in his first parish and since he answered the Call to the Ringsaker Church in Minnesota, this funeral, more than any other, communicated the pathos of life in this fallen world. Yet, even at this service, he read the words of promise:

> *"I am the resurrection and the life, he who believes in Me though he die, yet shall he live."* (John 11:25)
>
> He took a clump of prairie soil in his hand. He released it as he sprinkled it on the coffin, and spoke the words, from the Graveside Service of the Norwegian Lutheran Church, that recalled the creation of mankind: "Earth to earth, ashes to ashes, dust to dust!"

It seemed to Pastor Olson that he was planting a soul in God's Field – "The Field of Rings" – to await the fulfillment of "The Kingdom of The Rings."

After the funeral, Pastor Olson was still puzzling over Mrs. Ondestad's request to *meet the parents and the child* whom her grandson had saved when there was a knock at the door. He opened it and welcomed the funeral director who was holding a picture and a small notebook.

> "It was Per's," he explained, pointing to the title, *Poems On the Way Home.*

> Magnus thanked him and said that he would take it to Mrs. Ondestad later that day.

He had promised to help her, but *how* would anyone locate these unknown parents and a child in a city of more than one million people? He would tell her that this was an *impossible* request. But he decided that he would wait a few more days before he told her. She had enough disappointment for now.

Karl Victor had fallen asleep in Reidunn's arms. She looked at his plump, healthy frame and hugged him to her breast. He had been saved from a terrible death by the bravery of a stranger! She hummed a prayer of *thanksgiving* to the Lord and tried to hold back the tears. Again she had *witnessed* the *blessing* of the Ring, as it had been promised to her ancestor so many years ago.

> But *who* was the stranger who had given his life for her son? *What* was his name? *Where* did he live? *Who* were his people?

Lars suggested that they check with the police and the Coroner's Office for identification, explaining that they wanted to express their thanksgiving to the man's people.

When the Coroner heard their story, he released the information regarding the man's identity and the place of burial.

Northwestern Minnesota was a long way off, but they knew that through the church they could locate the pastor who had conducted the burial service.

So it was that within two weeks after Per's funeral, Pastor Olson received a letter which, to him, was an answer to prayer. Mrs. Ondestad had prayed that the Lord would allow her to meet the child and his parents. Well, he now had good news for her — the child and its parents wanted to come all the way from Chicago to meet her and express their heartfelt sorrow over her loss.

She was moved to tears by the kindness of their offer, yet she felt guilty letting them travel all that way and with the child. Though she was 82, she would rather make the trip to Chicago herself, than have these fine people go to all that trouble and expense.

It was near Thanksgiving time when a woman dressed in black, bowed under the heavy burdens of a difficult life and a recent tragedy, stood guarding her luggage at the Chicago and Northwestern Station.

Her large black bonnet hid the scars and deep wrinkles in her face, but it allowed enough light to reveal a kindly smile. *Kjerste Rinde Ondestad* was not afraid of the harried hustle of the Windy City. She was a *survivor* and knew how to look out for herself.

She had not informed the Hansons when she would arrive. Her letter simply said she would arrive "sometime around Thanksgiving."

It was two days before Thanksgiving when Reidunn opened her front door to see a woman in black who announced herself as *"The Grandmother of Per Ondestad."* She had a lilting Norwegian accent which seemed to give a song to her generous smile.

The Hanson family was expecting their honored guest and welcomed her with open arms.

> *"Velkommen Fru Ondestad!* ("Welcome Mrs. Ondestad!") We have been expecting you. Did you have a good trip? Please come in. Tove, please take Mrs. Ondestad's coat."

Lars secured her luggage and introduced Mrs. Ondestad to his family. Of course, three-year-old Karl Victor was shy. He peered at the visitor from the safe distance of his mother's skirts. However, soon he warmed up to the kindly lady with the beautiful smile. He didn't understand the deep meaning of her visit, but he did feel secure in her lap. Karl seemed to sense a special bond between them.

Lars and Reidunn were eager to hear Kjerste's story and the tale of her grandson, Per. But Mrs. Ondestad was more interested in hearing the exact account of the events on the day that her grandson had been killed. Eventually, she shared the sad story of his life and his feeling of rejection because he felt "unwanted."

The Hanson girls were old enough to understand when Kjerste related the sad story of Per's life. She told of his parents who lived together without marriage, so their son bore the shameful stigma of being a *"bastard."* Both of Per's parents had tried to dissolve their guilt and solve their problems with the "bottle."

> "Therefore," explained Kjerste, "Per felt angry toward his parents and alienated from others in our community."
>
> But she spoke tenderly of her own love for her grandson and how she prayed for him every day. She had asked the Lord to guide Per to "do the right thing."

Then, as she looked down at little Karl Victor, she knew that her prayers had been answered.

> She spoke with tears running down her cheeks. "Your son is alive, and my grandson died knowing that he had done what is *right* in the eyes of the Lord."

Kjerste stayed a few days and shared more of her own tragic story. She had been raised by godly parents who were faithful in worship and in the instruction of their children. However, as a young woman, she thought she was wiser than her parents. She did not heed their warning about marrying a man who was a "drinker" and not a member of her church. After all, she was sure that he would quit drinking if she asked him to, and would come to her church as he promised because he loved her!

Sadly, none of this happened. The drinking just got worse and his promises turned into ridicule as she tried to raise their children in the faith.

Brita, Tove, and Grace listened to every word that this kindly lady spoke. It seemed that she was speaking *wisdom* about things that they didn't fully understand. However, when they stood on their emotional tip toes and peeked into the future, they sensed that Kjerste's words were true.

In the days following Kjerste's visit, Reidunn's daughters had many questions for their mother! Some could be answered now, but others would have to wait for the right time.

34

To Escape the Melting Pot

"The melting pot was precisely for the spiritually stunted, those who no longer had qualities that let people see what they were or what they had been." (Waldemar Ager)

As Brita, Tove, Grace, and Karl Victor grew into young adulhood, Lars and Reidunn were pleased that their church and community had a strong youth program for their children and others of Scandinavian parentage. The young people had many opportunities to meet others who shared their ethnic identity and cultural values, as well as their Lutheran faith.

However, it caused Reidunn no little worry that every year there were more strangers moving into what had been a totally Scandinavian street. But it wasn't only the intrusion of many different ethnic groups and races into the cosmopolitan patchwork of the Chicago landscape which disturbed Reidunn. More serious for her was the proliferation of pagan religions and cults and the presence of competing Christian communities which were very different in language, liturgy, and custom from her own Norwegian Lutheranism. There were Roman Catholics, Baptists, Adventists, Orthodox, and the "English" churches —all threatening to steal "her" people.

Reidunn's protective, mothering instincts were aroused when she heard about her countrymen who had defected to heretical groups like the Mormons, Russellites, and Christian Science.

She worried about her children's future. How would they survive without being conformed to this world and lose their identity?

Philosophers could debate the effects of America's diversity on the nation as a whole, but Reidunn was concerned for her own children.

How would her family's future be affected?

What would all this diversity mean for her children and grandchildren? How would they be changed? What would happen to their Lutheran faith and their Norwegian-American culture? Would the new society become a "field of weeds?"

Though Lars shared many of her concerns, he reminded Reidunn,

"The new immigrants from eastern and southern Europe are not inferior to the Anglo-Saxon and Nordic/Germanic nationalities."

Still, when she heard about the foreign anarchists and revolutionaries who seemed intent upon destroying the United States of America, Reidunn was concerned for her children and empathetic with those who wanted to limit the new immigration.

As she reflected on these things, Reidunn became more convinced that her children must be educated in the schools of her Church. There, she reasoned, the faith and values taught at home and in church would be affirmed.

This was especially important to Reidunn because she had a vivid recollection of the beating her little brother received at the orphanage for just praying in Norwegian! She did not want any threat of violence to force her own children into the cauldron of the "Melting Pot." Reidunn was not ready to become an indistinguishable glob in the American "Melting Pot."

I Jesu navn går vi til bords
å spise og drikke på ditt ord.
Deg, Gud til aere, oss til gavn,
Så får vi mat i Jesu navn.
Amen.

In Jesus' name to the table we go
To eat and drink according to His word.
to God the honor, us the gain,
So we have food in Jesus' name.
Amen.

(The "Norwegian Table Prayer")

It wasn't long before Lars and Reidunn's eldest daughter, Brita, was matriculating at St. Olaf College in Northfield, Minnesota. Reidunn was pleased to hear of her new friends—most had Scandinavian names and one sounded German. None had strange sounding, "foreign" names.

Brita was also pleased with her professors and her courses. She assured her mother that she was being faithful in daily chapel and at evening prayers. This was the kind of report that the mother of a pretty 18-year old loved to hear!

Of course, there was more…but Brita didn't tell her mother everything!

She had met a handsome upperclassman who was fun to be with. He had taken her for a buggy ride on Sunday. Furthermore, he was the son of Professor Filkesager, one of the popular professors. Maybe she'd tell her parents about him when she came home at Christmas.

Professor Arne Filkesager was preparing his lectures for his class on American religious and political history. It was 1899 and the tidal wave of immigrants showed no signs of abating.

He wanted his students to hear some facts regarding immigration. He read aloud to himself:

"The nation is adding more than one-half-million newcomers each year. In 1873 there had been 459,803 hopeful arrivals. In 1882 this had climbed to 788,992. Throughout the '80s and '90s, the number of immigrants hovered at the half-million mark. In all, nearly 15 million Europeans have immigrated to United States in the forty years since 1860!"

Professor Filkesager continued reading his lecture notes aloud:

"Since 1880, many of these immigrants have been coming from the less developed areas of eastern and southern Europe. Some are questioning whether these masses will learn the English language and assimilate into American culture. The popular ideal among Anglo-Saxon Americans is the 'Melting Pot,' wherein all immigrant groups will forget their languages and their unique cultures and melt into the dominant Anglo society."

Arne paused as he remembered how the "Melting Pot" thinking was responsible for justifying the excesses of "100% Americanism." He had a vivid recollection of how children of Scandinavian and German immigrants in his own North Dakota parish were subjected to ridicule, verbal abuse, and punishment for speaking in their native tongue in public school, even on the playground.

This kind of "American nativism," which demonstrated hostility and disdain toward immigrant cultures and churches, had been increasing in intensity since the formation of the "American Protective Association" in Clinton, Iowa in 1887 and the "Immigration Restriction League" in the East in 1894.

Professor Filkesager continued reading aloud what he had prepared to share with his students:

"Many thought that the 'Melting Pot' seemed to be working, when the immigrants were primarily from Scandinavia, Germany, and the British Isles. However, the process of 'melting' isn't happening at the same rate with the new immigrants.

"What does this mean for America?" Arne was going to ask his students. "Does the nation need a new defining metaphor? Have the 'older' immigrants actually melted in…or, have they been transformed into something new and distinct from the Anglo majority?"

There were obviously more questions than answers.

Arne asked himself the questions he wanted his students to think about:

"*Could* America thrive with its great variety of disparate groups?"

"*How* can diversity be a positive factor in a functioning democracy?"

"*Would* the field of democracy remain fertile, or would it be poisoned by the variety of competing religious, moral, and political views?"

"*How* would America resolve the conflict between the idea of an easy tolerance toward differing beliefs, values, and opinions ("relativism"), and the need to stand up for honest communication based on a commitment to the Truth of Scripture?"

"*Is* the United States of America truly a Melting Pot?"

As he struggled with these issues, it seemed to him that America needed a different metaphor to describe the reality of what was happening in this nation where pluralism was the order of the day. The "Melting Pot" metaphor was not adequate!

But what metaphor would be more helpful to both explain the "American Experience" and guide the Nation into the future?

The answer to his question seemed to arise out of his own past.

Far had told him of two kingdoms in ancient Norway which were identified with the golden Rings. These were Ringerike ("Kingdom of the Rings") and Ringsaker ("Field of Rings"). Arne believed that the name of the first Kingdom suggested that the three rings were interlocked, whereas, in the second, he pictured the Rings lying separately scattered in a field.

Arne pondered this as a possible new metaphor of the American experience: "The Field of Rings."

It suggests, he thought, that each different ethnic group could be represented by its own ring. The "field" suggests the whole of American pluralistic society. Often rings touch or overlap with other rings. As each lay in the field, it does not have an exclusive right to its own space, but often shares part of its space with other rings.

"Arne's Field of Rings"

This new metaphor helped Arne to see how ethnic groups could retain their own identity within the "Field" of American society, but could also be influenced and modified in those areas where they overlapped with one or several different groups.

It will be interesting to hear how my students react to this new metaphor, "The Field of Rings," thought Arne. This may not be the best metaphor to define our nation, but it seems evident that without a new idea of self-understanding, the "Melting Pot" ideology will lead the nation into massive self-deception.

It will produce an attitude of unwillingness to acknowledge differences, and result in an inability to deal with them.

Yes! reasoned Arne. If the "Melting Pot" analogy becomes more widespread, it will encourage *relativism*—the denial that there is anything that is really true. And, *relativism* will eventually sow the seed of hatred for those who are different.

As he felt the golden Ring in the pocket over his heart, he wondered when the defining moment would come for America. He was startled as the clock struck 12:00 midnight. It brought him back to his preparations for morning classes.

35

Love Is Forever

"Many waters cannot quench love, neither can floods drown it."
(Song of Songs 8:7)

Professor Filkesager was still teaching both at the College and the Seminary, but was slated to move at the end of the semester to St. Paul, Minnesota, when the seminaries of the several synods would merge. He loved Northfield and the St. Olaf students, and it would be difficult to move and leave them behind.

So it was that when the Hansons visited their daughter Brita at St. Olaf College in the beginning of her second year, they were not able to meet Professor Filkesager. He had already moved to the new seminary campus in St. Paul. However, they enjoyed meeting his son, Brita's friend, Rolf, and the rest of his family.

58 *But the meeting of the keepers of the golden Rings would await another time.*

It was exciting for Brita to welcome her parents to St. Olaf and give them a personal tour of the campus. It was very special that she could introduce her parents to Rolf, his mother, and siblings. However, she was very disappointed that Rolf's father was not there.

She confided in her mother that she had a *strange sensation* that she had some *connection* with Professor Filkesager from somewhere in the past. This remark made more than a passing impression on Reidunn, but she kept it to herself.

Her thoughts went back to that fateful day at the Chicago World's Fair when Karl Victor was saved from a crushing death by stampeding horses.

> *Could* it be that Rolf's father was one of the men who had helped her that day?

In the miracle of her son's rescue, it *had* seemed to Reidunn that the Three Golden Rings had come together. But this thought was something that she could not yet share with Brita—only when the time was right.

Reidunn and Lars were very pleased to meet Mrs. Filkesager and her children, however. They certainly were a handsome family. Emilie was a gracious hostess who invited the Hansons for lunch — with the typical Norwegian disclaimer that she really didn't have anything to serve them. But the coffee and delicate *rosettes, sandbakels, kringla,* and delicious *lefse* served with her best silver and china revealed that Mrs. Filkesager was only being appropriately modest!

Rolf took a seat next to Brita, and Reidunn caught the radiant smile she gave him. It was evident that Brita was more than a little interested in Rolf. It seemed that *he* was also returning *her* favors. But nothing was said about this. Only Brita's younger sister, Tove, cast a teasing glance at her.

The table conversation focused on the "Big News" — the *assassination* of President McKinley at the "Pan-American Exposition" in Buffalo, N.Y., and the new President, Theodore Roosevelt. Many people were worried about this "Rough Rider" in the White House.

But Brita's thoughts were elsewhere. She was now a sophomore, and Rolf was a senior. They were in love, but too young to marry.

> What would *happen* to their relationship when Rolf went off to Seminary?

Rolf felt the Call of God to follow in the footsteps of his father and grandfather and become a pastor.

Brita was very supportive of Rolf's Calling but concerned that this would take four more years beyond college! Four years seemed like a very long time for someone in love. But Brita, too, was sensing God's Call. She felt the leading of the Spirit to serve as a missionary nurse. She would complete her studies at St. Olaf and take her nurse's training at the Deaconess Hospital in Minneapolis. There she could be close to Rolf at the Seminary in St. Paul.

It seemed like a good plan, but she still needed to complete *her* studies at St. Olaf.

59 At Rolf's graduation, *Reidunn* and Lars at last had the opportunity to meet Rolf's father, *Professor Arne Filkesager.* When Reidunn was introduced, she remembered what Brita had confided — a feeling of *"a connection"* with Professor Filkesager from somewhere in the past.

Yes, he *did* look like one of the kind gentlemen who had helped her and her children on that fateful day at the Chicago World's Fair.

> Reidunn's eyes widened. "Professor Filkesager, were you…" she hesitated, "were you at the Chicago World's Fair?"
>
> "Yes, I recall, I came for the special Chicago Celebration Day."
>
> With a note of eagerness in her voice, Reidunn continued her query, "Do you remember helping a woman whose child had just been saved from a terrible accident?"
>
> His face lighted up as he realized that this must be the woman whom he helped. "The event is indelibly imprinted in my memory. Yes! How well I remember!
>
> "I have often wondered about that lady and her children. It was a miracle how your son was saved from being crushed by that runaway team. The young man who gave his life was a real hero!"
>
> As Reidunn recalled that traumatic moment, tears began to stream down her cheeks. "I won't ever forget his bravery, and the kindness which you and the other gentleman showed us. I felt that…we were brought together…according to a plan."

Arne, too, had a sense of being part of a moment of destiny, as he recalled that day.

> He chose his words carefully. "It all happened so suddenly. Yes, it did seem that we were brought together by some unseen power. I have wondered, too, about the other man who helped that day.
>
> "It seems to me that he said he was with the President's party and I remember that he spoke with a strong Southern accent."

As they talked together, remembering that fateful day, both Reidunn and Arne *sensed a bond* between them that seemed to be from long ago.

But neither spoke of the golden Rings. The time was not ready for them to be revealed. Only in the unspoken language of the soul was each aware of the mystery which they shared and would one day pass on to their eldest children.

As Rolf and Brita walked and talked, the glow of young love hovered over them like a halo.

> It is the blessing of the golden Ring, thought Reidunn, as she watched them.

> It is the Garden of Eden revisited, thought Arne. They seem to be created for each other.

Yes, these two *were destined* to be the bearers of the Rings, but the mystery was not ready to be revealed.

And…they were not ready to receive it. For two young lovers the most profound mystery is the deep attraction they have for each other. Furthermore, in the case of Rolf and Brita, their concerns focused on the fact that there were still two more years to wait, and many turns in the road of life, before they could marry.

When Brita graduated from St. Olaf, Rolf was there by her side. They were still very much in love.

Rolf would serve a year of pastoral internship with Pastor Buckneberg in the Williston, North Dakota Circuit. The Seminary would not allow him to marry his sweetheart yet, but they talked about wedding plans when he graduated in two years.

Meanwhile, Brita had set her face toward the nursing school at Deaconess Hospital in Minneapolis. She was excited about this new adventure, but torn in her heart that her beloved would be far away for a whole year.

PART SEVEN

The Rings Come "Full Circle"

Armenian refugees receiving care at Aleppo, Syria

36

My Ways Are Not Your Ways

"So are My ways higher than your ways."
(Isaiah 55:9)

The nursing school and the hospital were run by Norwegian Lutheran Deaconesses. This was an order of consecrated women, mostly nurses, who had begun several hospitals among the immigrants in the U.S. and also staffed missionary hospitals in Madagascar, India, and Syria.

Brita's training included the study of the sciences, nursing skills, personal care for patients, and hospital administration, as well as daily Bible study, daily chapel, and introduction to the Diaconate. Frequently Sisters (Deaconesses) from other hospitals and from the mission fields spoke at chapel. The accounts of poverty, illness, and destitute conditions touched Brita's heart. But more than this, the Sisters shared that the people among whom they served were walking in "darkness" (without knowledge of God). They not only needed medicine for the body but also medicine ("light") for the soul, which only the "Great Physician" (Jesus) could give.

The desire to be used by the Lord to bring healing and hope to those who walk in darkness became a growing passion for Brita. This compassion for those who don't know Christ was a regular theme in her letters to Rolf. She loved him dearly, but she could not free herself from a sense of Calling to serve as a missionary nurse.

Rolf was understanding, but he wondered where this would lead. How could he expect her to deny the Lord's Call to marry him and serve as a pastor's wife?

He struggled with this question all during his internship until Holy Week (prior to Easter), when he was preaching at a service in a settler's cabin at Round Prairie, North Dakota. His text was Matthew 26:39, the Scripture in which Jesus is praying in the Garden of Gethsemane, anticipating his death on the Cross.

As Rolf read the text, it was as though these words were meant for him:

"My Father, if it be possible, let this cup pass from me; nevertheless, not as I will, but as Thou will."

The Lord had lifted his burden!

It was God's will that Brita should serve as a missionary nurse in Syria. He would accept it! By the power of the Spirit, he had been led to acknowledge, "Not my will be done but Thine, O Lord!" His love for Brita and their future was in the Lord's hands!

His letter was stained with his tears as he wrote to his beloved and told her the message he had been given from the Bible, the Word of God.

At Rolf's Seminary graduation, they both wept as they held each other in their arms. It would not be easy for either of them. Rolf would go to his first Call at Wildrose, North Dakota. Brita would begin her service as a Deaconess nurse at the Mission Hospital in Aleppo (near ancient Antioch), Syria.

Rolf and his family, as well as Brita's parents and siblings, gathered at the Great Northern Station in Minneapolis to send Brita off with their love and the blessings of the Lord. The pain of this parting could only be assuaged with tears and prayer.

It was *Arne* who prayed for Brita's safety and God's speed.

Then, touching his golden Ring in its hiding place over his heart, he closed his prayer with the words of the Norwegian blessing:

"Gud velsigne deg og bevare deg alltid!"
("God Bless You and Keep You always!")

60 Only Reidunn and Brita knew the secret which Reidunn had entrusted to her eldest daughter.... Brita would carry the golden Ring with her.

Reidunn had shared the story of the Rings and had given Brita the Ring inscribed with the word "MAZDAO" (*Wisdom*, or, *Spirit of Wisdom*). It was an awesome happening that—after 642 years—the Third Ring would return to the region of Antioch in Syria! Could this be a sign that all the Rings were soon to be *re-joined?*

37

Through the Valley of the Shadow of Death

"Even though I walk through the valley of the shadow of death, I fear no evil."
(Psalm 23:4)

The Anthony family had close ties with Armenian-Cilicia, the ancient Christian kingdom which was now included in the Ottoman Turkish (Muslim) Empire. *Gregory F. Anthony's* oldest son, *Alexander*, had met and married Zabel, the daughter of an Armenian merchant, R. Manukian, who had immigrated to the United States. The Manukian family still had many relatives in the city of Sis in southeastern Turkey.

As the war in Europe and the Mid-East was beginning in 1914, the Anthonys became concerned for the members of Zabel's family. Their anxiety grew after they heard the news that the Ottoman Muslim Empire had sided with Germany.

In January 1915, the *Chicago Daily News* reported that the Turkish army had attacked eastern Armenia and Georgia in order to connect Turkey with other Turkic dominions in central Asia.

> Though the Turkish effort failed, it is a portent of growing troubles for the Armenian population in eastern Turkey, thought Gregory. Alexander and Zabel must act soon to save her family!

Only with the assistance of Ambassador Henry Morgenthau were the Anthonys able to secure a passport. Though America was still neutral, the Turkish officials at the port of *Alexandretta* were very suspicious. Finally, the Anthonys were granted visitors' visas.

They arrived in the city of Sis on March 1, 1915. Though there were joyous reunions, Alexander and Zabel saw the look of fear in people's eyes. The threats expressed by recent Muslim immigrants from Bulgaria and Thrace were frightening.

> "We have come to take your lands and your houses," they said, shaking a clenched fist in the face of Armenian neighbors.

Ominous clouds of a *pogrom* (an officially planned massacre) were gathering on the horizon.

> Within a few days a messenger reported to the Manukian family, "There's trouble brewing in the neighboring city of Zeitun. It would be wise to leave as soon as possible!"

However, before they could pack their belongings, they heard gunfire and screams in the streets. Armenians were being murdered by their Muslim neighbors and the Turkish Army was making no attempt to *stop* the massacre. In fact they were *inciting* both Turks and Kurds to attack the Armenians. Alexander and Zabel heard that Christian churches were being desecrated, priests murdered, and men were being rounded up by the Turkish Army and shot.

Over the next few days, some foreigners were able to flee, but Alexander remained and tried to protect his wife and her family. Old men and boys, women and children were being herded together and forced to leave their homes. Young women were being raped and were forced by Turks and Kurds to become their wives or concubines. Children were taken from parents to be raised as Muslims.

The Turks killed Zabel's father, but they allowed Alexander to stay with his wife and family. It seemed apparent that the Turks were intending to annihilate the entire Armenian population in the five eastern provinces — nearly one-and-a-half million people! There was no way to get a message out to get help. All were being driven into the Syrian desert to die.

The terrible reality struck Alexander! My beloved wife, her family, and the Armenian people are destined for extermination.

He was warned by the Turks that if he stayed with the Armenians he and his wife would both die! There wasn't enough water or food. Every day hundreds were dropping from exhaustion. They were being driven out of their ancestral Armenian homeland toward Aleppo in Syria.

Alexander prayed that America or the Allies would learn of this tragedy and send help. But it seemed that the rest of the world did not know of this holocaust. When the "S. O. S." finally got out, diplomats from European nations, missionaries, and the American Ambassador, Henry Morgenthau, tried to stop the slaughter.

But the Turks ignored their pleas for mercy.

Gregory Anthony had not heard from his son for more than two months. The family feared that Alexander and his wife, Zabel, had perished in the *pogrom*. But Gregory believed they were still alive.

"I must try to find them!" he informed his wife. "I'll request the State Department to assign me to the Mid-East, where both French and British forces are engaging the Central Powers. Our reports indicate that a French force is seeking to aid the Armenian survivors and halt the slaughter."

Within the week, his request was approved and on May 17 Gregory Anthony was on his way as a "Special Envoy" to the Mid-East. His orders were to link up with a French Expeditionary Force on the Lebanese–Syrian border.

As he prayed for his son and the Manukian family, Gregory held the golden Ring. He was thankful that the inscription, "ASHEM" (*Truth*, or, *The Incarnation of Truth*), pointed to Jesus. The Ring was not an object of worship, but a reminder that Jesus was always near and ready to help.

It was in Him that Gregory put his trust.

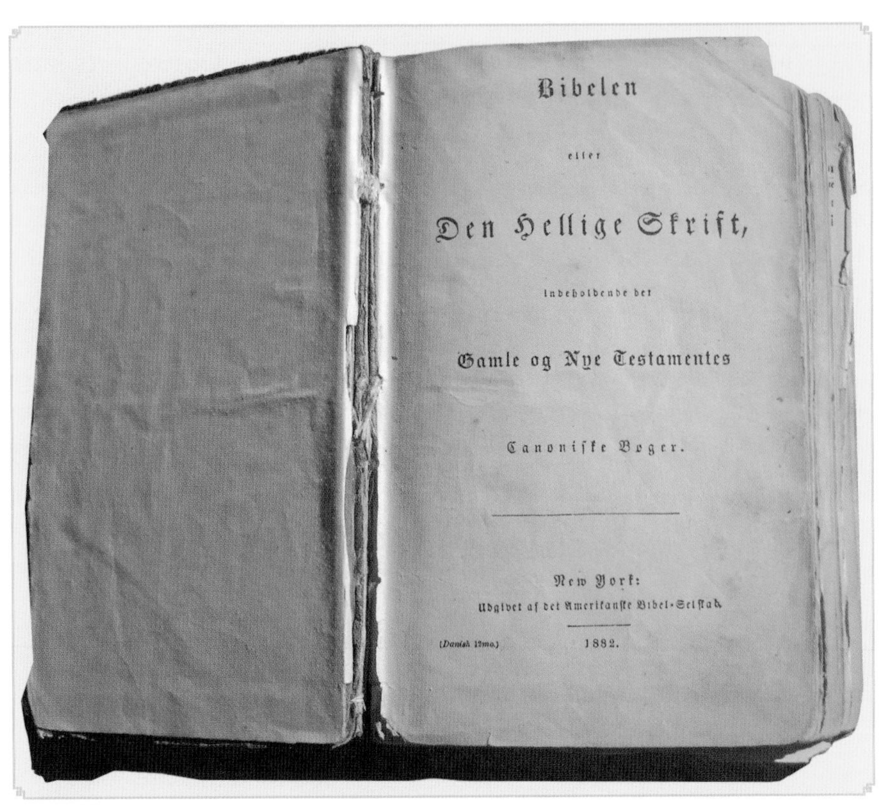
Bibelen

eller

Den Hellige Skrift,

indeholdende det

Gamle og Nye Testamentes

Canoniske Bøger.

New York:

Udgivet af det Amerikanske Bibel-Selskab.

(Danish 12mo.) 1882.

A Norwegian Bible printed in New York, 1882

38

Set the Believers an Example

"Set the believers an example . . .
in love, in faith, in purity."
(1 Timothy 4:12)

Pastor Rolf Eirik Filkesager was well liked by the people in his three-point Parish at Wildrose, North Dakota. He followed his father's advice and listened to the hearts as well as to the words of his people.

Within three years Pastor Rolf had earned the trust of his congregations, as well as of all in the community. He walked with them through times of joy as well as seasons of sorrow. He could be counted on to keep his word and be trusted with a confidentiality.

He loved his people and his work but he missed his beloved Brita. Though they both wrote regularly, the mail delivery from Aleppo, Syria, was intermittent at best. Sometimes there would be no letters for weeks, then, at other times the postman would deliver a whole bundle.

He wrote to her of the day-to-day events in his Parish and she wrote to him of the sick who were healed and the hungry who were fed. Occasionally, she spoke of some who had been wounded in warfare or in mob violence. He worried about her, but at the end of each day he surrendered her to the *protecting* presence of the Triune God.

When the first sounds of war out of the Austro-Hungarian Empire were heard, it seemed very far away. In 1914 most Americans felt safe behind two great oceans. Another war in Europe seemed to be very far away from American shores. However, for Rolf, turmoil in southeastern Europe and the Mid-East meant danger for his beloved.

By now, Rolf had served four years in his Parish. He loved his people and the High Plains. Brita had served as a Deaconess Nurse in Aleppo for four years. She loved her work with people who needed medicine for their bodies and food for their souls. Still, she felt very lonely at times. The Deaconess Mother House had asked her to stay for another term or until the war was over.

Meanwhile, Rolf had just returned to his office from a graveside burial service as the telephone rang. The voice informed him that he had a telegram from his mother. His father had contracted the flu and was very sick. He asked that Rolf come home as soon as possible!

It was a long ride from Williston, North Dakota to Minneapolis, but the fast night train made only a few stops. His mother, Emilie, and his sisters, were at the station. They boarded the streetcar for Deaconess Hospital. *Mor* explained that the doctor was worried about pneumonia. Arne was very sick.

Because of the quarantine, only Rolf was allowed in the room. *Far* was breathing heavily and could speak only a few words at a time, between gasps for breath. He seemed to have an urgent message for his son.

He motioned Rolf to his side. As he pressed a golden Ring into his son's hand, he told the story of the three interlocking Rings.

"Each Ring is inscribed with a mysterious word:

AHURO, meaning *God*, or Lord of All,

ASHEM, meaning *Truth*, or *The Incarnation of Truth*, and

MAZDAO, meaning *Wisdom*, or *Spirit of Wisdom*.

"These three interlocking golden Rings were offered by the Wise Men as a gift to the Christ Child. The Rings were separated during the Crusades. Two of the Rings were given to churches in Hedmarken, Norway by an Egyptian Crusader, as expressions of *thanksgiving* for help and healing.

"The Crusader had followed the 'Pilgrims' Way' through to the Nidaros Cathedral in Trondheim. There he had been washed at St. Olaf's Well and *healed of leprosy*."

Arne placed his hand on Rolf's shoulder.

In a hardly audible voice he whispered, "The bearers of the Rings and the nation will receive a special blessing. When the Rings are re-joined the whole world will be blessed. Tell this only to *your* eldest son when you pass the Ring to him."

61 With his last energy, Arne blessed his son and held Rolf's hand firmly until he had passed to his "Eternal Home" in The Kingdom of The Rings. Rolf embraced his father as he died. As he wept quietly, he placed the golden Ring in his pocket over his heart.

Then he called to his mother and his sisters, but made no mention of the Ring.

The funeral for Reverend Arne Filkesager was a time for both tears and joy. The "sting of death" was real but the assurance that he was Home in his "Father's House" brought joy amid the tears.

The funeral sermon was based on the Gospel text from John 14:1-6:

> *"Let not your hearts be troubled... I go to prepare a place for you ... and when I do... I will come again and will take you to Myself."*

This was the message of the Kingdom of The Rings, which Arne asked to be *proclaimed* at his funeral.

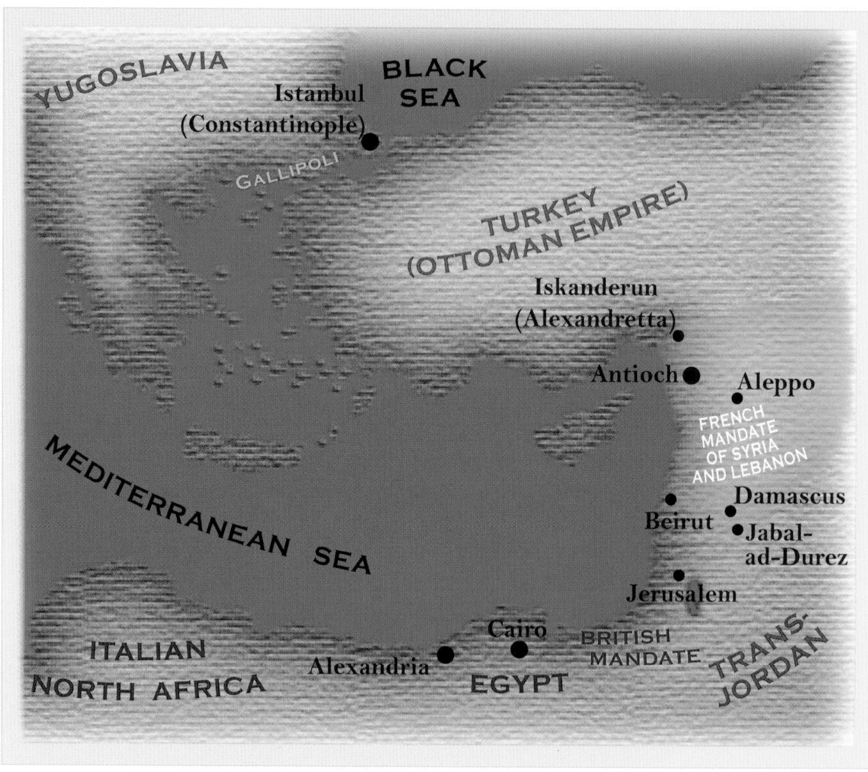

The Middle East, ca. post-World War I
("French Mandate" over Syria and Lebanon, and
"British Mandate" over Jerusalem, Trans-Jordan)

39

A War to End All Wars

"They shall beat their swords into plowshares. . . ."
(Isaiah 2:4)

It was March 1, 1915, only one month after Rolf's father's funeral. He had been busy writing notes of thanks to the many folks who had expressed their appreciation for his father's ministry.

There was a loud knocking at the door.

It was an urgent Union Pacific telegram from Brita's father, Lars Hanson! The message read:

> "*The Chicago Daily News* is planning to send a news correspondent to cover the tragic plight of the Armenians who are being driven out of their homes and lands into the Syrian desert. Let me know if *you* would be willing to do this. It is *possible* that this assignment may bring you to the Aleppo region where Brita is serving."

> This is an answer to my prayer! thought Rolf.

He was worried about his fiancée. He had prayed that a way would open for him to be with her. Now his opportunity had come. If his Parish would release him, he would accept the assignment.

His church councils understood their Pastor's desire and unanimously granted their approval for a leave of absence. The special prayer service for Brita and for his safety and health was an event the Pastor would not soon forget. Members of the Wildrose congregations were there in force at the Epping station on the day Rolf spoke his farewell with tears streaming down his cheeks. They wished him Godspeed and promised to pray daily for him and Brita.

> The question on many minds remained unspoken, Would he bring Brita *back* as his *bride?*

Rolf's heart's answer was too obvious to be spoken.

As a foreign correspondent for a large American newspaper, Rolf was given the opportunity to be attached to Allied military units. He was with a British convoy from the Suez Canal to Jerusalem, then he joined a French Expeditionary force in Lebanon and Syria. The unit's mission was to engage the enemy (Turkish troops) and to find and help the Armenian refugees who were being forced out of their homes and lands in eastern Turkey.

As the unit moved along the coast to the ancient site of Antioch, then circled east toward Aleppo, they passed the bodies of many men, women, and children who had perished in the holocaust. Then they found a group of starving and thirsty refugees who were very thankful for the food, water, and medical attention provided by the French soldiers.

Among this group was an *American* who was carrying his *wife*. Rolf saw that the woman was near death and needed immediate medical attention. He knew they were near Aleppo. There would be help at a hospital there. Rolf knew that if he could get them to the Mission Hospital, perhaps the Deaconesses could save the woman's life.

The man was exhausted, but Rolf and his assistant carried the woman to the ambulance. A local man knew the way and offered to lead them.

Rolf felt the golden Ring against his chest and was encouraged.

> He recited Psalm 46:1 to himself, *"God is our refuge and strength, a very present help in trouble."*

The woman was still breathing when they entered the hospital compound. Rolf asked for a nurse. Brita heard his voice! Their eyes met.

> Brita was at the bedside of a patient. She called out in a soft, but an emotion-filled voice, *"Rolf!"*

He ran to her side and held her close for a moment, then motioned to the stretcher.

> "Can you help this woman? Her husband has carried her from the city of Sis. She is very sick!"

62 Rolf caught a glimpse of something on a chain around *Brita's* neck. She put it quickly inside her blouse and continued touching the woman's forehead.

> "She has a high fever, and her pulse is very weak! She needs liquid!" Brita reported.

The Deaconesses were tending to many refugees. They had been streaming into Aleppo for the past few days. The tragedy was beyond description. Some reports were that more than one-and-a-half million Armenians were being driven from their homes to die in the desert.

Mr. Gregory F. Anthony had left with an advance unit of the French Force who went in the direction of Sis to find and help survivors. He held the golden Ring in his hand as a reminder of God's presence and prayed that he would find Alexander and Zabel alive. He was not with the unit which had spotted an American carrying his wife. He did not know that Rolf had taken them to the Mission Hospital in Aleppo.

Gregory was distributing water and bandages to survivors and kept asking about a tall American and his wife. But his inquiries were met with blank stares. The survivors were in a state of shock. No one had seen them, it seemed. Perhaps they had been shot in the massacre. But Gregory would not give up the search!

Meanwhile, two days had passed and the Deaconesses had done everything they could for Zabel, but she still hovered between life and death. As Rolf gathered with Brita and the other nurses for morning prayers, it seemed that there was no hope that Zabel would survive. Everyone knew the limits of their own healing powers.

They had come together, trusting that the Triune God is the source of all healing power and that He promises His ever present help in times of need.

63 Just as the "Matins" service began, a tall figure slipped into the back of the chapel.

> As they sang the familiar versicle, it seemed to *Brita* that the presence of the Lord was there with them. *The Blessing of the Rings is happening!* she felt it as they sang:

> O Lord, open thou my lips,
> And my mouth shall show forth Thy praise,
> Make haste, O God, to deliver me.
> Make haste to help me, O Lord,
> Glory be to the Father, and to the Son,
> and to the Holy Ghost!

Rolf, too, sensed that the promise of the Rings was being fulfilled in their very presence.

Gregory, in the back of the chapel, had the same feeling that he had at the Chicago Columbian Exposition when he helped the young mother, and her small son who had been saved from a tragic death. It seemed to him that the three golden Rings were coming together.

> Each kept his thoughts to himself, but gave verbal thanks to the Triune God as they heard the excited report of Alexander. Zabel had opened her eyes and spoken his name! "She is ALIVE!"

Gregory clutched the Ring in his pocket over his heart. He remembered that the inscription "ASHEM" meant *Truth*, or, *The Incarnation of Truth.*

> He wondered when The Incarnate Christ would *return*. Perhaps the "Coptic Secret" would be revealed that day.
>
> Could it be, he thought, that the three Rings would join together *here*, near the ancient city of Antioch, as a sign of Christ's return and the fulfillment of the belief that this was "The war to end all wars"?

The Rings knew the answer—the keepers would still wait for the promised fulfillment.

64 *The Rings were separated again.*

Gregory left with Alexander and Zabel as soon as she was able to travel. Rolf asked to bring Brita back, but the Deaconesses could not release her because of the urgent need for nurses in Aleppo. It was a difficult parting, each understanding that for the time being each must return to his and her individual Callings.

They both wept. Would they see each other again was the unspoken question.

As they embraced, the Rings touched.

40

When Will He Come?

"Of that day or that hour, no one knows,
not even the angels in heaven, nor the Son,
but only the Father."
(Mark 13:32)

Maroun heard the joyous cry, "She is ALIVE!" echoing down the halls of the Mission Hospital in Aleppo. He didn't understand English, but he did understand exuberant joy. He had been brought to the Mission Hospital with a severe bullet wound and the Deaconesses had nursed him back to health. He was soon ready to be released. These nurses were like angels of mercy. He was living proof that God worked his miracles through these dedicated women.

Many weeks before, he had been wounded in battle against the Turks. The French unit he was serving with had brought him, nearly dead, to this oasis of healing in Aleppo, Syria. Maroun was one of thousands of Arabs, both Christians and Muslims, who were in revolt against the dictatorship of the Ottoman Turks. They were being aided in their revolt by both British and French military units. Maroun was serving with the French Expeditionary Force. He had been wounded in battle near the ancient city of Antioch.

He was a Maronite Christian from the mountains of Lebanon. Here, in spite of Muslim persecution through the centuries, they had maintained their faithfulness to Jesus Christ, the Savior and Son of God.

Maroun was especially thankful that his Church still worshipped in the language that Jesus spoke, Aramaic. When the liturgy was being recited, he would close his eyes and see the image of Jesus in the midst of the congregation, talking to them as He had spoken to His disciples centuries before.

Now it was 1916, and the Turks who had sided with Germany were attempting to quell the Arab revolt. The French and British were battling to help the Arabs. The Turks had been pushed back to Alexandretta, but they were now regaining the offensive and were shelling the city of Aleppo.

As in prior bombardments, Brita and the other Deaconesses had moved the hospital patients to the cellar for protection. Now Brita helped Maroun to a hiding place in the cellar. It was near the secret place where she kept the golden Ring with the inscription, "MAZDAO," meaning *Wisdom*, or, *Spirit of Wisdom*.

When the Turks took the city, they ordered the Deaconesses to bring all the patients from the cellar. The nurses were forced to evacuate the hospital, because the Turks wanted it for a command post. But Brita did not bring Maroun out of the cellar, for to do so would mean his immediate execution. She and the other nurses hid Maroun in a recess of the cellar beneath a pile of blankets, sheets, and other hospital supplies.

65 Because she was afraid the Turks would take the golden Ring if she wore it or carried it, she revealed its location to *Maroun* and asked him to keep the secret of the Rings and carry the Ring to safety

when he escaped. She explained in her broken French that she had written down the story of the Rings and placed it with the Ring in its hiding place.

The Deaconesses were ordered by the Turkish authorities to leave Aleppo immediately. They would be carried by horse-drawn wagon to a neutral site and exchanged for Turkish prisoners. There was no time to pack or to bring anything. They were herded into the wagon and bumped away into the night. Brita prayed that Maroun would not be discovered, but would be able to escape with the golden Ring.

Under the shroud of night, Maroun, with the treasured Ring hidden in the lining of his robe, crawled from the cellar and escaped the Turks. It was some days later that Maroun struggled up the rocky path to his native village of Aslout in the Lebanon mountains. He was met by his wife, Noora, and his two-year-old son, Sharbel. He recounted how the Deaconesses at Aleppo had cared for him and nursed him back to health, but he didn't mention the golden Ring or its story. This he had promised to keep secret until the other Rings were discovered or until he gave this Ring to his own son.

What joy it was for Maroun to return to his family and his village! Now there was even more profound meaning for him as he attended the Maronite Church and heard the very language of Jesus as the priest spoke the ancient words of the liturgy.

Now that Maroun knew the story of the three golden Rings, the *Trisagion* (the three-fold praise of the Triune God) in the liturgy had new and deeper meaning for him:

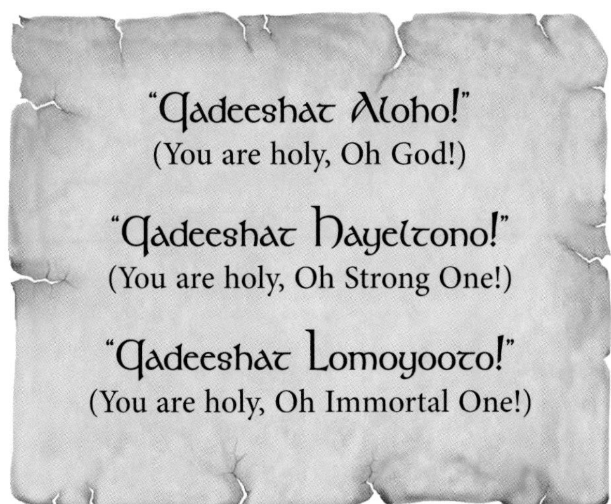

Now he had the new privilege of holding next to his heart the golden Ring that was given to Jesus by the Magi!

He vowed he would take it with him when he made his pilgrimage to the Church of the Nativity in Bethlehem, next Christmas.

The Church of the Nativity, Bethlehem

Maroun had thought often of the promise he had read when he opened the small chest where the golden Ring rested. He believed that the Ring would bring a blessing to him and his family, but he yearned for the time when the three Rings would be re-joined to bless all nations.

Where were the other Rings and who held them in trust?

He prayed that the Lord would give him answers to these questions. But as time passed, there seemed to be no answer to Maroun's petitions —only more war and unrest in his homeland. It began again with a rebel attack on the French installations at Mt. Jabal ad-Durez in 1925.

(The League of Nations had given France a mandate over Syria and Lebanon in 1920, after the end of World War I in 1918.)

However, many Arabs resented French control and broke out in rebellion.

But Maroun had great respect for the French because of their aid in the war against the Turks and their support through the centuries.

The Lebanese spoke of France in such terms of endearment as: *The Sweet Tender Mother of the Maronites.*

But he and many other Christian Arabs were falsely accused of being "French collaborators." Their villages were attacked by roving bands of Islamist radicals. It became increasingly dangerous to live in Lebanon and Syria. For himself, he was not afraid of these radical Islamists, but he feared for the safety of his wife and children.

After much prayer and with the blessing of his father and the priest, Maroun made plans to immigrate to America.

66 It was 1927 when Maroun and his family set sail from Beirut on the ship named *Carpathia II*. They saw to it that their chest of belongings was secured. It included the family Bible, personal treasures, clothing, bedding, dishes, and a small wooden chest. This held a secret which Maroun guarded. Neither his lips nor his actions would reveal the secret of the Ring, which he had pledged to protect.

Still, he wondered, Where are the other Rings? When will the Three Rings come together again? Could it be that in America the Rings would join together to usher in the fulfillment of "The Kingdom of The Rings"?

In the midst of his questions, he remembered Jesus' words: *"Of that day or hour no one knows... only the Father."* (Mark 13:33)

Yes! Maroun believed this word of Jesus, and his mind was at peace again.

The Saga Must End . . .

For Now

"*Den Store Hvide Flok*" ("Behold a Host")

41

"Maranatha" — "Come, Lord Jesus!"

"He who testifies to these things says, 'Surely I AM coming soon.' Amen, come, LORD Jesus!"
(Revelation 22:20)

It was some years later, after Rolf and Brita had married and had their own sons and daughters, that they were preparing to journey to Europe and the Middle East on the *S. S. Carpathia II.* They learned that this ship was named for the liner that had rescued survivors from the *Titanic*. Remembering that tragedy, Rolf and Brita were moved to share the story of the Rings with their eldest son, Eirik, named after his great-grandfather. However, they thought it best to reveal the secret as they visited at the bedside of *Bestemor* (Grandmother) Reidunn.

So it was that on a beautiful Sunday in the season of Pentecost Rolf, Brita, and Eirik gathered at Reidunn's bedside to share together the presence of the Triune God in the Lord's Supper.

Each sensed the closeness of "the Christ," since all believed the words of Jesus, the Savior, read by the Pastor: *"This is MY body... this is MY blood."*

This moving experience of Jesus' presence through the sacred act of Communion is a powerful confirmation that Jesus' promise—repeated three times in the final chapter of the Book of Revelation—is true: *"I am coming soon!"* (Revelation 22:7, 12, 20)

At the close of the Communion service, Reidunn asked the Pastor to lead them in singing the treasured Norwegian hymn, *"Den Store Hvide Flok"* ("Behold A Host") which depicts the vision of the Kingdom of God, The Kingdom of the Rings revealed to St. John and recorded in Revelation 7:9-17.

As her family sang the words to this beloved hymn, tears welled up in Reidunn's eyes. She couldn't see the music; but the words came from her soul as she sang this moving hymn.

Following the Communion service, Brita, Rolf, and Eirik listened intently as Reidunn recounted the saga of the Rings. She told them of the blessing which was promised to those who were the keepers of the Rings. This promise was soon to come with the passing of the First Ring to her *grandson*.

> With this new sense of his place in destiny, Eirik asked the same questions that had been on his parents' minds for a long time: "*What* had happened to the other Rings? *Would* the three Rings come together again? *When* will The Kingdom of The Rings be fulfilled?"

Before she answered, Reidunn reached out for the Ring. It was the first time that she had held this Ring with the inscription "AHURO" (*God*, or *Lord of All*).

67 She handled it tenderly, and studied it carefully, before placing it into her grandson's hand. Then, grasping his hand with both of hers, she pressed it to her lips. It was the sign of the profound blessing which would come from the Triune God Himself.

All were silent as Reidunn struggled to formulate her response.

> Finally, a soft whisper came from Reidunn's lips: "***Soon!*** The Kingdom is *coming*...***Soon!***"

Soli Deo Gloria...

Holy, Holy, Holy!

Author's Concluding Commentary

I have written this saga with the intention that the reader will encounter the content and message on several levels. These include the Spiritual/Theological, the Historical, the Ethical/Cultural, and the Personal levels.

On the Spiritual/Theological level, I employ the traditional symbol of the Triune God—the three interlocking rings—as the underlying metaphor of the saga. The fictional connection of this symbol with the Magi's Gift of Gold to the Christ Child is used to communicate the primary theological message—namely, the ubiquity, power, and hiddenness of the Kingdom of God ("The Kingdom of The Rings") in everyday life and history, and the immanence of Christ's Second Coming.

This is a compelling message because we live in a world where the signs of "The End" seem to be evident on every hand. The conclusion of the saga leaves the question open—"*When* will The Kingdom of The Rings be fulfilled?" However, it suggests that "the End" and fulfillment is near. (*"Soon!"* says the leading character on her death bed.)

This saga also has a Historical purpose and message. Because the assumption is that history is *"His-story,"* the broad sweep of time from the thirteenth through the twentieth centuries is tied together by the nearness of the Kingdom of the Triune God ("the kingdom of the three interlocking golden rings"). Because history is moving to fulfillment in the Second Coming of Jesus Christ (signaled in the book by the joining together of the three Rings), history has a linear, not a cyclic or evolutionary pattern. In other words, the Kingdom of The Rings remains the constant reference throughout the span of time.

The "Rings *metaphor*" serves to tie history together, so it can be viewed as a unity.

A secondary Historical purpose in writing this saga (wherein history and fiction come together in a single literary form) is to stimulate the study and appreciation of history by tying it to a fictional story.

This story has an Ethical/Cultural purpose as well. The characters confront ethical and cultural issues (i.e., slavery, civil war, immigration, ethnic rivalries, "Melting Pot" assumptions, conflict with Islam, world war, racial issues, alcohol abuse, etc.) which remind us of challenges confronting our contemporary world. The Rings, *in their testimony to the Triune God and His Word,* are a reminder that in spite of the changing attitudes of the culture, the standard of absolute, unchanging Truth remains.

On a Personal level, the purpose of this saga is to help readers to see themselves and their ancestors *mirrored* in the story, and to come to a deeper understanding of their own identity and of the "American Experience" of their immigrant ancestors. The saga *focuses* on individuals who are swept up in the tide of the significant immigration from *Norway* in the nineteenth century (CA. 850,000) as a type of *all* immigrant groups who have historic ties to Europe and the Middle East. Like other immigrants, the Norwegians, in their struggle to adapt to this "Promised Land" and also to retain their identity, have left the marks of their toil, tears, tragedies, and triumphs on the warp and woof of American society.

In this regard, I have attempted to reveal the personal and ethnic destructive effects resulting from the underlying assumptions of the "Melting Pot" which emphasized conformity. I have substituted "The Field of Rings" as a more adequate metaphor of the "American Experience" of the immigrants.

My prayer is that this saga will encourage each reader in his/her faith in the "Triune God," who is symbolized by the three interlocking golden rings, and that it will encourage the *study* of Scripture, as well as the sagas of the Western World, the history of our nation, and our own personal family stories.

***Duane R. Lindberg,* PhD**

List of Historical Persons During the Time of the Saga

Thirteenth Century and Before

Jesus the Christ

The Magi, "The Three Wise Men" (Three distinguished "foreigners," i.e., Gentiles, from the "East")

Saint Mark, Evangelist, Missionary to Egypt

The Knights Hospitaller of St. John — founded in eleventh century

Baybars I, Muslim ruler of Egypt, Mameluke dynasty, 1223–1277

Bohemund VI, Crusader King of Antioch, 1237–1275

de Lusignan, Amalric, Crusader King of Cyprus, 1285–1310

Eriksson, Leif, Explorer, discovered North America (Vinland) in CA. AD 1000.

Frederick I Barbarosa, Holy Roman Emperor, 1123–1190

Haakon IV Haakonsson, King of Norway, 1204–1263

Haakon V Magnusson, King of Norway, 1270–1319

Hugh III, Crusader King of Cyprus, 1267–1284

Mamelukes, Muslim Rulers of Egypt (came to power in 1250)

Olaf I Tryggvesson, King of Norway, introduced Christianity in southern and western Norway, 968–1000

Olaf II Haraldson, King of Norway, continued the conversion of Norway to Christianity, martyred, recognized as a Saint in both Western and Eastern Churches, 995–1030

Sigurd I, "The Crusader," King of Norway, led an expedition to the Holy Land, 1107–1130

Fourteenth, Fifteenth, and Sixteenth Centuries

Charles V, Holy Roman Emperor, 1500–1558

Christian II, Elected King of Norway but imprisoned by the Danes, 1481–1559

Constantine XI, Byzantine Emperor at fall of Constantinople, 1404–1453

de Lusignan, Guy, King of Armenian-Cilicia, 1342–1344

de Lusignan, Leo, King of Armenian-Cilicia, 1374–1375

Engelbrektson, Olav, Roman Catholic Archbishop of Norway, 1480–1538

Frederick I, King of Denmark and Norway, CA 1536

Haakon VI Magnusson, King of Norway, 1340–1380

Jakob, Bishop of Hamar when the Hamar Cathedral was destroyed, 1563

Johnson, Arnstein, Pastor, Ringsaker Church, Norway, CA 1536

Luther, Martin, Reformer of the Church, 1483–1546

Olav av Ringsaker, Sokneprest (priest), CA. 1349

Knights Hospitaller of St. John of Rhodes, 1310–1522, of Malta after 1530

Seventeenth, Eighteenth, Nineteenth, and Twentieth Centuries

Ager, Waldemar, editor and author, 1869–1941

Anderson, Rev. Bersvend, pioneer pastor and editor in the Red River Valley of the North and in Alberta, Canada, temperance leader, 1821–1917

Bjørnsen (Benson), Bjørn, immigrant farmer from Norway to Iowa, 1855

Brown, John, abolitionist, hanged at Ft. Sumner, 1800–1859

Buckneberg, Rev. Ingvald, pioneer pastor in western North Dakota, 1872–1948

Cleveland, Grover, President of U.S., 1837–1908

Darwin, Charles, naturalist, author, *Origin of Species*, 1809–1892

de Crevecour, J. Hector St. John, farmer and author, 1735–1813

Eielsen, Elling, lay preacher and pioneer pastor in Illinois, Wisconsin, and Iowa, 1804–1883

Handel, George Frideric, composer, 1685–1759

Harstad, Rev. Bjug A., pioneer pastor, teacher, editor in North Dakota, Minnesota, and Washington, 1848–1927, Founder of Lutheran secondary schools and college, President of the "Little Norwegian Synod" (1918–1921)

Hauge, Hans Nielsen, Norwegian Revivalist and entrepreneur, 1771–1824

Hegel, Georg W. F., idealist philosopher and author, 1770–1831

Heg, Col. Hans Christian, Commander of the 15th Wisconsin "Scandinavian" Regiment, Union Army, Civil War, 1829–1863

Ingersol, Robert, American "free thinker," lecturer, 1833–1899

James, Jesse, American outlaw and bank robber, 1847–1882

Kvitne, Styrk Anderson, poet, 1854–1940

Larsen, Rev. Dr. Lauritz, pioneer pastor, seminary professor, President, Luther College, Decorah, Iowa, 1833–1915

Lawson, Victor, publisher, *Skandinaven* and *Chicago Daily News*, 1850–1925

Leibniz, Gotfried W., philosopher, mathematician, and author, 1646–1716

Lincoln, Abraham, U.S. President, Emancipation Proclamation of Slaves, 1863 and Homestead Act, 1809–1865

Morgenthau, Henry, U.S. Ambassador to the Ottoman Empire (Turkey,) 1856–1946

Muus, Rev. B. J., pioneer Norwegian Lutheran Pastor, Founder of St. Olaf's School (College), 1832–1900

Oglethorpe, James, Founder of the Colony of Georgia, 1696–1785

Roosevelt, Theodore, President of U.S., 1858–1919

Salzburgers, Lutheran refugees from Austria who settled in Georgia, beginning in 1733

Saugstad, Christian T., pioneer Norwegian Lutheran Pastor in Minnesota and Canada, author, President, Free Lutheran Church, 1838–1897

Scott, Dred, American slave who unsuccessfully sued for his freedom in 1857.

Semler, Johan, German theologian and Biblical critic, 1725–1791

Skordalsvold, Johannes. J., poet and author, CA. 1840

Turner, Fredeick Jackson, professor and author, 1861–1932

Veblen, Thorstein, professor and author, 1857–1929

Wesley, John, Founder of the Methodist Church, 1703–1791

Whitman, Walt, American poet, 1819–1892

Whitefield, George, English preacher and evangelist, leader of the "Great Awakening" in the U.S., 1714–1770

Timeline of Fictional Rings Carriers

"AHURO" (*Lord of All*)

SAGA #		YEAR
67	Reidunn blesses Ring, gives to Eirik F.	1933
61	Rolf F. gets ring; to Aleppo, SYRIA	1915
59	Prof. Arne F. meets Reidunn	1897
48, 53	Arne F. to Chicago	1893
46	Arne to Dakota	1882
45	Arne to St. O. (page 95)	1875
37	Arne, Ring	1866
34	Eirik to Texas	1854
33	Arne av F.	1788
	Eirik av Filkesager, Norway	1777
19	Arnstein av Filkesager, Ringsaker, Norway	1531
10	Ringsaker Church, Norway	1269

"ASHEM" (*The Incarnation of Truth*)

SAGA #		YEAR
63	Greg Anthony at Aleppo, SYRIA	1915
49, 53	Greg Anthony at Chicago W.F.	1893
43	Greg Anthony at Constantinople	1878
45	Greg Anthony III, Newberry, SC	1868
31	John Anthony, Georgia	1734
30	Leopold Anthony, Salzburg, Austria	1732
29	Mark Anthony, Vienna, Austria	1529
28	Gregory Anthony II, Rhodes	1453
27	Gregory Anthony, Egypt	1450
26	Fatima of Alexandria	1383
25	Farouk of Egypt	1375
24	Guy de Lusignan, King of Cilicia, Armenia	1343

"MAZDAO" (*Spirit of Wisdom*)

SAGA #		YEAR
66	Maroun carries Ring to USA	1927
65	Brita reveals Ring to Maroun	1918
62	Brita at Aleppo, SYRIA	1915
60	Brita Hanson gets Ring	1911
50	Per Ondestad at Chicago W.F.	1893
47, 53	Reidunn at Chicago W.F.	1893
40	Reidunn Haraldson at Mother's grave	1866
38	Petra Haraldson & family leave Norway with Ring	1855
22	Harald the Sexton to Ringerike, Norway	1567
13	Hamar Cathedral, Norway	1269

8 Hugh III King of Cyprus

1–7 Marcarius of Alexandria, Egypt 1269 AD

Glossary — Religious and Theological Terms Used in the Saga

Throughout the book there are general Christian theological terms referenced, as well as specific Norwegian Lutheran Church history terms. For those readers unfamiliar with these items, the following glossary is included for easy access.

Advent — The church season including the four Sundays prior to Christmas.

Breviary — A book containing Psalms, readings, and prayers of the Divine Office.

Chancel — Part of the church building where the altar stands.

Confirmation — The rite by which baptized persons renew and confirm their baptism and profess their commitment to Jesus Christ and His Word.

Conventicle Act — The law enacted by the Dano-Norwegian government declaring lay preaching illegal.

Diaspora — The scattering of a people with a common background.

Diet — The formal assembly of princes and electors of the Holy Roman Empire.

Gospel — The good news concerning Jesus Christ the Savior (Romans 1:6).

Grace — God's undeserved love through Christ Jesus (Rom. 3:24).

Haugean Theology — That Christian teaching which emphasizes a personal and "living" faith in Jesus Christ.

Haymarket Anarchists — The anti-government protesters who rioted in Chicago's Haymarket Square on May 4, 1886.

Lent — The 40-day period from Ash Wednesday to Easter excluding Sundays.

Lepers' Window — That opening in the wall of the church near the altar through which the priest could give the Communion bread to lepers.

Matins — An early morning liturgical service.

Parochial — Relating to a church parish or to a restricted outlook on a particular matter.

Pietism — That religious movement which seeks to emphasize a living faith and the importance of devotion to religious duties and practices.

Princes' Confession of Faith — The Augsburg Confession presented to Emperor Charles V by German princes supportive of Martin Luther at the Diet of Augsburg in 1530.

Prophetic — That which predicts or foreshadows what is coming.

Rationalism — A philosophy which teaches that human reason is the source of ultimate truth.

Rationalistic Preaching — The practice of basing one's religious opinions or teaching on what one thinks is reasonable rather than on God's revealed Word.

Revival — A stirring up of religious faith by fervent evangelical preaching at public meetings.

The Reformation — The great religious reform of the Western (Roman Catholic) Church begun and led by Martin Luther when he posted his 95 Theses on October 31, AD 1517.

Salvation — Deliverance from sin and the judgment on sin through baptism and faith in the saving work of Christ (Mark 16:16).

Second Coming — The promised return of Jesus Christ to Judge the world and to fulfill God's plan for mankind and for all creation.

The Small Catechism — A brief summary of the chief doctrines of the Christian faith written by Martin Luther to be used by fathers as a guide in the instruction of their children.

The See of... — The official jurisdiction of a bishop or archbishop.

Sexton — One who has charge of the material care of a church building.

Social Idealism — A philosophy which believes in the temporal possibility of creating a perfect human community.

Synod — A union of congregations of the same faith for the purpose of promoting and preserving the faith.

Theses, The 95—The statements regarding the church practice of granting Indulgences (divine forgiveness of temporal consequences of sin) which Martin Luther posted on the Castle Church door in Wittenburg, Germany on October 31, 1517.

Three Interlocking Rings—Historic Symbol of the Trinity, which is often sewed on altar, pulpit, and lectern cloth hangings.

Tree Claim—Additional acres of land which a homesteader could receive if he planted trees on it.

Vinland—The Norse name for that part of North America about the Gulf of St. Lawrence and New England which was discovered and explored by the Norsemen in ca. AD 1000.

Discussion Guide: Questions and Meditations For Readers

OVERVIEW

- What is the most significant thing you learned by reading this book?
- Has something you read changed your mind about anything?
- What three words would you use to describe this book?

PART ONE

- What is the meaning of "The Kingdom of The Rings?"
- What is the significance of the Three Interlocking Rings when considered as a unity? When considered as individual Rings?
- What is the eschatological ("End Times") meaning of the promised coming together of the Rings?
- Between AD 1095 and 1291 Christians carried out seven Crusades. What was the religious purpose of the Crusades?

PART TWO

- Norway's "Age of Greatness" was in the Twelfth and Thirteenth centuries. What caused the tragic end to this period of greatness?
- Why did pilgrims journey to the Nidaros Cathedral in Trondheim during the Middle Ages? When and why did these pilgrimages cease?
- When Marcarius returned to Cyprus after he was healed of leprosy, the second Ring "ASHEM," was still in the possession of the Christian King of Cyprus. Why was the message of the Second Ring so offensive and threatening to the Muslim General, Farouk?

PART THREE

A.

- The Muslims were defeated in their attempt to capture Vienna in AD 1529. What are the implications of this Christian victory for western and northern Europe?
- The Anthony family, keepers of the second Ring, immigrate to the Colony of Georgia in the company of the Salzburgers. Where are the Salzburgers from and why did they immigrate to America?
- The leading figure in the religious revival of Norway in the Nineteenth century was Hans Nielsen Hauge. What did he do to stimulate the re-birth of the nation?

B.

- In the Dred Scott case, the Supreme Court denied the personhood of the slave. Since 1973, the killing of the unborn has been justified by the Courts for a similar reason. What was Eirik reminded of when he reflected on the birth and baptism of baby Johan Nelson?
- Magnus and his relationship to Gyda's family illustrates the reality of "class distinctions" in Norwegian society. How does this "play out" in our nation?
- Do you think that belief in the Triune God (symbolized in the book by the three interlocking rings) influenced the Fathers of our nation in the structuring of our *tri-partite* government?

PART FOUR

- What is the source of comfort and hope in the face of sudden, tragic, untimely death?
- For most Norse immigrants, the church was the center of their social and spiritual lives. Issues which divided many Norwegian-American communities were the attitudes toward the "election of the saints by God," the role of the public schools, and the abuse of alcohol. What do you think about these issues today?

PART FIVE

A.

- What event celebrated the rebirth of Chicago after the Great Fire of 1871? When was it held?
- How does the story of Ivar Ondestad and his family illustrate the truth of Exodus 20:5 and 34:7?
- Why are some sinners like Amund converted and others like Ivar are not?

B.

- When Per saved Karl Victor from a tragic death, his sacrifice signaled the nearness of the three golden Rings ("The Kingdom of The Rings"). Have you experienced a time when the Kingdom seemed very near?
- Do you agree with Gregory F. Anthony III that human government is necessary in a fallen world? Can any form of government produce the "perfect society"?

PART SIX

- How is the presence of the Triune God affirmed in the words of Scripture declared at Baptism (Matthew 28: 19)?
- Do you share Reidunn's concern to try to maintain your family's values, faith, and identity in the midst of our society today?
- How do you respond to Arne's questions?
  - Can America thrive with its great variety of disparate groups?
  - How can diversity be a positive factor in a functioning democracy?
  - How can America resolve the conflict between the idea of an easy tolerance toward differing beliefs, values, and opinions (relativism) and the need to stand up for honest communication based on commitment to the Absolute Truth of Scripture?

PART SEVEN

- The nearness of the three golden Rings at Aleppo gives Christians the assurance about what?
- It is important to remember that NOT all Arabs are Muslims. Many are members of ancient Christian communities like the Coptic, Syrian Orthodox, Maronite, Chaldean, as well as Greek Orthodox and Roman Catholic. The Maronite Christians of Lebanon use the Aramaic language (Jesus' native tongue) as their liturgical language. The ancient prayer of the Church, petitioning the Lord to come soon is spoken in Aramaic, *"Maranantha!"* ("Come Lord Jesus!") What does this signify to you? To others around the world?
- This saga of "The Kingdom of The Rings" is intended to encourage all Christians to know that the Triune God is always near to us, powerful to help, gracious to forgive, and faithful to His promise to take us to our Heavenly Home. In your own personal walk of faith, what has been your experience with this promise?

Bibliography

Ager, Waldemar T., *On the Way to the Melting Pot*, translated from Norwegian by Harry T. Cleven, 1st edition, Prairie Oak Press, Eau Claire, WS, 1995.

Bakken, Petter, et al., *Veldre Bygdebok,* Veldre Historielag, Haaves Boktrykkeri, Brumunddal, 1974.

Blegen, Theodore C., N*orwegian Migration to America,* The Norwegian-American Historical Association, Northfield, MN, 1931.

Cross, F. L., editor, *The Oxford Dictionary of the Christian Church,* 3rd Edition, published in the United States by Inc., NY, 1997.

de Crevecoeur, J. Hector Saint John, *Letters from an American Farmer,* E. P. Dutton & Co., NY, 1912.

Derry, T. K., *A Short History of Norway,* George Allen & Unwin Ltd., London, 1968.

Encyclopedia Britannica, William Benton Pub., Chicago, 1963, vol. 6:831 and vol. 16:109. Used by permission.

Hansen, Marcus Lee, *The Immigrant in American History,* Harper & Row, NY, 1940, 1964.

Hreinsson, Vidar, *The Complete Sagas of Icelanders,* Leifur Eiriksson Publishing, Reykjavik, Iceland, 1997, "Introduction" by Robert Kellogg.

Kvitne, Styrk Anderson, unpublished poem, "When Life's Storms," from Personal Collection of E. Mardell Lindberg, written by her Grandfather.

Lee, Art, *The Lutefisk Ghetto* (*Life in a Norwegian-American Town*), Adventure Publications, Cambridge, MN, 1978.

Lindberg, Duane R., *Men of the Cloth*, Arno Press, a New York Times Company, NY, 1980.

_____, "Norwegian-American Pastors in Immigrant Fiction," 1870 –1920, *Norwegian-American Studies*, Vol. 28, The Norwegian-American Historical Association, Northfield, MN, 1979.

Lovoll, Odd S., *The Promise of America: A History of the Norwegian-American People,* University of Minnesota Press, Minneapolis, MN, 1984.

_____, *A Century of Urban Life: The Norwegians in Chicago before 1930*, The Norwegian-American Historical Association, Northfield, MN, 1988.

Luther, Rev. Dr. Martin, *The Small Catechism,* 1529.

Malmin, Rasmus, and Norlie, O. M., and Tingelstad, O. A., *Who's Who Among Pastors in all the Norwegian Lutheran Synods of America 1843–1927*, Augsburg Publishing House, Minneapolis, MN, 1928.

Mitchell, Samuel Augustus, *Mitchell's New General Atlas*, S. Augustus Mitchell, Jr., Philadelphia, PA, 1860. (Republished by the Minnesota Historical Society, St. Paul, MN, 1994.)

Nelson, E. Clifford and Fevold, Eugene L., *The Lutheran Church among Norwegian Americans*, Augsburg Publishing House, Minneapolis, MN, 1960.

Norlie, O. M., *History of the Norwegian People in America*, Augsburg Publishing House, Minneapolis, MN, 1925.

_____, *Norsk Lutherske Menigheter i Amerika 1843–1916*, Vol. I and II," Augsburg Publishing House, Minneapolis, MN, 1918.

Ormoy, Ragnhild, *Ringsakboka II Mellomalderen,* Ringsaker Historielag, Brumunddal, Norway, 1992.

Overland, O. A., *Illustreret Norges Historie, Folkebladets Forlag,* Kristiania, Norway, 1888, vol. 1 and vol. 3 (inside front cover).

Shaw, Joseph M., *Bernt Julius Muus,* Norwegian American Historical Association, Northfield, MN, 1999.

Skordalsvold, Johannes J., from poem: "To Our Real Heroes" in *History of the Norwegian People in America* by Norlie, O. M., Pastor, Augsburg Publishing House, Minneapolis, MN, 1925.

Tranberg, Anna, *Ringsakboka III Korn og Klasseskille*, Ringsaker Historielag, Brumunddal, Norway, 1993.

Turner, Edward Raymond, *Europe 1789–1920*, Doubleday, Page & Company Pub., NY, 1922.

Turner, Frederick Jackson, *The Frontier in American History*, H. Holt & Co., NY, 1920.

Veblen, Thorstein, *The Theory of the Leisure Class,* Macmillan Co., NY, 1899 (re-issued Viking Press, NY, 1945).

Walker, Williston, *A History of the Christian Church,* Charles Scribner's Sons, NY, 1918 (copyright 1946 by Amelia Walker Cushing and Elizabeth Walker).

Wells, H. G., *The Outline of History,* Garden City Books Pub., Garden City, NY, 1920, Doubleday & Company, Inc. 1949.

Weisberger, Bernard A., *Reaching for Empire,* Part Five, 131, included in *The Life [Magazine] History of the United States, 1890–1901,* Time Incorp., NY, 8:95.

Whitman, Walt, from poem: "Democratic Vistas" in *Leaves of Grass and Selected Prose,* Doubleday & Co., NY, 1924.

Resources

Photographs and Classical Paintings

Chicago History Museum, Rights and Reproductions, Color Reproduction of Broadside: Chicago Day, at the World's Columbian Exposition, 1893. Thanks to Angela Hoover.

The Image Works, New York, NY, with special thanks and appreciation to Sarah-Maria Vischer-Masino, Researcher.

Paul Bunyan Museum, Akeley, MN. Courtesy, President Frank Lamb.

Quotations

Page xv–xvi: Robert Kellogg, *The Complete Sagas of Icelanders*

Page 9: *Quran*, Sura 2:194; THE KORAN, reproduced by permission of Penguin Books Ltd., London. Thanks to Lottie Fyfe.

Page 55: *Dallas Times,* Dred Scott Decision. (Extinct. Public Domain) Thank you to the History and Archives Division, Dallas Public Library.

Page 108: Johannes J. Skordalsvold, poem, "To Our Real Heroes."

Page 113: Styrk Anderson Kvitne, unpublished poem, "When life's storms sweep."

Page 156: *"I Jesu navn"* (Norwegian Table Prayer), public domain.

Lyrics

Messiah, George Frideric Handel, 1741, public domain.

"Matins Liturgy," *Lutheran Book of Worship,* Augsburg Publishing House, Minneapolis, MN, 1978, used by permission.

Hymn, *"Den Store Hvide Flok"* ("Behold A Host!), *Service Book and Hymnal,* Augsburg Publishing House, Minneapolis, MN, 1958, used by permission.

Trisagion (Qadeeshat), Used by permission by Rev. Fr. Rodrigue Constantin of the Holy Family Maronite Catholic Church, St. Paul, MN.

Credits
Photography, Maps, and Artwork

Page No.	Citation	Source/Permission
Frontis-piece	"The Beauty of Norway's Fjords"	Photograph Erik Lindberg
Title	"General view, Trondheim (Trondhjem)"	The Image Works (EMEP0206345)
iii	Re-enactment: Soldiers; King Olaf II blessed before the Battle of Stiklestad, 950th Anniversary	Dr. Lindberg Family Collection
v	"Bohemund and Dogobert Sailing"	The Image Works (EAKG0898321)
viii	"Lake Mjøsa from Rute 33 looking NE-SE"	The Image Works (ETPM0815128)
xiii	The Hopperstad Stave Church (12th c. replica)	Photograph by Dean Sorum, Moorhead, MN
xiv	"Olav II Converts People"	The Image Works (EMEP0071384)
Prelude	"Guided by a star, the three Magi are led to the Bethlehem stable where Jesus has been recently born 1st century."	The Image Works (EMEP0191576)
2	"Egypt, Alexandria. St. Mark's Cathedral, Coptic Easter Ceremony"	The Image Works (EPHD0460403)
4	"Procession-of-the-Crusaders" 1841, detail by Jean Victor Snetz (1787–1870 French)	Bridgeman Art Library/London Stock Photo 475-2368; used by permission.
6	Map: Egypt/Syria/Mid-East (Journey of Marcarius, ca. 1267)	Original Art by Forge Toro
8	"Single Rings and Three Interlocking Rings" graphics; also pp. i, 48, 60, 87, 90, 100, 186, 204, 212, and Cover.	Art by Desta Garrett
12	Statue: King Olaf II, Stiklestad	Dr. Lindberg Family Collection
13	Map: "The Pilgrims' Way" (*pilegrimsleden*)	Original Art by Forge Toro
14	"The Lepers' Window" (recreation) Hopperstad Stave Church (12th c. replica)	Photograph by Dean Sorum Moorhead, MN
15	The Ringsaker Church	Public Domain
16	The Nidaros Cathedral	Dr. Lindberg Family Collection
18	Flisaker Farm, Ringsaker, Norway, birthplace of author's grandfather	Dr. Lindberg Family Collection

Page No.	Citation	Source/Permission
22	The Ruins of the Hamar Cathedral	Dr. Lindberg Family Collection
24–25	Map: "The Kingdom of Norway" 1239–63	Original Art by Forge Toro
32	Map: Journeys of the House of Anthony, 15th and 16th centuries	Original Art by Forge Toro
35	"Martin Luther at the Diet of Worms, 1521"	The Image Works (EAKG0007980)
37	"View of Cathedral of Cologne, Germany, 1880–90"	The Image Works (EALN0820749)
38	Vista of "The Promised Land"	Dr. Lindberg Family Collection
40	Map: "Advent of the Rings in America"	Original Art by Forge Toro
44	"Haugeans Praying"	The Image Works (EAKG0249789)
54	Map: "The Western Campaign of the Civil War"	Original Art by Forge Toro
63	Fort Atkinson	Dr. Lindberg Family Collection
63	Map: "Upper Sioux Agency"	Original Art by Forge Toro
71	"Family Trunk, 1855" Mrs. Duane R. (E. Mardell) Lindberg	Dr. Lindberg Family Collection (Photograph by Martha Stone)
72	Typical Norwegian Bride, ca. 1855	From O. A. Overlund, *Illustreret Norges Histeorie, Folkebladets Forlag*
78	"The Red River Lumber Company Sawmill"	Paul Bunyan Museum, Akeley, MN Courtesy, President Frank Lamb
80	"Paul Bunyan"	Paul Bunyan Museum, Akeley, MN Courtesy, President Frank Lamb
81	The Loggers of "Camp No. 5"	Paul Bunyan Museum, Akeley, MN Courtesy, President Frank Lamb Photo: Arrow Printing Inc., Bemidji, MN Thanks to Stan Haley, Pres., and Connie Knutson for photo enhancement
81	"Logs Piled High!"	Paul Bunyan Museum, Akeley, MN Courtesy, President Frank Lamb
85	*Basilica Sancta Sophia (Hagia Sophia)*	Photograph by Andrew Lindberg Adapted by Forge Toro.
88	"Storm Clouds Gathering"	PHOTO 24 / EXACTACOLOR; used by permission
107	Map: "Northby Parish"/"Dakota Territory"	Original Art by Forge Toro

Page No.	Citation	Source/Permission
110	"The Prairie Winds"	"Prairie and Sky," photograph by Cris Fulton, 2012
114	Stained Glass Window, Allen Memorial Hospital, Waterloo, Iowa	Dr. Lindberg Family Collection
120	Map: "The Journeys of The Rings to Chicago"	Original Art by Forge Toro
124	Color Reproduction of Broadside: "Chicago Day, At the World's Columbian Exposition, 1893"	Chicago History Museum, Rights and Reproductions; used by permission. With thanks to Angela Hoover
130	Board of Trustees including Founder, Rev. B. J. Muus, St. Olaf's School (St. Olaf College), 1866	Photograph by O. G. Felland, St. Olaf Faculty and Librarian; the Christian Lindberg Collection.
134	Iconic Jesus from wall of *Basicilica Santa Sophia (Hagia Sophia)*	Photograph by Andrew Lindberg, Adapted by Forge Toro.
138	"Crowd Scene. Chicago World's Fair, 1893"	The Image Works (ESZP0092355)
140	Bronze Sculpture, Ministering to a Patient Allen Memorial Hospital, Waterloo, Iowa	Dr. Lindberg Family Collection
148	Three Golden Interlocking Rings, Hanging Altar Parament	Photograph by Dean Sorum, at The Lutheran Church of Christ the King, Moorhead, MN Used by permission. Praise Banner, Copyright PraiseBanners. Used by permission. Thank you to Dusty Emerick.
159	"Arnie's Field of Rings"	Concept, Dr. Lindberg; Art by Desta Garrett "Fields" photo, FOTOSEARCH k7759073
166	"Wounded Armenians, Aleppo, Syria, February 28, 1919"	The Image Works (ERVL0632508)
172	Norwegian Bible, 1882	Dr. Lindberg Family Collection
176	Map: "The Middle-East Post WWI"	Original Art by Forge Toro
182	Iconic Jesus from wall of *Basicilica Santa Sophia* (*Hagia Sophia*)	Photograph by Andrew Lindberg Adapted by Forge Toro.
184	"Interior, The Church of the Nativity; Bethlehem, c. 1888; Illustration from *The Life and Times of Queen Victoria,* Vol. 2, by Robert Wilson (c.1888); Unknown (creator), Robert Wilson"	The Image Works (EHIP5810354)
191	"God-like Sun Rays at Top of Clouds"	The Image Works (ECLS0010344)
213	Dr. Duane R. Lindberg	Dr. Lindberg Family Collection
215	Gerald Christian Nordskog, Pres. NPI	Photo by Brent Nims

About the Author

Duane R. Lindberg was born and raised in the Scandinavian hinterland of northwestern Minnesota. His paternal grandfather was born on a Viking Age farm in Ringsaker, Norway near the burial mounds of ancient kings.

Duane received his BS in Chemistry from the University of North Dakota, a MTh from Luther Seminary, St. Paul, a Doctor of Divinity degree from the American Lutheran Theological Seminary, and an MA and PhD in American Studies from the University of Minnesota. His dissertation was published by Arno Press, a New York Times Co., in 1980 under the title, *Men of the Cloth* and the *Social Cultural Fabric of the Norwegian Ethnic Community in North Dakota.* His articles on this topic have also been published in "Norwegian-American Studies" and in "The Scandinavian Presence in North America," *Harpers Magazine Press.*

Following a brief career as a research chemist and as an officer in the US Army Chemical Corps, Dr. Lindberg studied for the Lutheran ministry and served congregations in North Dakota and Iowa.

In addition to his 50 years of pastoral ministry, Rev. Lindberg has served as the Presiding Pastor (Bishop) of the American Association of Lutheran Churches from 1987 until his retirement in 1999. As Presiding Pastor, he was instrumental in founding the American Lutheran Theological Seminary and served as adjunct professor in areas of church history and systematics. He also taught medieval history at Upper Iowa University.

Duane and his wife Mardell reside in Waterloo, Iowa. They are blessed with five children and eleven grandchildren. In their retirement, the Lindbergs are active in their church and the American Association of Lutheran Churches (AALC). They volunteer in their community through the Sons of Norway, Rotary, and Valley Lutheran School. They are encouraging their grandchildren in their commitment to their faith and in many activities, including academics, sports, music, and the study of the Norwegian language and culture.

A Word from the Publisher

Gerald Christian Nordskog

Near where I have lived for the past two decades is a winding road called the "Norwegian Grade," up and over a mountain separating two plains/valleys—on the north side Santa Paula valley, with the mountain in between, to the south side the plains along the Pacific Ocean coast in Ventura County, California. It was built by Norwegian immigrants who carved it out to bring their crops to market quicker and easier upon settling here at the turn of the twentieth century.

My paternal ancestors settled in New York and Iowa, entering America in the 1880s–90s leaving a Norse farming village called Nordskog (North Woods) in northern Norway. My maternal family ancestors (Ferrara) came from Sicily and Genoa, Italy very early in the twentieth century past the Statue of Liberty and through Ellis Island.

According to Dr. D. Lindberg (pages 46, 193) there were 850,000 Norsemen who caught the "America Fever" in the "Great Migration of the Norwegian People to America." The Norwegians (Nordskogs) of my great-great-grandfather were a prolific family—my grandfather Andrae (Arne) was one of a quiver full of siblings. He founded the first record production company on the westcoast, Nordskog Records in Santa Monica, CA and was the first general-manager of the world-renown Hollywood Bowl. He also ran for Vice-President of the USA in 1932.

My dad's sister, my Aunt Gloria Nord(skog) was a famous skating star in the USA (roller) and mainly in Europe (ice), who lived in England most of her career, and was asked to give a Command Performance for Queen Elizabeth of England.

My dad, Bob Nordskog, was an entrepreneurial industrialist, and also was inducted into the Motorsports Hall of Fame as a powerboat racer and promoter. As I read this book, I recalled an exaggerated statement my father used to repeat: "Ten Thousand Swedes were chased through the weeds by one Norwegian"; but Lindberg does describe the historical event on pages 26–27.

I am thankful for my Norwegian and Italian heritage—some Irish/English too. I am grateful that the captive Christian women from the Viking excursions into Europe, became wives, tamed their husbands and many led them into the Christian faith. We all can be blessed by knowing King Olaf I and King Olaf II and others pursued changing the Norwegian Viking culture to one of western civilized Christianity around the first millennium!

Dr. Duane Lindberg, a Norwegian, is a historian and a theologian and a visionary as well. He has studied and taught the Scandinavian heritage, world history, and God's Story throughout his life as a pastor and university instructor. (See his biography on preceding pages.) He wrote this historical and evangelical novel while at his lake cottage in Minnesota...polishing it in his home in Iowa. I was reminded and learned abundantly more about the history of the last millennium by reading his book. I applaud the great research, reasoning, and writing he has accomplished in this *The Kingdom of the Rings!*

> "*And he said unto them, When ye pray, say, 'Our Father which art in heaven, hallowed be thy Name. Thy kingdom come: Let thy will be done, even in earth, as it is in heaven.'*" (Luke 11:2)

One reservation: This Italian-Norwegian's theology is persuaded toward the historic Post Millennial eschatology of victory. Nordskog Publishing believes that we are now and have been—since the ascension of Christ to the right hand of our Heavenly Father, He having conquered the enemy on the cross—joint-heirs and ambassadors of Christ who *now* reigns. He will bring the world under submission through the effective work of the Holy Spirit eventually to convert the hearts of the nations, so that *every knee will bow and every tongue will confess that Jesus Christ is Lord* (Psalm 72:17; Isaiah 45:22-23; Romans 14:11; Philippians 2:10).

Psalm 110 teaches us that Christ will reign from heaven, in the middle of His enemies, through His volunteers—the body of Christ—until His enemies are vanquished. Paul the Apostle, in this context says that the last enemy is death. Jesus must remain in heaven until He conquers death (1 Corinthians 15:20-28). His will, His kingdom comes to earth as it is in heaven. This singular accomplishment thus vindicates God saving man from his sin, shaming his adversary the devil (Luke 7:35).

That we may differ on the future end of the world is not surprising. Yet we concentrate on those things we have in common. As with Paul the Apostle we look to *"the unity of the faith and of the knowledge of the Son of God, to a perfect man, to the measure of the stature of the fullness of Christ."* We, of course, fully agree with and embrace God's working in history toward the Second Coming of Christ when He finally and ultimately fulfills all things. Upon His sure incarnation and life on earth as fully man while fully God, we look forward to and cherish in our hearts, and then the new earth and new kingdom will be forever and for all eternity. MARANATHA!

> *"I am Alpha and Omega, the beginning and the end, the first and the last. Blessed are they, that do His Commandments, that their right may be in the tree of Life, and may enter in through the gates into the City....*
>
> *"I Jesus have sent mine Angel, to testify unto you these things in the Churches: I am the root and the generation of David, and the bright morning star. And the Spirit and the bride say, Come. And let him that heareth say, Come: and let him that is athirst, come: and let whosoever will, take of the water of life freely....*
>
> *"He which testifieth these things, saith, Surely I come quickly, Amen. Even so, come Lord Jesus. The grace of our Lord Jesus Christ be with you all, AMEN.—THE END"*
>
> (Revelation 22:13-14, 16-17, 20-21)—Geneva BIBLE—1599

Dear Rings-Reader,

As Arne prayed for Brita's safety and God's speed,
at the end of Saga 59, he closed his prayer—
and I end this Noble Novels book,
with the words of the Norwegian blessing:

"Gud velsigne deg og bevare deg alltid!"
("God Bless You and Keep You always!")

Jerry Nordskog
July 4, 2014

"Whatsoever things are... noble,
...think on these things."
Philippians 4:18

ORDER FROM NORDSKOG PUBLISHING

West Oversea: A Norse Saga of Mystery, Adventure, and Faith

by Lars Walker ***Sailing West to visit Lief Eriksson but blown off course to strange lands.***

"Walker understands the unique Norse mind-set at the time of the Vikings' conversion to Christianity and westward explorations. This is a saga that will keep you on the edge of your chair – and make you think." –John Eidsmoe, *Author*

"It is refreshing to read popular fantasy built on a foundation of solid research and love of the medieval Icelandic sagas." –Dale Nelson, *Touchstone*

"Action, excitement, and the sheer fun that reading can be." –Gene Edward Veith, *Author*

"I cannot give a high enough recommendation to Walker's Norse saga." –Hunter Baker, *Author*

PB 5½" x 8½" 296 PP ISBN 978-0-9796736-8-9 2009, 3d Printing 2013 $13.95

Another World by Philip Stott

An action-filled novel that combines Biblical and scientific themes with heart-racing adventure.

Japh hears a scream in the night, a devastating crash, and flight becomes the only option, beginning a chain of events which will change the entire course of history.

Now, at every turn, evil has overtaken the world, leaving the few decent people left with imminent peril the only constant. As the heavens threaten and the earth trembles under tribulation, its very existence remains in question. And will humanity survive?

"May all who read this account of the first world's terrifying ruin by flood be driven to seek refuge from the judgment that is yet to come by fire." –Barry Beukema, *Ontario*

PB 5½" x 8½" 284 PP ISBN219219978-0-9796736-9-6 2010 $12.95

Jungle Sunrise by Jonathan Williams

"A captivating novel written by an Xtreme Team missionary who risked his life to find and assist native people in the remote jungle of Peru. He unlocks the secret of how to begin life anew as the book's central character moves from a depressing, directionless life to an incomparable adventure. Do not start reading until you have some time because you won't put it down." –Paige Patterson, *President,* Southwestern Baptist Theological Seminary

"They discover the ultimate meaning in life through trials and tragedy." –Jerry Rankin, *President,* International Mission Board, SBC

PB 5½" x 8½" 230 PP ISBN 978-0-9824929-8-7 2010 $12.50 [Audio book available.]

Close to His Heart by Leonora Pruner

"A superbly researched historical romance set in 18th century England. Jane Austen fans – who have wondered what Lydia Bennett's life might have been like if she had had a grain of good sense and had fallen into the hands of an honourable man – will love this story." –Donna F. Crow, *Author*

"Both Grace and Lord Buryhill long for a loving, faith-minded spouse. Misunderstandings shatter their marriage until Grace's loss of memory offers an opportunity for renewal – if they can forgive each other. A beautiful world of romance that will leave you with a sense of joyful hope." –Kay Marshall Strom, *Author*

PB 5½" x 8½" 384 PP ISBN 978-0-9824929-5-6 2010 $13.95

In the Aerie of the Wolf by Leonora Pruner

Young Anne Crofton's family sells her into marriage to a man she's never met. In the home of Lord Wolverton, Master of the Wolf's Aerie, she finds herself thrust into danger, betrayal, and sword fighting in a castle with secret passageways. With courage, faith in God, and a personal resolve to be a good wife despite her heartache, she seeks Biblical wisdom in the pursuit of true love. You will become lost in another time and place and won't want to put the book down.

"What a triumph! Leonora's best book ever. A gripping love story with the page-turning pacing of a Gothic romance and fairy-tale evocations of *Beauty and the Beast*. A heart-stopping tale set in the wilds of 18th-century Yorkshire with Pruner's superb period detail and spot-on theology." — Donna Fletcher Crow, Author, *A Very Private Grave*

PB 5½" x 8½" 368 PP ISBN 978-0-9827074-8-7 2011 $13.95

UPCOMING – *The White Knight, the Lost Kingdom, and the Longing Heart*

An epic-size ideal romantic adventure. With abundant imagination and great Biblical sensibilities, Judy Carlson takes up the ancient story of the Eastern Islands, now overtaken by the mysterious and evil Lord Regent. The battle to restore righteousness, liberty, and justice takes place just as the White Knight's Prince Lael meets the intriguing and beautiful sea princess. This unique, yet fairy-tale story, will engage, entertain, and edify with Godly counsel readers of every age. Perfect for homeschool literature study or family reading aloud.

Nonfiction books PRESENTED BY Nordskog Publishing

Meaty, tasty, and easily digestible Biblical treasures!

The Fear of God: A Forgotten Doctrine

by Arnold L. Frank, D Min

Gives the reader both a godly rebuke and an impassioned plea to hear the Word of God and the wise counsel of the Puritans that speak about the fear of God, which precedes the love of God.

Expanded 2nd Edition includes Scripture Index and Study Questions.

ISBN 978-0-9796736-5-8 PB 6″x 9″ 228 pp 2008 $16.95

Died He for Me: A Physician's View of the Crucifixion of Jesus Christ

by Mark A. Marinella, md, facp

"The death of Jesus for our sins is the heart of the Christian faith. What does a physician have to say about that death? In this important new book, particularly intriguing are the details of the death of Jesus as found in the Old Testament, written hundreds of years before." —Jerry Newcombe, DMin

Spanish Edition— *Por Mí, El Murio* 2009 **$14.95**

ISBN 978-0-9796736-6-5 PB 6″x 9″ 144 pp 2008 $13.95

Truth Standing on Its Head: Insight for an Extraordinary Christian Walk from The Sermon on the Mount

by John N. Day, PhD

Dr. John Day, Bible scholar and pastor, begins with the paradoxical Beatitudes and takes us through our Lord's greatest Sermon in depth, offering readers a "mind-expanding and life-transforming" experience. How can the meek inherit the earth? How are the persecuted blessed? While these are not things that we naturally associate with happiness, this is Jesus' startling opposite-from-the-world way of bringing us into the most blessed and happy life —an extraordinary Christian walk.

ISBN978-0-9824929-3-2 HB-Casebound 6″x 9″ 192 pp 2009 $18.95

God's Ten Commandments: Yesterday, Today, Forever by Francis Nigel Lee, llb, DJur, DCL, PhD, ThD

"God gave man Ten Commandments. Every one of them is vital, in all ages. God Himself is the Root of the Moral Law, and perfectly reflects it. It is the very basis of the United States and every other Common Law nation in the world." —Dr. Francis Nigel Lee

"Dr. Lee is a man deeply devoted to God. I am happy to commend to your reading Dr. Lee's work." —The Honorable Roy S. Moore *former Chief Justice, Alabama Supreme Court, and President of the Foundation for Moral Law Inc.*

ISBN 978-0-9796736-2-7 5″x 8″ 128 pp Extensive Appendix including God's Eternal Moral Law Chart PB 2007 $11.95

Loving God with All Your Heart: Keeping the Greatest Commandment in Everyday Life

by Susie Hobson

This small book offers a huge practical encouragement for grounding yourself in the Bible and developing a deep personal relationship with God as the firm foundation for living and serving and experiencing ultimate and unfailing love. You will love Susie's personal testimony.

ISBN 978-0-9824929-6-3 Casebound 5″x 8″ 120 pp 2010 HB $15.95

Loving God Prayer Journal

by Susie Hobson

This thick Journal opens flat with plenty of space to write, place for date, and Index in front to record prayers and answers to prayer by date. Across the bottoms of the pages are Scriptures with encouraging commentary by Susie Hobson.

ISBN 978-0-9831957-2-6 2011 HB-Casebound 6″x 9″ 288 pp $18.95

New... **Publisher's 15% Discount on two-book companion set** **LG-SET ISBN 978-0-9831957-7-1 2011 $15.95 + $18.95 = $34.90 - 15% = $29.70**

A Whole New World: The Gospel According to Revelation by Greg Uttinger

"Greg Uttinger's book is refreshing for its brevity; it does not confuse the reader in the minutia of exposition. It de-mystifies Revelation by focusing the reader on the big picture. I encourage anyone to read it. The blessing on those who read, hear, and keep the message of Revelation (1:3) was referring to its core message—that we serve the risen, victorious Lord of time and eternity. Uttinger's book is faithful to that 'Revelation of Jesus Christ' (1:1)." —Mark R. Rushdoony, *President*, Chalcedon Foundation

"The author clearly and simply puts forth a very realistic interpretation, taken from Scripture as a whole. He deciphers symbolism from the Word of God and concisely explains the glorious future all believers cherish in anticipation of God's ordained 'Whole New World'." —Gerald Christian Nordskog, *Publisher*

ISBN 978-0-9796736-0-3 5″x 8″ 100 pp 2007 PB $9.95

Nourishment from the Word: Select Studies in Reformed Doctrine by Kenneth L. Gentry, Jr, ThD

This book is a welcome collection of shorter writings for serious Christians following the Biblical encouragement to "be a good servant of Jesus Christ, constantly nourished on the words of faith and of sound doctrine" (1 Tim. 4:6). Dr. Kenneth L. Gentry, Jr. provides a banquet of nourishing entrees too seldom found on the menu of the modern church to help hungry believers grow in understanding.

Dr. Gentry's deep study of Holy Writ, and his precise and gentle, loving style of communicating make this book a must for pastors and laypersons alike who want to follow Jesus lovingly, obediently, and wisely. We need to consume the meat and not just the milk of theology. Wisdom is the principle thing, so says the Word of God. Come, eat, and be satisfied.

ISBN 978-0-9796736-4-1 PB 6″x 9″ 188 pp 2008 $15.95

More Featured Books from . . .

The Virgin Mary In the Light of the Word of God by Dr. Labib Mikhail & Dr. Nasser S. Farag

A book that presents insight from Scripture about the honor due to blessed Mary, the mother of Jesus, while exalting Christ Jesus as the only Way, Truth, and Life!

"This is a relevant study clarifying Mary's role and significance. I highly recommend it as a balanced and Biblical portrait."

– **Dr. James Massey**, Dean Emeritus, Anderson University School of Theology
"One of the 25 most influential preachers of the past 50 years." *Christianity Today*

ISBN 978-0-9827074-9-4 PB 5.5″x 8.5″ 176 PP 2011 $12.95

From Mason to Minister: Through the Lattice by Neil Cullan McKinlay

A captivating and poetic memoir of the author's spiritual journey—from Scotland to Canada to Australia—in his quest to "find the Truth and know the Living God." While neither an apologetic nor a polemic, he corrects much misinterpretation and misunderstanding of Freemasonry. Inspiration from Masonic teachings on Solomon's Temple, the arch, and keystone led him to a deep study of the Bible and of "the Stone the builders rejected," Jesus Christ. You will be uplifted and delighted as you follow the author in the discovery of his calling.

ISBN 978-0-9827074-7-0
HB 6″x 9″ 208 PP 2011 $18.95

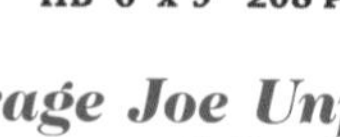

Your Average Joe Unplugged A Humorous and Insightful Devotional by Joseph D. Schneller

Through 30 daily devotionals and a half-dozen humor articles, the author presents honest, often humorous encouragement for your Christian pilgrimage through this fallen world. And all throughout he shows how, by Christ's grace, our everyday lives can have eternal impact.

ISBN 978-0-9831957-1-9 PB 5.5″x 8.5″ 116 PP 2011 $11.95

Young Heart *Our new line of character-building books for children and youth.*

With My Rifle by My Side
A Second Amendment Lesson

by Kimberly Jo Simac
Illus. by Donna Goeddaeus

HIGHLIGHTED BY GLENN BECK ON TV & RADIO

This is more than just a picture book. Written in verse with full color illustrations throughout, it tells two stories at once: a boy's initiation into rifle safety and hunting; and his awakening to the solemn necessity of firearms for preserving personal and national liberty. This book also teaches the role of the Colonial Minutemen and of all who have defended our country throughout history. The appendix for parents and grandparents contains gun safety guidelines, links to programs for children, and quotations from our Founders to introduce a 2nd Amendment study.

"This is the message children need to get—and adults, too."

–**Larry Pratt**, Ex. Dir., Gun Owners of America

2011 Christian Small Publisher Book of the Year

ISBN 978-0-9827074-4-9
HB 8″x 10.5″ 48 PP $18.95

John Locke
Philosopher of American Liberty
by Mary-Elaine Swanson

Why Our Founders Fought for "Life, Liberty, and Property"

Foreword by David Barton of *WallBuilders*

Magnum opus by the accomplished scholar, biographer, and author of *The Education of James Madison: A Model for Today*, co-author with Marshall Foster of *The American Covenant: The Untold Story*, presenting the much-needed truth about John Locke, the most read and quoted thinker of our Independence era. From original sources Mrs. Swanson documents Locke's true Biblical Christianity as the source of his ideas, demonstrating that our Founders understood "the pursuit of happiness" as the Bible's protection of property, and that the Bible is the underlying foundation of civil law and liberty proclaimed in the phrase "the Law of Nature and Nature's God."

FULLY INDEXED AND FOOTNOTED
PB 6″x 9″ 432 pp **ISBN 978-0-9831957-3-3 $19.95**

Rebuilding Civilization on the Bible: Proclaiming the TRUTH on 24 Controversial Issues

The call of the Bridgeroom is going out to His Body. This book will help you to be an effective part of the coming revival of the Church and a new reformation to bring true Biblical Christianity to the nations.

The vital documents in this book are the culmination of 37 years of the work of hundreds of Christian theologians and pastoral and lay leaders from a broad variety of denominations, who met together to restore "the faith once delivered to the saints" and hashed out statements of **Biblical Truth** on **24 controversial** topics, beginning with the Eternal and Inerrant Word of God.

The 24 resulting documents in this book offer a plumb line for *restoring the Church to God's Word* and *God's favor to the Church!*

ISBN: 978-0-9882976-8-5

Price: $19.95

Binding: 6″ x 9″ Paperback, 352 pp., Illustrated; Appendix

Imprint: Nordskog Publishing Inc.

Category: Theology/Current Affairs

4562 Westinghouse St., Ste. E,
Ventura, CA 93003
805-642-2070 • Fax 805-642-1862
www.NordskogPublishing.com •
Jerry@NordskogPublishing.com

About the Authors

Jay Grimstead, D.Min., author; founder-director of COR. Masters & D.Min., Fuller Seminary. Leader & Area Director, Young Life Campaign, 1957 to 1977.

When he was called by God to hold the principles of the Bible alongside the Church as a prophetic plumb line, he organized theologians and Christian leaders to stand for God's Truth and to create Theological Documents defining and defending key points of historic Christianity. In 1977, Dr. Jay founded the International Council on Biblical Inerrancy. In 1984, he founded the Coalition on Revival, and in 1991, COR formed the Church Council movement.

Eugene Calvin Clingman, D.Min., co-author and contributing editor. Bachelor in Theology, Berean Bible College, San Diego; D.Min., Heber Springs Theological Seminary. Eugene has served as associate and as senior pastor, and with the U.S. Center for World Missions. With COR since 1999, he is now Executive Administrator of the International Church Council Project.

Thy Will Be Done

When All Nations Call God Blessed

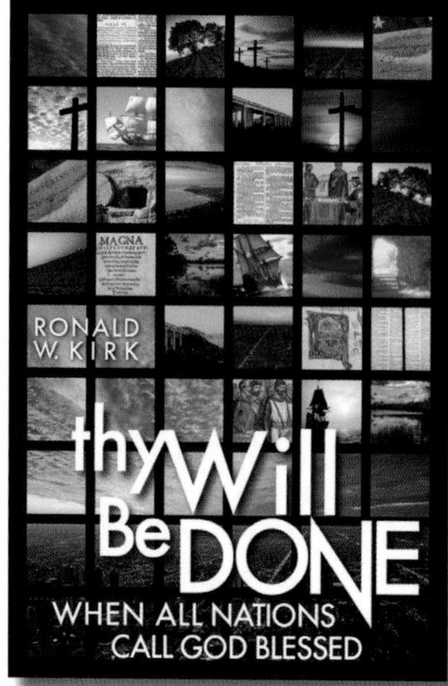

ISBN 978-0-9882976-5-4
PB 6″ x 9″ 250 PP 2013 $ 17.95

Order from

4562 Westinghouse St., Suite E
Ventura, CA 93003
❊ www.NordskogPublishing.com ❊
805-642-2070 ❊ 805-276-5129

by Ronald W. Kirk

This book applies Biblical truth in every field to give readers a realistic and powerful depiction of a sinful world redeemed and transformed by Christ this side of eternity.

Biblical principles guide a comprehensive and practical approach to a fulfilled Gospel life and the earthly tools needed for the Great Commission. Let us hasten the day!

"Ron Kirk comprehensively applies the Lordship of Christ to all areas of life."

Dr. Peter Hammond
THE REFORMATION SOCIETY

"If each of us did commit to being salt and light, what would our communities look like then?"

William J. Murray
RELIGIOUS FREEDOM COALITION

"This book examines how we ought to conduct ourselves individually, as family leaders, as church members, and as citizens to restore God's Kingdom on earth."

Kendall Thurston, MURPHYS, CA

"If only God's people would read and learn and apply, for transforming the generations to come!"

Jay Dangers, NEW HOPE UGANDA

RON KIRK MET JESUS CHRIST during college, and graduated in 1974 from the University of California, Berkeley as a professional landscape architect. Since 1980,

Ron has studied and taught the Biblically and historically identified applied-faith theology and philosophy outlined in this book. Its principles have now long proven themselves in the curriculum and methods of pioneering day and home schools founded and administered by Ron, the first being The Master's School. In 2013, Ron joined the missionary staff of New Hope Uganda to provide training and curriculum to its new teachers college, bringing a rigorously Biblical system of education to the nation's schools.

Married since 1971, Ron and Christina have five children, five sons- and daughters-in-law, and twelve beautiful grandchildren, all walking with Christ.

American Heritage Christian Church ordained Ron as a minister in 1984.

To see all of our exciting titles and
view book contents, and to get ebooks
go to:
www.NordskogPublishing.com

If you like solid and inspiring content,
get our free eNewsletter,
The Bell Ringer.
Get it here:
www.NordskogPublishing.com/eNewsletter

We also invite you to browse the
many short articles, poems, and testimonies
by various perceptive writers—
here:
PublishersCorner.NordskogPublishing.com

Ask the publisher about upcoming titles
and e-book versions, and a discount
when you purchase multiple books.